TOUCHES OF
WONDER AND TERROR

Here are eight stories of science fiction and fantasy to stir your emotions, amuse you, or give you a night of uneasy sleep. There are fun-loving aliens on tour, a vision quest in the Badlands of North Dakots, a protocol hostess with a most unusual employer, and a cursed knife blade uncovered by children.

A space traveler is seduced by a musical, cosmic voice, and a film critic discovers true realism. A warrior learns what valor really is, and a woman climbing a dangerous mountain is aided by a strange being from the past. Great reading from a master wordsmith!

Borgo Press Books by JAMES C. GLASS

Imaginings of a Dark Mind: Science Fiction Stories
Sedona Conspiracy: A Science Fiction Novel
Toth: A Science Fiction Novel
*Touches of Wonder and Terror: Tales of Dark Fantasy and
    Science Fiction*
Visions: A Science Fiction Western
Voyages in Mind and Space: Stories of Mystery and Fantasy

TOUCHES OF WONDER AND TERROR

TALES OF DARK FANTASY AND SCIENCE FICTION

JAMES C. GLASS

James P. Glass

THE BORGO PRESS
MMXII

TOUCHES OF WONDER AND TERROR

FIRST EDITION

Published by Wildside Press LLC

www.wildsidebooks.com

DEDICATION

For short story writers near and far—
you know who you are.

CONTENTS

AUTHOR'S FOREWORD

A writer becomes a published author by writing, rewriting, and sending work to editors for their consideration. It is a process, taking months or even years before there are positive results. At first there is the form rejection slip which tells the writer nothing helpful for improving the work. Next best, often seen in the small press, is the checklist offering broad general hints about problems with the work. ('The idea is old', or 'The Story moves too slowly', *etc*.) Hand-written rejections with specific comments, when they begin to happen, tell the writer the work has been noticed and is being encouraged. Throughout this process the rejection slips received are the dues a writer is paying to be published. It is a process that continues throughout a professional career. A writer should learn from editorial comments and is well advised to apply them to the work, but often the writer has moved on to other projects and the rewriting doesn't get done.

Such is the case for the stories in this collection. All are earlier stories of mine that came close to selling, but had problems and received helpful suggestions from editors for doing the necessary work. It has been an interesting experience to rewrite these stories now, after publishing so many other stories over the past twenty-three years. The rewriting has been extensive, some storylines totally changed from the originals, and I present them here for the first time. Reader comments are most welcome, and can be delivered to my web site at www.sff.net/ people/jglass/

Thanks go to editors and former editors such as Stan Schmidt, Kris Rusch, George Scithers, Charles Ryan, and Patrick Swenson for their useful comments in the past, and to my editor, Rob Reginald, for putting together this volume.

WHEN HARRY MET BOB

Harry met Bob on the Brin Mesa trail along red rock buttes and spires west of Sedona, Arizona. It was a winter day: clear blue sky, bright sunshine, a cool breeze, and the temperature near sixty. Harry had made the final climb up rock and slippery skree to a ridge which sloped down to a wooden bench and a panoramic view at the end of the trail. Just below the ridge, where he now sat on a flat rock, he had an even better view of the Verde valley, its monumental buttes and pinnacles of layered sandstone, limestone and basalt stained red by iron.

His breathing was heavy from the climb, a consequence of the high gravity, and he cooled himself in the shade of a shaggy Arizona Cyprus bordered by Manzanita and one hearty prickly pear cactus. *Pristine country*, he thought. *It has beauty, clean air and a delicious solitude. No wonder this is touted as the new-age capital of the country, maybe even the planet.*

A man was climbing up towards him, moving clumsily on the rock and bent over with effort. He wore jeans, a yellow chamois shirt and black, cowboy hat. His breathing was audible from twenty meters away, and his aura was deep blue from the effort. Suddenly he looked up and smiled. He had a pleasant old face, round and flushed.

"Almost to the ridge. You doing the loop?" asked Harry.

"Absolutely not," said the man. "This is far enough for me. I'll take another photo, and then I go down again." The man stuck out a hand. "I'm Bob. Only got here yesterday, and I'm one of those foreign flatlanders you hear about."

"Harry," said Harry, and he shook Bob's hand. "It's over five thousand feet here. At my age I take it easy the first few days. You wintering, or just here for a weekend?"

"A month this time. I got lucky and found a small house uptown."

"Been here before? You are lucky. The portal has filled up on me twice. I've been here a week, and two more to go. Some interesting geology here. I was a geologist at home. Don't see these kinds of formations there."

"You're retired?" asked bob, brightening.

"Yep," said Harry. "The white hair gives me away every time. You?"

"Two years ago. I was an organic chip engineer for Telarts, mostly for these things." Bob took a palm-sized module from his shirt pocket and opened it. It was a Model 20 Jaziril Telecom, still state-of-the-art.

Harry felt like he'd found a kindred spirit. "I have an older model. It's sort of backwoods where I live."

Bob smiled. "Small universe," he said. "You here alone?"

"Never got married," said Harry. "Never had the time, or stayed around long enough."

They both laughed. "I had a wife, but she went elsewhere," said Bob. "Got tired of my little pranks, I guess. Look, if you don't mind company I could show you around. I don't know geology, but I've been studying the culture here; fascinating, and nothing like it at home."

"That's what I hear," said Harry. "Sure, it'd be good to see the most important things instead of just wandering. Takes me a few minutes to get into town. The only place I could find on short notice is in Oak Creek."

"No problem," said Bob, then, "Get yourself a Sedona newspaper. It comes out Wednesday and Friday and lists everything going on. Let me know what interests you. We could start tomorrow by hitting a few art galleries and some of the tourist shops. There's exceptional primitive art here, and interesting foods. It's a great place for indigestion."

"One of the delights of increasing age," said Harry, and they both laughed again.

They exchanged addresses and telephone numbers, and made a date for the following day.

* * * * * * *

Time went quickly for Harry and Bob. They were the perfect traveling companions, interests broad and complementary, both of them eager to explore new things.

They began with the more mundane shops: western clothing, Native American arts and crafts, fine jewelry in silver and gems. They admired pottery, carvings in sandstone and alabaster, flutes of cedar, but purchased nothing. Bob was temped by an F-sharp flute. Eventually he assembled a substantial collection of books about the area: geology, early history, sacred sites, vortices, and the new-age culture in the town.

Harry made no purchases until they hit the new-age shops, and he spent hundreds of dollars at a single mineral and crystal store near the edge of town. There were phantom and rutilated crystals of quartz, a plethora of thumbnail specimens of rare crystals from around the planet, all of which he carefully packed away in a small bag. Harry traveled light. For amusement he also purchased a book on the meditative and medicinal value of crystals, many of them supposedly tuned to a specific musical note and Chakra, whatever that was. Bob explained it all to him later.

Bob seemed more interested in odors, buying a large selection of incense sticks and cones, a brass burner, several vials of essential oils and an aromatherapy lamp. Even Harry had to admit that after several days of using these products, Bob's odor was distinctly pleasant.

"To learn the geology, one has to hike and climb," said Harry.

"To learn the culture, one has to experience it," said Bob in return.

Bob had to experience as many alternative medical techniques as possible. There was ear coning, acupressure, emotional clearing, reflexology, reiki, myofascia, quantum touch, rolfing, shiatsu, celestial touch massage, cranial-sacral, aromatherapy, transformational navigation and, worst of all, lymph drainage therapy! He tried most of them while Harry waited outside closed curtains, inhaling delicious odors and studying geological survey maps.

They went on long hikes together and visited sites touted for their mysteries. Near the airport they made a short climb to a mesa and found a young couple in a standing embrace inside a small circle of stones. The woman's eyes twinkled as she smiled and hugged her partner. "Absorbing some energies," she said to them, and then the couple hurried away.

"Believers make the stone circles, and unbelievers kick them away. This is supposed to be an electric vortex site," said Bob.

The panoramic view was grand, stretching east to Bell Rock and far west to high buttes. "I read about it," said Harry. "The Schuman resonance is supposed to be at seven or eight cycles per second, the earth charging and discharging due to global atmospheric electrical activity. They haven't figured out the earth grid stuff, or why the area here is so accessible to us, but then I don't understand all of it either."

Bob smiled. "Yeah, well, the way they present it is good for the tourists. Bell Rock out there is another electric vortex site, they say, but Cathedral Rock is a magnetic type, and there's supposed to be an interdimensional window that aliens and angels come through."

"Oooo, angels," said Harry.

They hiked the trail into the sacred area of Boynton Canyon and took photographs of a knobby spire called Katchina Woman. The spire was said to occasionally sport a blue aura, but the color was wrong. "South of here are the Palatki Indian Ruins, and beyond them there's supposed to be a secret, buried military base, and UFO's flying around. People say they've seen Humvees and men in black out there where there are no roads. Black helicopters, too," said Bob.

Harry shook his head. "This is what happens when people have an untrustworthy government and naughty tourists who don't obey the rules."

Bob slapped his shoulder. "Oh come on, Harry, lighten up. This is a place to have some fun."

So Harry lightened up and even allowed his own sense of humor to surface. Bob's infectious enthusiasm made it easier for him to stop thinking like a scientist all the time. Without being conscious of it, the two of them were becoming close friends for many years to come.

Late one day they made a nervous climb on steep, rough rock up a buttress sprouting delicate, multiple spires and shelves. In a slot framed by two massive columns towering high around them they scrambled their way up to a high saddle for photography. Others were coming behind them, for Cathedral Rock was a landmark of the area, and visited frequently. Harry got one of his best pictures of the trip there, and the view was breathtaking. Suddenly he held up his arms and twirled like a child. "Oh, oh, I'm magnetic," he said, and Bob laughed.

"Do you actually have to leave so soon?" asked Bob. "You're really having fun now."

"Well no, I don't. I'm retired, remember?"

"You traveling with Aurora, or Trans-Di?"

"Aurora."

"Me too. Why don't you extend your stay a week, and we can take the same slip back," said Bob.

Harry thought for only a few seconds, then, "I'll do it. What else do I have to do these days? I'm still learning how to be retired. When do you leave? I'll call my reservation in tonight."

"Never mind," said Bob. "You can do it from here." He took his Model 20 out of a camera bag, made contact. Harry punched in his reservation code and did the rest.

Bob took back his Jaziril 20 and nodded at the puffing climbers now nearing their position at the panoramic viewing site of Cathedral Rock. "You know," he said, eyes twinkling, "I think we can have some real fun with this place."

"Oh, oh," said Harry.

* * * * * * *

And so there was another week and a half of fun in the high country of northern Arizona. They ventured out a bit, drove to Flagstaff and artsy Jerome, and visited nearby Indian ruins. A long tour by jeep took them to more ruins and a huge sinkhole formed by the collapse of a limestone cavern ceiling. The driver on the tour refused to talk about black helicopters or UFOs in the area. Sworn to secrecy, he said.

A day before their departure they had an expensive dinner together in uptown Sedona and walked nearly two miles to the Spiritual Center to hear a special lecture on UFOs. A kindly, white-haired man talked about alien visitations and showed photographs of their saucer-shaped spacecraft. There was even a photo of such a craft sitting in the driveway of a man who claimed continual contact with the many alien societies living on planet earth.

Harry whispered to Bob, "Atmospheric entry had better be slow in that thing. And what are all the spherical balls around the hub?"

"That is where they store their alcohol," said Bob. His expression was serious, but his eyes said otherwise.

A matronly woman seated in front of them turned around with an admonishing glare, silencing them.

They walked back down the hill to town in the light of thousands of stars. "One hundred eight alien civilizations indeed," said Harry, staying in the mood. "The number can't be more than forty, tops"

"I've counted twenty-three," said Bob.

"That's more like it. And that picture of the alien, the one with the long earlobes, I've been wondering about you. Why is it *you* don't have long earlobes?"

"I have them trimmed every Thursday," said Bob, and sniffed primly.

Bob smiled, and sighed audibly. "Seriously, Harry, I'm going to miss this place. I missed it after the last time I was here. It has been even more fun being here with someone I could share it with."

"So why don't we do it again next year?" said Harry.

"You serious?"

"Absolutely. Let's exchange addresses and keep in touch. Plan ahead. I haven't had a massage yet, and we'll both be ready for a good rolfing by next year."

They shook hands on it, went back to their cars in a happier mood, and then home to pack.

Departure the following morning was complicated by their choice of location for it. Bob came to the rescue, finding two young men who, for a fee, would return their cars to the uptown lodge lot for them. They picked the men up at the lodge at sunrise, drove 179 and Back o' Beyond road to the Cathedral Rock trailhead.

Both of their backpacks were stuffed full. The young men looked at them curiously, and then drove the cars away, leaving them alone at the trailhead.

"Now I wish I hadn't bought all these books," said Bob, looking up at steep rock.

"Give me some of them. We'll sort it out at the other end," said Harry.

They repacked the bags quickly and went up the short but steep trail over rocky knobs and loose scree to a gentler slope around a buttress to the Cathedral Rock high saddle viewpoint. Passing the lower viewpoint they'd seen two vans pulling into the trailhead lot below; other hikers would soon be joining them. Bob looked at Harry. "We could get our travel permits revoked for doing this."

"Not likely," said Harry. "People see things here all the time, and more often than not their reporting isn't accurate or taken seriously."

Bob and Harry grinned at each other like two naughty children, and hurried on.

When they reached the high viewpoint no other hikers were in sight. They took two final pictures of each other, with twin walls of red rock in the background. Bob took out his Model 20 Jaziril and tapped a key. Behind them the air seemed to shimmer, as if suddenly heated.

"Here they come," said Harry.

A group of four hikers had come around a buttress base and were ascending the faint trail over smooth rock twenty meters below them.

"Now," said Harry, grinning.

Bob tapped the Jaziril three times. There was an explosion of color, an iris of air opening wide and shimmering brilliantly in emerald green.

"Aurora would be very unhappy if they knew we were doing this," said Bob.

There was a shout from below.

"I know," said Harry, "but they won't hear about it from me." He gestured Bob forward to the bright vortex of green. "After you, angelic one."

"And you need to have your earlobes trimmed," said Bob.

They hoisted their packs, and stepped inside the bright glow.

There was another shout, and then a scream from nearby as the five-dimensional Branegate closed behind them.

BADLANDS DREAMING

"You're crazy to go out there alone."

John Natani bristled, Italian blood boiling, but his Indian half forced him to remain calm. "That's why I'm paying for a long distance call, Joe. I want you to go with me. It's only a few days, like when we were kids. You remember the place."

At the other end of the line, Joseph Eaglestaff sighed before answering his childhood friend, remembering how the elders had called them a dreaming pair. "That was a long time ago, John. I'm the one with finals coming up in a week. You're the one who dropped out of school. What you do is your business."

"I don't want to be an engineer, Joe."

"So switch majors like I did. Ask around, and see what else you're interested in. It's either that or stay on the reservation and collect welfare, or move into town for some crummy job nobody wants. You don't need a vision-quest to make that decision for you; just think about it."

"I will, when I make Ihamblecza—in the badlands."

"The heat will boil your brains out. You won't think of anything. This is the twenty-first century, John. Quit listening to old men and wapiyapi. They live in the past. Take charge of your own life."

"You hate your own people," said John, even though there had been times, as a half-breed, when he'd not been treated as one of them. But now his parents were dead, and it didn't matter anymore.

"I won't even answer that," said Joe. "There's no future for me on the reservation, and I'm getting out. You do what you want."

"I will," said John, and he started to hang up the phone.

"John, be careful out there," said Joe quickly. "Even the old ones knew when to quit trying. Don't kill yourself for a dream. John?"

"Yes?"

"I'll be thinking about you."

"Sure," said John, and he hung up the phone.

* * * * * * *

The drive north and west was stifling under a searing North Dakota sun in August. Wind from the north brought dry air that sucked moisture from John's body, leaving his skin covered with a light frosting of salt, and making him feel itchy all over. He gassed up the old jeep at a discount station in Medora, and headed west a few miles before turning north on an old fire road skirting the edge of the national park, up towards high cliffs and buttes banded in red, black and yellow.

Here was his place of silence, peace and solitude, a place to make his vision quest as the old ones had done in the Black Hills far to the south and long before his birth. But here was his place, near his home, near the miserable land on which his people now lived with alkali water and stunted grass.

He could not identify with those who fought to return to the sacred hills. His land was here, burning hot in the sunlight.

The road became shallow ruts in tall buffalo grass, and then there was no road at all. The jeep bounced up the hill until John saw cottonwood trees to the east and traversed towards them, buckling himself into the seat and feeling the weight of the vehicle shift wholly to the downhill tires. The Little Missouri River came into view below, a muddy trickle shining mirror-like in the summer sun. He parked the jeep at a precarious angle between two trees and got out to chock the wheels with dead branches.

He threw his pack on the ground and checked the contents: a pair of gallon plastic bottles filled with water, three chocolate bars, and a package of Fig Newtons. It was enough for maybe three days, but he felt guilt. The old ones had gotten along on far less. He closed the pack and ate one candy bar while he cinched up, then covered the jeep with a green tarp and secured the four corners to trees with nylon rope. He hoisted the pack on his back, adjusted the straps, and then started down towards the river, looking back once to check the jeep. It was not visible twenty yards from the trees. When he reached an old road paralleling the river, the long walk began.

In nearby Medora that afternoon and for three days thereafter, the officially recorded high temperature reached one hundred and four degrees.

John followed the road for five miles, his mind a blank, eyes staring at the rutted bentonite, and scoria chips ahead of him. He didn't notice the heat at first; wind blowing down from the high, colorful buttes cooled him. The road veered upwards to the north, crossing a sandy saddle strewn with the bones of some hapless, small animal, and he stopped there for a moment, breath suddenly quickening. Ahead of him lay a green valley of buffalo grass, a trickling stream carving jagged, rust-red gashes across it towards the high plateau rising on the other side, and up one ridge dark shapes were moving rapidly. Even at this distance he could hear their coughing and growling. The buffalo were here, and it was a good sign.

He quickened his step down into the valley as the road changed to trail to a single rut to a faint line of bent and crushed buffalo grass meandering past a prairie dog town long abandoned, and up a long draw towards the high plateau above him. The draw became a clay shelf, strewn with bits of petrified wood from another age; the climb was suddenly steep, his feet slipping, and sweat running into his eyes. Near the top he stopped to remove his pack and sip from the water bottle.

The ground moved.

Five yards to his right a bentonite cliff thrust upwards twenty feet to the high plateau and all along the edge the buffalo herd suddenly appeared, rushing by and growling at the man below them. John Natani felt fragile in the presence of such massive animals. He was curiously unafraid. Two bulls moved by, large as his jeep, ignoring him, then several cows and a calf, the rest of the herd thundering by beyond the edge. John's heart quickened when a cow lurched to the edge, glared down at him angrily, and pawed at the clay with sharp hooves as a calf pressed against her. A part of him screamed in fear, another part freezing him calmly in his place, raising his arms towards the frenzied animal and speaking to it.

"I come to find the buffalo woman; I seek Ptesanwin. Lead me, so I may make Ihamblecya."

The cow had no chance to answer. Behind her the monstrous lead bull suddenly appeared, head lowered, one terrible horn disappearing up the female's anus, and she jumped screaming, scrambling ahead of her tyrant and away from the cliff edge. The ground trembled again, and was still.

John took the few remaining steps up to the high plateau and saw the herd moving quickly across it towards the west, through ripe buffalo grass covering the treeless plain to the horizon. When he passed them at great distance, two hours later, they were paralleling his course. John Natani found significance in this. The Ptepi were with him, and Ptesanwin would be near. He lowered his head and trudged onwards across the endless plateau.

When he reached the end of the grassy plain the sun was high. His lips and tongue felt swollen, and pack straps chaffed his shoulders raw. He stopped for a moment, took a long pull of warm water from the bottle, hoisted his pack once more and began picking his way carefully down narrow, sloping clay ledges into a canyon with no name. One moment a gentle breeze was cooling his face, but as he dropped below the edge of the plateau it seemed the furnaces of hell were unleashed upon him. His first breath of hot air rising from the canyon floor made him gasp, and his eyes were suddenly dry. There was no water in this canyon, but it had seen better times of green forests and sparkling streams. Along the bentonite shelves that were the canyon walls lay silicified remains of giant trees that had once cast shade here. Volcanoes to the south and west had killed them with ash and poisonous gases, and now their crystalline bodies glistened in the sunlight. Small Junipers clung tenaciously to scoria outcroppings in the gray clay, a hopeful sign of life and splash of green in a world of alkaline white, red and gray.

John moved across the clay, feeling it crackling beneath his feet, listening for a sound of other life and hearing nothing. The canyon laid barren, dead beneath him. Loneliness descended like a heavy cloud, urging him to turn away from this evil place. But it was a place of cleansing, he told himself, a place for turning inwards, asking questions, exploring goals and motivations. A place for Ihamblecya.

He climbed to a sandstone shelf near the canyon rim, scrambled up onto it and removed his pack. There was a commanding view of the canyon towards the west, and what breeze there was he would feel here. John removed his shirt and headband; let his black hair spill over his shoulders. He took a long pull from the water bottle, stowed it carefully in his pack and turned, sitting cross-legged to face the west rim of the canyon. Behind him, from somewhere out on the high, grassy plateau, there was a coughing sound. John smiled, raised his arms and closed his eyes to a descending sun, knowing he was not alone. As the heat seared his flesh, he began to pray.

It was ritual, prayers taught to him by mother and grandfather. He repeated them over and over until his mind drifted along with the words, observing but not hearing, present but somehow detached from the incantations. The words began to lose meaning as his mind drifted away, wandering far from the canyon heat, back to the dusty roads and grasslands of the reservation, a place of belonging far removed from the college campus he had despised and fled.

John was filled with a sense of regret, of failure. He'd only stayed a month, leaving before first exams. Of what use to his people would he be as an engineer? They didn't need computers or high technology; simple work and dignity had been enough for thousands of years. A corner of his mind nagged at him. Of what use are you to your people just sitting here on a rock and talking to the wind and snakes and trees of stone? Why are you really here? John felt hot sweat running into his eyes and mouth, opened the water bottle and took another long drink from it. "Ptesanwin, wise one, please speak to me. Show me the way I must follow."

He watched a blood-red sun descend beyond the western rim of the canyon, and ate a few of the Fig Newtons to silence his noisy stomach. A night breeze chilled him, but he did not put on his shirt and shivered on the ledge until the breeze subsided. His tongue felt swollen again, and he drank more water, holding it in his mouth for a long time before swallowing.

Behind him on the grassy slopes near the canyon, a coyote family emerged for the night's hunting, greeted each other with a symphony of yelps and howls that filled him with a sense of oneness with all life. Soon after, he heard the scratching of toe-nails on rock, saw dark shapes moving among the petrified logs and stumps below him, then a yip and low growl as one of the furtive creatures sensed his presence. "Miyacapi, little four-legged ones, tell Ptesanwin I am here." He prayed until a full moon had crossed the star-filled sky, and as the coyotes returned to their dens he succumbed to the exhaustion of unanswered prayers and fell into a dreamless sleep.

By the evening of the following day he had used up all his food and water, and he was consumed by doubt. His body was stiff and aching; dry lips had cracked open, and when he licked them he tasted blood. His mind seemed a blank. There were no answers, no thoughts, voices or visions. He was not worthy or ready, or Ptesanwin was a myth for ignorant people of the distant past. There was a coughing sound and low growls from the plateau behind him; the buffalo were still there, agitated. It was rutting season. "Ptesanwin, where are you?" he whispered. Even the coyotes avoided him that night, and he fell asleep with tears in his eyes.

He awoke when the sun was high. He was drenched in sweat. His vision was blurred by a white veil before his eyes, and there was a buzzing sound in his ears. His heart was pounding, skin turning cold, instinct screaming within him to find shade. He scrambled from the ledge and over rocks towards the canyon floor. Stepping over a rocky log, he felt a searing pain when something struck his leg. He looked down numbly as the venomous snake struck him again in the same place, and he staggered backwards onto a flat of alkali sand in shock. The snake glared at him a moment, then crawled back under the log. John felt no malice, sensing a purpose in the pain already moving up his leg. Perhaps this was his answer; he would die in this place rather than live in the white man's world. In a coldly rational way he realized this was likely in his weakened state. But a part of him wanted to live, while the remainder dwelled in self-pity. He limped across an alkali flat and along game trails towards a Juniper-covered escarpment jutting out over a scoria-lined canyon filled with thick underbrush. The escarpment was near an occasionally used horse trail, and shade was there. His death could be comfortable; more than he deserved for an ill-spent life. Ptesanwan would hide her face from him, and smile as he died. This was truth. Tears came. Must it be this way? He pondered the question, and felt numbness creeping into his groin. *Please don't let me die*, he thought. *There are things I should do—but what are they?*

He found a shady hollow beneath two intertwined junipers and crawled into it, dragging his violated leg behind him. Someone had camped here. He found match sticks and a piece of aluminum foil. The vacationers were gone and usually it was only rangers or ranchers who ventured this far into the backcountry. Perhaps they would check the buffalo herd, and come within signaling distance. The numbness was now in his abdomen, and he knew soon he would begin the fight to breathe as paralysis reached into his chest to suffocate him. To sleep was to die. John pushed himself up into a sitting position, back against a juniper, and stared out at the rolling hills and colorful buttes. The country he loved so dearly was killing him. Or was he killing himself? Was there no place for him in the world? Must he be thrown out? He felt sudden anger. *I have done nothing wrong*, he thought, to which his mind answered, *you have done nothing at all.*

A red sun touched the western rim of the canyon and shadows lengthened around him as John Natani fought to live, consciously willing his chest to rise and fall, forcing air in and out of parched lungs. He despaired, but then a Wambli came, and he wondered if it had been sent by Ptesanwin to sustain him. He had grown sleepy with the effort of breathing when suddenly the great bird was there, sitting on a tree branch a few feet above his head and staring darkly down at him. At first he'd thought it was a hawk, but then saw it was a young, golden eagle, and his spirits rose. He dared not speak to the bird, for fear it would leave him. *Wingflapper, sacred one, carry a message for me. I wish to live.* The bird watched him closely for a while, holding John's attention as he struggled to breathe, then suddenly lifted into the air with a single downward thrust of its wings, and flew majestically away towards the southeast.

Darkness came. John felt tranquility, a resignation to what was happening, a sense of plan, of purpose, and he rode the feeling like a leaf in dry wind, closing his eyes, letting himself fall into a dream-state near consciousness. In his dream he saw small children laughing and kicking at a rubber ball in a field of buffalo grass. He warned them to beware of snakes and they smiled at him, black eyes sparkling mischievously, and then he awoke, gasping for breath. He rubbed his eyes, willing himself to stay awake. Breathing seemed easier now, but he was tired, and so terribly thirsty. His tongue seemed to fill his entire mouth.

Rutting sounds came from the east; he heard them more often now, and once he saw movement at the canyon rim. The coyotes were strangely silent this night, and yet he sensed life nearby, watching him. Even fear could not hold his attention;

exhausted, he fell into a deep sleep, and dreamed about the children.

When he opened his eyes he was on his back staring up at a full moon shimmering past gnarled juniper branches. There was a cool breeze, and yet his body was drenched with sweat. The image of playing children lingered in his mind as he hovered on the edge of consciousness, and he felt strangely happy, even though breathing remained an effort. He had been awakened by something: a touch, or a sound. It was there again, along with a rank, wild odor, sharp in his nostrils. He sat up against the tree, wanting to sleep, peering through branches with fluttering eyelids, as though drugged. Beyond the branches, dark shapes moved in the moonlight, down bentonite slopes towards a grass-filled hollow near where he sat. They came in single file, grunting and growling, and the brittle clay crunched loudly beneath sharp hooves. When they reached the grass, some began rolling on their backs, kicking spindly legs with pleasure. John felt the ground tremble beneath him. This is a dream, he thought. He crawled quietly from beneath the tree, and sat cross-legged at the edge of the grass. *Ptesanwan, I am here.*

The herd seemed oblivious to his presence and continued to graze peacefully. John ignored them, for his eyes were fixed on two enormous bulls descending a clay bluff. Between them a white cow glowed beautifully in the moonlight. They moved slowly, majestically, in a straight line through the herd, the other animals moving respectfully aside to let them pass. The path they followed ran directly towards John, and he was suddenly wide awake and filled with fear. The animals came to the edge of the grass and stood before him, the shimmering cow flanked by two gargantuan bulls with lolling tongues, and menacing, amber eyes. Their hot, rank breath flooded his senses. He closed his eyes with fright.

"John Natani," said a voice.

He opened his eyes. Before him the bulls stood closely together, drooling. Between them, clothed in a simple white robe, stood a young woman. Dark, Amerind eyes gazed out from a finely chiseled face framed by the robe's hood. Her skin glowed like polished marble in the moonlight, slender arms caressing the shaggy manes of the sentinels who pressed closely to her.

"Ptesanwan," said John.

"I am called that by some," she replied. Her full lips moved, but the movement was not that of the words he sensed in his mind. Her speech was soundless, and somehow he was not surprised.

"You have lived through a dangerous day," she said seriously.

"The Wambli you sent helped me to survive."

"The bird sought an easy meal; I did not send him. When he saw you would live he flew away, and I heard his anger, just as I have heard your confused prayers."

"You have come to me," he said, wincing. With the few words he had spoken his dry lips were bleeding again.

"I come to water and sweet grass, away from the crawling people. We will sleep here this night. I hear your voice, and many others. You are full of self-pity. Must I stand before you? You do not listen to your own heart."

The rebuke was knife-edge sharp in his mind. Was this a dream? He thought not, and summoned his courage for the moment.

"Ptesanwan, I ask for no material thing, only advice on the direction of my life. I wish to be useful."

"Are you not useful now?" she asked, and scowled at him.

"I have no job, and I've dropped out of school. I don't have any goals, and I—"

"—You care about the people, and show love for them, yet you say you are not useful. This is a foolish statement. To give your love is to give all. Your accomplishment is the respect you have for others."

John's disappointment was heavy in his heart, but he feared argument with the vision before him. "Is there nothing more?" he asked gloomily.

"There is, but you have already decided your course. You

need nothing more from me, and you are weary from your quest. The people will tend to you, and then we will all rest."

He was commanded, and confused. John nodded his head wearily and looked up at the finely chiseled features and glowing skin. The words escaped him before he had a chance to think. "You are very beautiful," he said. "I wonder if you are a dream."

She smiled then, and his heart quickened. "Your mind has chosen the image you see," she said. "It is interesting." She looked deep into his eyes, and then suddenly slapped the shoulders of the massive bulls beside her. "Tend to him, and I will find water."

The bulls moved closer to him, amber eyes glaring. Only weakness kept him from scrambling away to the safety of the trees. Their foul breath was hot in his face, and he closed his eyes.

The bulls began to lick him.

Two great tongues licked at his body, moving him from side to side with a lulling rhythm, quickening his circulation until he felt tingling in his legs and hips. There was a gurgling sound; he opened his eyes and saw the white cow pawing at the ground near him, water bubbling from the depression she had made. He crawled to the place, bulls following, still licking him, and he tasted the water. It was sweet, in a land where nearly all water was alkaline. He drank his fill of it, while the bulls continued to massage him until it seemed he was a glowing flame between them.

"Come lie with me, and you will be warm tonight," said a voice in his head.

John crawled to where the cow had settled down on dry needles beneath a juniper tree, and snuggled against her belly while the bulls pressed in close to them. She nuzzled his head as he drifted into sleep, feeling the softness of arms around his neck and smiling again as he found the children still there, playing with the ball and calling to him to join their game.

He awoke alone beneath the tree, surrounded by grass crushed flat beneath the weight of sleeping buffalo. Two rangers on horseback encountered him as he climbed up out of the canyon. He told them only about his ordeal with the snake, and they put him on a horse, themselves riding double and upwind from him to escape the terrible odor he emanated.

On the long ride back across the high plateau they saw the buffalo herd grazing quietly hundreds of yards from their trail. John searched in vain for the white cow. The rangers asked John what he did, and he said he was starting university, and they asked what he would study, and he said he intended to teach elementary school, and they joked about the poor pay for teachers and rangers. It was several minutes before John fully realized what he had said to them. He was filled with both sadness and excitement, sending out a silent promise to someday return with children for Ptesanwan to look upon, and as they rode, a Wambli swooped low over them, heading east into the rising sun, leading the way.

THE MODULATION OF
BENNY KINGMAN

One light-second away from his body, Benny Kingman's soul modulated with the universe. Conscious of shrieks and wails, the soft murmurings of clashes between light and dust, he heard the squeals of particles spinning madly in frantic pursuit of freedom from nearby Sol. On top of it all was the deep throb of the megawatt carrier wave rushing towards the receiving dish at Solar Four. The passage of time was infinity, but now in his third transit Benny could relax, allowing himself to be swept along in black space filled with cosmic voices. In real time it would be less than an hour before he would open his eyes again to the lights of the lab.

The first transit had been a slow nightmare, a cacophony of modulation driving him into a panic he had barely overcome when back in his body on earth. His heartbeat had become so erratic they had aborted the run, bringing him back instantly. He remembered wondering if they hadn't lost a part of his soul, if even now a part of him could not be recalled from its manic dash into the solar system. Both Janet and Doctor Cox had assured him he was still Benny, their most important member of The Team. They said his safety was their number one concern, but he had felt a sense of loss as if he were now somehow incomplete, a carefully protected tool of Solarian Systems, Incorporated. He was Benny the tool, chosen to carry out a project costing billions of dollars even before the first transit.

In a way it was his own project, an extension of an idea from his private researches on modulated signal storage in super-conductors. But the concepts of mapping the micro-currents of human consciousness and modulating a carrier wave with them had come from others. Nobody had thought a person could actually experience a transit on a beam of light and remember it. Benny had proven them wrong.

Now Benny modulated with the electronic voices of the universe, finding new ones nanosecond by nanosecond. He could only speculate on the faces behind the yammering. There was a high-pitched call, descending in tone, perhaps a burst of distant lightening in a Terran storm or the plaintive call of a dying star. When he died someday, would his soul burst forth as a single packet of energy to become a permanent transient in the universe? If so, then perhaps stars had souls and life was nothing more than pure energy, with Benny Kingman an infini-tesimal part of it.

Time returned as the voices disappeared, and there was an instant of black void as he interfaced with the robot that was his receiver on board Solar Four orbiting only a thousand miles above the lunar surface. His vision came on, scanning the infra-red and visible spectrum to inspect each indicator of the control panel in front of the seated robot known as HTSI, the acronym for Human-Robot-Syntheses-Interface. One by one the indi-cator lights went out as he proceeded through the interface veri-fication list, the last two switches reset manually by each of the five-digit hands of HRSI. Months in space had had no effect on the intricate articulation abilities of either hand, he was happy to see, since such delicate repairs remained an unsolved problem of the project.

There was the usual pause as he touched the receiver switch, the hint of panic at blocking the stream of photons that was his mind. There was the usual elation when he hit the switch cutting him off from earth without a flicker in his conscious-ness as he continued to swirl in the superconducting circuitry of HRSI. *I am energy*, he thought.

Benny turned HRSI left to a second console on which his

problem would be indicated, as programmed before launch of Solar Four. He scanned the systems indicators and found the problem in seconds: there was a heater failure in propellant tanks one and three. Through the interface he checked voltages and currents. The tank one problem was trivial, the heater functioning perfectly, but a thermistor-epoxy bond had somehow broken, giving a false temperature reading. It was easily checked from ground control, if you had it, and nothing you couldn't fly with if you didn't mind meaningless warning lights. But what if the warning then became real? He switched to tank three, and indeed the problem there was serious. There was no current, the heater dead and no possibility of repair from earth. Until now. This was what HRSI was all about: the dispatch and storage of human intelligence at light speed to effect real-time diagnostics and repairs on deep-space probes remote or lost to contact with earth. An intuitive, thinking and learning system, Benny and HRSI were one entity, physically and mentally, on-board Solar Four. Alone, and cut off from earth base.

HRSI climbed from its chair in the airless compartment, jacked in the umbilical cable for EVA, and then took a tool-kit from one wall and opened the port to the blackness of space. It clambered outside, a metallic skeleton with bucket-head, two optical sensor slits glowing red in sunlight reflected from the lunar surface, only the delicate fingers on each hand giving the machine a remotely human quality. It climbed aft to the fuel tanks, found a thermistor hanging by an epoxy thread, patched it in place with strips of titanium-fiber glass composite tape, then found the broken heater coil on tank three, lugged the broken ends together and spot-welded them in place. The total repair time was twenty minutes. Back inside, port closed, Benny/HRSI ran a new systems check until satisfied the heater would take full current, then pressed the ready/transmit button with a metal finger.

The voices of space engulfed him as if glad to have him among them again, a part of the whole. He thought of his apartment, routine evenings with his one pleasure of working on his robotic toys, weekends passing slowly. He had no relatives, no friends. To others, outside of work, he was invisible.

A moaning modulation struck him and he felt instant sadness, as if someone close to him had died. *Talk to me*, he thought. The universe chattered back in squeals and white noise, and the moan was gone.

Blackness, and then moist heat, and his clothes stuck to him. His eyelids fluttered in bright overhead light. Something soft and warm pressed on his forehead. He opened his eyes as Janet pulled back her hand, smiling. Blond hair framed her square face, full lips, eyes the color of turquoise.

"Welcome back, spaceman. You did a super job out there, even better than expected. How do you feel?"

Benny rubbed his eyes. "It's bright in here. It hurts."

"Here, sit up," said Janet, and she put her hands under his shoulders. He smelled perfume. He was lying on a soft couch, wires trailing away from the multiplexer helmet still on his head, and he was sweating profusely. He sat up; dangling his feet over the edge of the couch as Janet carefully lifted the helmet from his head and placed it on a table. "Better, now? Your face is flushed. Want something to drink?"

His face was flushed from her touch more than anything else. Benny nodded, and Janet got him a glass of water which he gulped noisily. "It couldn't have gone better," she said brightly. "Jerry just phoned from Houston Control and called it a hundred percent. No more moon business, he said. We've got a unanimous go ahead from the company to activate the Jovian probe. You're going to Jupiter, Benny. Nice job."

"I'm getting used to it, now. All the different signals, I mean. I try to pick out different ones and imagine where they're coming from. It makes the time go faster."

Janet laughed, a beautiful sound. "All of that in just over a second. Time really is relative, isn't it?"

"Yeah, but the signals are all different, and they keep me company. It's really strange."

"Put it in your report, Benny. Jerry will want to know all

about it." She handed his hairpiece to him.

Always Jerry Cox. Janet was in love with the man, would never know the terrible crush that Benny had on her. "When is Doctor Cox coming back?" he asked.

"Late tomorrow. Can you have your report ready by then?"

"Sure." Benny slipped the wig over the transparent dome of his skull, the polymer-cast micro circuitry of a neo-cortical pickup net nestled between bone and brain to feed his mental self to the multiplexer and amplifiers and finally the big carrier wave.

"Why don't you take off early and get some rest?" said Janet. "The next few days are going to be pretty frantic around here, and we want you at your best. We're counting on you, Benny. You're the most important person on this project."

Janet smiled, and returned to fiddling with the helmet. He left her standing that way in the stark laboratory room and walked quietly out of the Solarian Systems complex into Atlanta sunlight. He stalled away an hour with a sandwich and coffee at Gerraldo's, and then caught the bus to College Park and made the one mile walk down Fayetville road to his little condo among condos in the trees. The neighborhood was in decline since the great rush to urban renewal in the twenties, the once fashionable condos now mostly rentals inhabited by lower-middle income folks like him. It was a dignified decline, the yards well kept, and paint fresh, the crime rate non-existent.

The phone was ringing as he let himself in, getting his evening off to a bad start.

"Hello?"

"Yes, hello. This thing has rung twenty-three times before you answer. Are your legs broken?"

"I just got home from work, mom, this very instant. You should call later."

"I should call later. You should call your mother who is sick, that's what you should do. Ester calls me three times a week, and from New York, yet. You who lives close never call me at all."

"Atlanta is a long way from Miami, mom, and Ester married a bank president. How are you?"

"I'm terrible, if you care. I need oxygen all the time now. The air in the city is poisonous, and no decent person should have to live here. Why don't you call your mother?"

"The project takes all my time, mom. I get home late and get up early. Work and sleep, that's it, just to make a living."

"And why is that? You, the genius. All the things you've invented, Ester says you should be rich by now. I think that company is stealing from you; you know what I'm saying? Talk to Ester and Frank about a loan, and make your own business before it's too late. They maybe you can afford to see your mother once in a while. And find a nice girl. You should be married by now."

"I'm sorry, mom. I'll try to call more often, but right now I've got to get a report done that's due tomorrow. I'll call this weekend, I promise."

Her voice seemed to soften. "Okay, you do that. And don't let those people steal your soul. You keep some ideas for Benny and give Frank a call. I've talked to him."

"Yeah, mom. Thanks."

He hung up the phone and sighed. Everyone was trying to run his life, and usually succeeding. Still, there was a sinister element of truth in what his mother had said about the company. Much of HRSI had been designed and prototyped at his own kitchen table, on his own time. All he had to show for it was a modest salary and a thousand dollar a month bonus that was half a month's rent. He went to the kitchen and stared at the pile of chips and boards on the table there. Rising from the mound of debris was a human hand with long fingers, the latest HRSI articulator now covered with a fine polymer. How much would that be worth as a prosthetic if he owned the patent to the interface? It all belonged to the company. Even Benny Kingman.

He worked on his report until midnight, and finished it.

* * * * * * *

Benny sat on the couch and drank a glass of orange juice while Janet fussed with the helmet. She smiled when Doctor Cox came into the room, but Benny didn't. Cox looked at Benny seriously, as if he cared. "How you don', guy? Ready for the big one?"

"Just another transit, I guess. I feel okay."

"Don't take it too lightly, Benny. Jupiter is a noisy place electromagnetically, and there's a lot more beam spread at that distance. We don't want you wandering off on us, do we?"

Always that condescending tone in his voice, as if he were talking to a child. Benny swallowed the last of the orange juice. "You just point me in the right direction and I'll get the job done. Let's get at it."

Janet frowned at him, looked at Cox and then brought over the helmet and lowered it onto Benny's head. She leaned him back on the couch and strapped him in place. "Good luck," she said close to his ear.

"Yeah, sure."

Cox looked down at him. "You okay this morning? You seem miffed about something."

Maybe now I should ask for a raise, he thought. *Maybe now is the time to talk about royalties.* "Nothing," he said. "I just want to get on with it."

"Okay, then. Here we go. Breathe deep and relax, breathe and relax...." Cox's voice droned on, designed to soothe. Benny focused on the monotony of the sound, the rise and fall of his chest, the hum of the helmet coming on, multiplexing the signals coming from his brain, multiplexing Benny Kingman with sixty cycle to disk, then down the hall to the room where the giant klystrons glowed purple and it was very hot, and—

—he wondered why he had suddenly become so concerned with money, because it really wasn't important at all. They were all together again, and there was news, if only he could figure it out. If only he could communicate. I'm flying along at the speed of light, a complex distribution of photons like the rest of you and I would like to talk. I would like someone to listen to me.

There was white noise, and then a long screech like an injured bird. Harsh words without meaning. It was a quantum electro dynamical language, universal, crossing borders between rock and dust and hot gas. I am energy, alive, going on a journey. Come with me, share the experience while we can before our paths diverge and you are gone.

The screech was gone, replaced by pops and cracklings of colliding dust particles and the high pitched roar that was the torn flesh of a star swallowed by a black hole in the center of the galaxy. For a nanoinstant, Benny felt terror. I cannot help you. The murmurings returned, along with whistlers from the swirling storms of Jupiter and the buzz of charges trapped by magnetic fields, and then something new. It was high-pitched, a three note pattern, descending, ascending, holding, then a repeat followed by a pause. Quickly it was back again: a G, then F or maybe F-sharp, back to G, again a short plaintive burst of energy, clear and undistorted. It had not traveled far.

You are no star or swirling dust, he thought. *There is no violence in your voice. Life is energy, I am energy and I hear you. Stay with me while you can, but soon I will be where I cannot hear your call.*

The new modulation became a warble, up and down, a delicate articulation of something lovely, something alive reaching out to him and Benny felt excitement, new self awareness as if a part of him had just caught up with the complex of photons nearing Jupiter. Over the cracklings, screams and low moans Benny focused on that one beautiful tone without understanding its source or meaning, yet feeling a happiness he'd never felt before. He clung to it as a drowning man clings to a floating scrap of paper, his mind racing in a rage of feelings, pouring himself outwards, downwards, inwards, the tone changing with him, speeding up the pattern, adding subtle new modulations. Surely this was intelligence, but saying what?

There was black void and sudden silence. The voices were gone, and he was alone again as the receiving dish of the Jovian probe routed him along a myriad of optical fibers. He was buried alive in a waveguide, and then the control panel was in front of him, changing colors as he went through the systems check. It had been only a tone, a music that had stirred his soul into empathy—for what? What had he felt? Loneliness? Suffering? It had responded to him, changing as he thought at light speed. Now it was gone and he was locked in a mechanical toy of his own invention, a thing of metal, sensors and superconducting microelectronics. Benny struggled for control, worried about what Janet and Cox might see at the other end of his ethereal lifeline. There could be heart irregularities, as in his panic during the first transit. They might immediately abort the test; there was too much at stake here and a part of him wanted desperately for it to succeed. Another part of him wanted to be free in space with the others, especially the one making that beautiful sound.

He shut off the receiver and completed the systems check, activated the Langmuir probe for a particle density measurement, rotated the magnetometer to get a field vector scan for a portion of the orbit. Soon he would transmit, and in thirty minutes real time be staring up at the lights of the laboratory again. He would have a sandwich at Gerraldo's and go home to an empty apartment. A thought occurred to him, something so contrary to the program that he felt fear, and then elation. The receiving antenna was at his control. He could make a quick antenna scan of the space around him, out of contact with earth. In the robot, would he cease to exist, even in the superconducting memories? If I am energy I cannot die, he answered to himself. I can only change form. Still, moving the antenna was risky, a mechanical process requiring fine-tuning for re-lock on earth, but programmable. It was a calculated risk, in search of cosmic music.

A metallic finger moved to the control panel, keyed in a one hundred-eighty-degree antenna about-face from earth, followed by a scan along the plane of the ecliptic in an ellipse reaching ninety degrees above and below the plane, followed by return to earth contact and immediate transmission. The hand of the robot paused, and then plunged to the control panel.

There were crackles, moans and white noise, and then, for only an instant, the sweet modulation of something living, searching for him still, a frantic cry, white noise, nothingness, blackness, and then the cry again, fading in the babble of the universe as he was suddenly hurled unwilling on the never-ending journey back to earth, screaming to whoever would listen.

"Don't go!"

Jane was shaking him when he opened his eyes. "Benny, Benny! Come out of it. Wake up!"

He blinked his eyes, saw Cox glaring down at him. "What the hell happened out there? We nearly lost contact with the probe!"

Benny rubbed his eyes, sat up and lied for the first time in his life. "Nothing happened," he said calmly. "Everything went fine, but I think you brought me back a few seconds early. It surprised me."

"We're barely getting magnetometer data, the signal's way down and you're telling us nothing happened? The antenna has moved while we were out of contact, and we didn't do a thing here." Cox, hands on hips, gave him a dark look of suspicion.

Benny looked straight into the man's eyes. "I'm telling you, nothing happened. It was perfect, all of it, No problems. Check the lab receiver. The problem must be there."

"No," said Cox thoughtfully. "It could also have been reflections. Europa made a transit just below you when we lost lock. A reflection could have scattered from the probe and confused the power-sensor servo. The signals are so weak at that distance."

"I felt no confusion or signal loss. I was ready to transmit when you suddenly jerked me back. The problem has to be at this end." Benny was surprised by the calmness and sincerity in the sound of his voice.

"Whatever," said Cox. "I'm going over this gear with a fine-toothed comb before it's a go again. And I'm committed to a complete test by Friday to keep our funding on track. That's if you're up to it, Benny. We need you at a hundred percent."

Benny smiled at Cox and shook his head slowly. "I told you I feel fine, and I'm ready to finish the job. Now when do we go?"

Cox thought, eyes darting around the room. "I'll bring in another receiver tonight and check it out. We can be ready by the day after tomorrow."

"Fine," said Benny. "I'd like to take tomorrow off and get some rest for it, if that's okay?"

"Sure," said Cox, still looking grim. "Janet and I will handle everything here and you take care of yourself."

"I'll do that, Doctor Cox, and I'll see you both Thursday morning." Benny got off the couch and walked out of the laboratory, leaving them arguing about deadlines, and maybe about him. He went to Gerraldo's for a sandwich and coffee, and then took the shuttle home. The phone was ringing when he entered the apartment, and he let it ring itself into silence. He took the receiver off the hook and left it that way.

Benny cleaned up his table, made a careful record of his tests on the new HRSI articulator and put his notes in the bottom of a bureau drawer. He cleaned his apartment from top to bottom and washed two weeks' worth of breakfast dishes, went outside and walked to a park to sit on a bench for two hours, watching the birds pursue their lives. Beautiful music filled him up. For the first time, it seemed, he noticed the trees and flowers and green grass. It was all beautiful, and the sunlight felt warm on his face. At dusk he returned home, locked himself in and sat in an overstuffed chair staring at a blank television screen, not consciously aware of thought, but in a deep day-dreaming state he could not recall when he finally went to bed.

The dream he remembered had sounds: screeches and wails and a beautiful warbling tone that made his heart sing even in deep sleep. It was a dream of music, an orchestration of cosmic proportions, passionate and angry, but with gentle subtle harmonics speaking of an energy unending, changing in form, of life everlasting in an infinite whole. He awoke twice, willing himself to sleep again, and returning to the music.

At daylight sleep fled. Benny ate toast, drank coffee and the walls closed in on him. He caught the shuttle to downtown Atlanta and spent the day lost in crowds of people, alone in a sea of humanity, each drop pursuing a private course. He did not, could not feel he was a part of it. Somehow he felt alien, could not make conscious contact with another person who would respond to him, yet something out there in the blackness of space *had* responded to him, had cried out in despair when he was rushed away.

Towards evening he shivered at the shuttle stop for half an hour before his shuttle arrived, going straight to his apartment and climbing into bed in darkness, fully clothed. Mercifully, sleep came and he dreamed about flying free in the vacuum of deep space, surrounded by voices calling to him, and then a pure, melodic tone.

Towards morning, rising to a state near wakefulness, he made an important decision about his life.

* * * * * *

"The receiver checks out fine," said Cox. "I've massaged the program to lock the antenna except on our command, so we shouldn't have the problem we had last time. The orbit adjustment was right on the money and you'll have a perigee at twelve-hundred miles above the surface of Europa at the end of the charge density mapping sequence. The spectrophotometer and emission spectra measurements are entirely up to you and HRSI on any surface features you find interesting. Otherwise, enjoy the ride. Put everything else out of your mind, Benny, and focus on those measurements. NASA has big money riding on this job. Are you ready for it?"

"Let's get going," said Benny softly, the shadow of the helmet falling on his face as Janet lowered it over his head. He breathed in her perfume deeply and exhaled once, twice, forcing himself to relax, controlling his excitement, his anxiousness to depart. Janet looked closely at him, put a hand on his and squeezed.

"You come back to us, now," she said, frowning.

Why? He thought. "I'll be fine," said Benny, "and I buy dinner tonight for all of us."

"It's a date," said Janet, without a smile. Benny closed his eyes, breathing deeply again as the multiplexer hummed into life, drawing him out of himself, mixing, modulating the being of Benny Kingman, and preparing him for the powerful carrier wave now beaming towards Jupiter from the roof of the laboratory. "You take care of yourself," he mumbled. And his last waking sense was the smell of her, and then—

—he was a complex of photons hurrying at light-speed towards a planet that had failed to become a star, towards a tiny nearby moon with a surface like etched, cracked glass, and around him was the hiss of plasma wind.

The sun cried out to him in a burst of protons from a flare, moaning in its rapid dispersion within the earth's magnetic field, and then he was hurtling outwards alone in the early stage of transit. Somehow it was different this time; he had a clearer sense of consciousness, of self, as if suddenly the whole Benny were participating in the event. He did not feel alone. *I'm not just along for the ride*, he thought. *This time there is purpose.* His subconscious core bathed itself in the timeless, meaningless hiss, patiently yet alertly, expectantly awaiting what was certain to come after he escaped the earth's magnetosphere.

An eternity later it came to him, the shrieks and wails from afar, the symphony that thrilled his soul. Yes! I am here again. *Hear me*, he thought, knowing full well that for most of them outside the narrowly focused beam he rode it would never be so. But there was another he waited to hear, something close that sang in pure tones rising and falling sweetly ahead of him in his crawl towards the probe, so near and yet so far, a tiny distance to be reached over an infinity of time's passage. He waited, impatience growing, willing it to happen. *I have returned for a reason*, he thought, *and you must still be there.* He remembered his feeling during that modulation, and—

—It burst upon him like a chorus of flutes, trilling, and then sliding up to a single high frequency and down again to frolic in lower registers. So strong, so pure without distortion as if it were riding on the droning wave-ship that carried him. He was happy, content, and delirious with feeling, all in an instant, yet he knew it would pass quickly as it had before, even in retarded time. *Can you feel the carrier wave; are you answering to it or the tiny modulation that is me? I cannot communicate. I am only photons.*

The song was gone.

He was a machine again.

For a moment the robot sat inertly in front of the control panel while the modulated currents that were Benny's conscious mind whirled in superconducting circuitry, searching blindly for interface, prodded and pushed by a program written on a cluttered table far, far away. The panel lit up in blue, green, yellow and red as he fought to remember his tasks, remembering, inching HRSI's articulator to the panel and running through the checklist stored in the brain of the machine. Something was terribly wrong. Something was missing. He studied the panel, recalled his last transit, the steps in the sequence, and an articulator moved across the panel. A thin finger paused above a status switch. Antenna Op. The light was off, yet it was not on the checklist. But it *had* been, before now. He punched in an antenna ready command and got a rude error signal. The antenna was locked in, frozen in place. Now he remembered. *There won't be problems like last time,* Cox had said. *I massaged the program.*

Benny/HRSI punched Transmit Ready, hammering it off as soon as the red light appeared. *They will be watching carefully, now. Control yourself. No emotions from what's left of Benny or they'll abort the mission. Total control, and I'll have an hour from contact break off to get it done. So give them something to do.* He shut off the receiver, activated the Langmuir probe, the rotating crystal spectrometer, and brought the guiding telescope image to a focus on the screen in front of him. He rotated the device to a plain on the Europan surface only a microsecond away. He keyed in an auto-scan in ten degree steps. The spectrometer diligently obeyed.

HRSI jacked in the umbilical and stood up to open the EVA port, looking straight down at the surface of Europa and up to find the antenna turned a hundred and eighty degrees away from it. *If you're going to lock the antenna on me I guess I'll just have to do a manual override*, he thought, and gave the orders to HRSI. The machine pulled a tool kit from the wall and clambered outside to grasp the antenna base. *So strong, so clear*, he thought. *It must be coming from the surface of Europa.* He found the servo and disconnected it, loosened eight bolts to free the fist-sized goniometer at the base. The antenna moved, and he was committed.

They would know in thirty minutes that he had lost them. He had lost himself, his only being now swirling in the superconducting mind of the machine. Sixty minutes real time for light to travel to and from earth from here. He stood up, grasped the antenna and turned it towards Europa, searching for a pure tone. At this distance what was the solid angle at the surface? What was the arc length: meters, or kilometers? The antenna moved roughly, with agonizing slowness. A cacophony of screams from the star that had failed to be, and then he was looking at the little moon's surface, north to south, west to east. Slowly, lost forever from earth, he searched for a warbling song.

And was surprised when he found it.

The signal was so strong he experienced a momentary lapse of consciousness and identity that frightened him even as he locked the goniometer in place. He crawled to the port. HRSI was suddenly sluggish and dropped the tool kit, dumbly watched it float away. One arm locked as it tried to slide inside, jamming it in place. Benny screamed the mental commands, heaved the machine out and tried again, overload input garbling all he tried to say. The machine finally tumbled inside in disarray. Benny found himself upside-down, staring at the control panel, an articulator outstretched, thumping madly at switches.

And although he had planned to do it, it was only on his third try that he punched TRANSMIT with the antenna still pointing at its chosen target on Europa, and dumped the superconducting memory of the machine.

* * * * * * **

He was a life-giver, and the colony was growing again after a dormancy of a thousand years. The heat of chemical reactions softened the buried gourd, a single root carrying energy meters beneath the bottom of the frozen crevasse, absorbing the new moisture there and carrying it to the long stalks and tendrils of the colony. There were many like him, and Benny was a part of them all, swirling in organic superconducting minds awakening as one to begin the new cycle. Tendrils reached out to touch and entwine, sharing warmth, stroking each other to stimulate the pulses of once soil-locked Europan water flowing to the coiled, meter-high stalks where already the swellings had appeared.

Nearby the first flower had opened, spreading a lavender head in search of light spewing from a distant yellow star. Its giver warbled a song of new life. Benny shared the pleasure, the exhilaration of being, the harmonics of awakening to self-consciousness, awareness of touch and surging currents and the deliciousness of the heat within him. They were one, welcoming him, and yet the life-givers were individual in the songs they sang. The configurations of their currents were different, but joined together in a resistance less whole to produce a symphonic statement of pureness and beauty that burst forth from the icy fissure to sail away among the stars.

A stalk quivered, and then there was a sudden spasm. Benny reached out one long tendril of his new body and felt a crack in the swelling there, felt the velvety petals folded in a cone, pushing outwards like a spear. The cone spread open as it emerged, and he placed the tip of the tendril at its center as the colony hummed a single, throbbing tone. The gourd pulsed, and he felt the surge of hot liquid within him, the first drops emerging from the tendril's tip. Drop by drop he fed the new flower as a chorus rose in triumph around him. *I am a giver of life, and this is my gift to you.*

The flower drank greedily, quickly, until the stalk from which it grew suddenly stiffened, straightening out, and pushing the bloom upwards to the edge of the crevasse. The tendril fell away after a final caress. Benny felt joy, pride, and fulfillment of purpose, and the others joined him in an ascending, trilling melody to celebrate the birthing.

TRICKS

The lights had been on for one minute and Brenda was already sweating. The cool breeze from the air-conditioning vent above her head had little effect. Norm saw it and rushed to her, powder brush in hand. "Nerves, dear? You're making streaks," he gushed.

Brenda looked up from her notes while Norm fussed over her. "Just do your job," she said, and he gave her a pouty look. She was already plugged in and Arlene's voice was suddenly there.

"He's settled in the Green Room. Brenda, and so is Tasha. They were doing a deep breathing thing when I left."

"What's the mood? Will they talk?" said Brenda. Norm looked at her expectantly, and then realized she was talking to her mike.

"No problem with Drax and that ego of his, but Tasha seems quiet," said Arlene. "Beautiful little thing, but she needs some sunshine and food. You might have to drag her out at first. I show two minutes to air time. Getting Drax now. Go easy with him, Brenda. After all your on-camera arguments with him, and the stuff in the magazines, it's no secret what you think of his work."

No secret, indeed. Her campaign against graphic humiliation and torture of women had focused on Drax's films and nearly bankrupted the man, yet he'd been quick to accept Arlene's ratings-hungry invitation. Too quick, she thought. Arlene called her paranoid when she ordered an armed guard to be present in the studio for tonight's show.

Drax had been cordial enough when he'd arrived, coat draped European-style across broad shoulders, but he leaned too near for his greeting and she smelled his foul breath.

"Thank you for this opportunity, Brenda. Despite our differences I have always been strongly attracted to you. There is nothing more exciting to me than a woman who has both talent and strength."

"Alas, we do poorly as slaves," said Brenda, and turned away from him. Tasha had given her a horrified look. The poor girl probably spent half her time chained up in the play dungeon Drax was rumored to have in his bleak mansion in the hills. Brenda wanted to buy her a hamburger and put some color back in her face.

Norm stepped back to inspect his art, limply flicked the brush at her and went back to join the other camera man in the gloom off-set. A few technicians and security man Cassidy lounged on metal bleachers at the back of the studio and were the only audience. The show was live, and it was now exactly midnight. Brenda checked her face in the monitor. No streaks.

The set was simple, a long, narrow desk with facing chairs on a dais and a backdrop panel painted black and covered with stars and nebulae. The lighting was kept low to keep a somber mood during the show, since Brenda's interviews were seldom happy occasions and often provocative.

She eased back in her chair, arranged the note cards in her lap and licked her lips, looking up as the red light on center camera went on. Norm counted down the last few seconds on his fingers, and then pointed at her. "Good evening," she said, and looked straight into the camera. "I'm Brenda Morelos, and this is Midnight Journal. Our guests tonight are award-winning horror film director and actor Andrew Drax, together with his lovely co-star of three films, Tasha Dent. Our subject for this midnight hour is fear: what causes it, how it is translated to the screen, and why people flock to theatres by the millions to be frightened out of their wits. And I can think of no better person to discuss this than the director and star of 'Rivers of Blood', Mister Andrew Drax."

Arlene pulled aside a corner of the backdrop curtain and Andrew Drax strode onto the set, smiling thinly and extending his hand towards her. Tall, gaunt yet handsome and now dressed in black pants and turtleneck with a cape draped over one arm, he leaned over as Brenda forced herself to raise a hand to him. He took it in his own slender fingers, kissed it, and she felt something sharp rake across her palm, making her shudder. He grinned close to her face, and she saw two small fangs in his mouth. Brenda recoiled and laughed as Andrew turned to snarl at the camera. "Always in character," she said. "Welcome to our show, Andrew."

Drax sat down in the chair opposite her, their knees almost touching. He fumbled at his mouth with his right hand, removed the fangs, and held them in his palm for a camera close-up. "Custom made, sharp and hard enough to punch holes in pop cans. A realistic trick, don't you think?"

Brenda checked the palm of her hand. There was a narrow, red welt there, but the skin wasn't broken. "And frightening," she said. *Rude*, she thought.

"The teeth? Not at all. If you saw me wearing them all evening at a party you'd find them amusing, perhaps absurd, and even boring. Another demonstration, if I may. Shake hands with me. Yes, just hold out your hand."

Brenda did so timidly, and Drax sniffed the air near her fingers. *A strange reaction*, she thought.

"You hesitate," said Andrew. His face seemed flushed under the lights, his eyes a dark brown near black. "Why?"

"I—I'm not sure what's going to happen next."

"Ah, but of course you've met my right hand, so we'll try the left one." He withdrew his left hand from beneath the cape in his lap and thrust it forward. It was grey, veined red with long, gnarled fingers and nails like bear claws. Brenda jerked her hand back so hard her note cards fell on the floor in disarray, and she heard laughter from the gloom beyond the set. Her heart pounded in fury and then Arlene's voice was in her head again.

"Quit frowning, Brenda. This is the King of Horror, so play along, laugh it off. This is GREAT stuff!"

Brenda laughed nervously. "I just aged ten years. What *is* that thing?" *You arrogant prick!*, she thought.

"A glove", said Andrew, pulling the thing from his hand. "Molded silicon rubber, with some artistic embellishments. Even the nails are soft, yet it frightened you." He held it out for another close-up.

"I'll say it did. Here, let me get myself together again." Brenda retrieved her note cards and ordered them in her lap.

"Nice touch," said Arlene in her ear.

"What *did* frighten me, Andrew?"

"Surprise—surprise at seeing something totally outside your everyday experience, a thing unknown to you, a thing unexpected. It could be a normally friendly dog that acts fierce, or a sudden thumping in the basement of your house in the middle of the night, or vampires in dark alleys. We fear what is different, the things foreign to us that we don't understand. Add to that the possibility of physical injury or death and you have horror."

"And you are called the King of Horror right now," said Brenda, forcing a smile.

"Thank you," said Andrew. "I owe a lot of it to my cast and crew. They are wonderful, all of them."

Brenda ignored his condescending smile. "It seems to me the horror is in the violence, torture and death. There's a lot of that in your films, Andrew. I've often wondered why people pay money to see that."

Andrew made a teepee with his hands and rested his chin on it, boring into her with coal black eyes. His smile had disappeared. Brenda felt her face flush, and she glanced at her little audience in the studio. Cassidy saw it and raised an eyebrow at her.

"Catharsis," said Andrew.

"I don't understand." Norm was waving at her. One minute to commercial break.

"All of us fear injury or death. Even you, Brenda. Add that to another basic fear, the anticipation of pain with a slow, agonizing death coming as a release. It's the anticipation that's horrifying, and it's all happening to someone else up there on the screen, not to you sitting comfortably in the audience. The thing you fear kills someone, but you survive, you go home safely, untouched by that which terrifies you. It is a catharsis of the fear that haunts you. You have triumphed over it." Andrew's nasty smile returned.

Many would call it gratuitous violence and gore, with the victims predominantly women. Let's talk about this when we come back." Brenda turned quickly to the camera. "This is Brenda Morelos for Midnight Journal, and we'll return after this announcement."

The red light on camera center flicked off and Norm rushed to her with his powder brush for a touch up. Drax required no work, for his face, though flushed, was dry.

Andrew leaned forward, and their knees touched. Brenda shivered at the contact. "You still don't think much of my films, do you, Brenda?"

"I think they encourage violence and torture of women by unstable people, Andrew. I've been very vocal about that."

"And quite influential, I must say," said Andrew softly. He leaned closer and sniffed the air near her again. "Many of my best scenes have been cut from the last two films to get an R rating, specifically *because* of your influence. Are we going to talk about that? Will we discuss the products boycott you've urged on your followers, keeping my work off television and forcing me to seek foreign investors for my films? Others do what I do. Why do you persecute *me*, Brenda? I'm really quite fond of you."

"I didn't intend to talk about the negatives this time. I think I've done enough." Brenda studied her note cards, not looking at him.

"Good, so then we'll stick to fear. By the way, you'll be pleased to hear that I'm retiring from film-making."

"What?" Now she looked at him, her mouth open in surprise. "Will you announce that during this segment?" Her heart pounded with excitement.

"Of course, if you bring it up." Andrew grinned at her.

"Watch Norm, Brenda, and keep down the hostility," said Arlene in her ear. "Great, so far, and I'm getting Tasha in two minutes for entrance before the next break."

"Got it," mumbled Brenda. Norm was counting down, and then the red light was on as she faced the camera.

"Welcome back to Midnight Journal. We're discussing fear and horror in film-making with Andrew Drax, director of 'Rivers of Blood'. Tell me, Andrew, what is your definition of gratuitous violence, the kind of thing that some people accuse you of having in your films?"

Andrew looked strangely pleased by her question. "Gratuitous violence serves no purpose; it does not advance the story. I've always been careful to avoid it. Any student of film will tell you the violence I use is always an integral part of the plot."

"And why so much violence directed against women? I'll be asking Tasha how she likes being the object of so much torture."

Andrew laughed heartily, but it wasn't a pleasant laugh. "I'm sure you'll find men and women equally represented. As a woman you naturally recall the female victims more vividly because you identify with them, and also their fears. Childhood fears, especially."

"Childhood fears?"

"Oh yes. In this there are differences between men and women. For example, a little boy is taught to—"

"Keep him going," said Arlene. "Stall if you have to. Drax must have locked the door coming out of the Green Room and Tasha isn't answering to anything. I have to get a key."

"—and that sub-conscious fear of failure, linked to the father, can lead to a dangerous, paranoid personality," continued Andrew. "Like it or not, little girls and boys are treated differently, with different expectations."

"Hang on. I'll have her out in a minute. Watch Norm," said

Arlene.

"And then there are fears from unique childhood experiences. Can you think of one from your own childhood, Brenda? Andrew was studying her now, smiling faintly, eyes glittering disturbingly in the lights.

Momentarily distracted, she quickly said, "I was attacked by a neighbor's dog when I was four. I've been afraid of dogs ever since then."

"It's a common fear, Brenda, and you can be reminded of that instant, that horrible moment, with simple things." Andrew put the little fangs back into his mouth, leaned over and popped two contact lenses into his eyes with one hand. When he looked up his eyes were yellow with red capillaries crisscrossing the whites. He bared his fangs and hissed at her a foot from her face. His breath smelled metallic, and Brenda leaned back to escape it.

"Memories?" said Andrew.

"Not really. It's not the same," she said tiredly.

"Damn, she's asleep. Keep him going," said Arlene. "Two minutes to break."

"Oh dear, now I've bored you," Andrew said sadly. "Terror is such an individual thing, so difficult to achieve." He slapped his knee, and then shrugged. "Perhaps it's time for me to move on to other things, refresh myself, and get back to the roots of my art."

"Yes," said Brenda quickly. "You said during the break that you're retiring from films? Can this be true, after all the success you've had? I would think—"

"EIYEEEEEEEE!" Arlene's scream shattered her inner ear and Brenda jumped, startled, reached for the earphone. "Oh my God, my God, my God, oh—oh—the blood. She's soaked in blood! And her poor throat—Norm, someone, get back here!"

Bleachers clattered as two men rushed from the studio.

Andrew was leaning close, sniffing again, his little faux fangs sparkling. "Is something wrong? You were just startled by something."

"I—oh, I just got word that Tasha Dent won't be joining us. She has suddenly become ill." Brenda's heart was thumping, and sweat burst from every pore in her body.

Andrew Drax sniffed at her again and smiled, his face two feet from hers. She could smell his terrible breath and something else, a sharp, musky odor. "Poor Tasha. She is such a fragile thing, but she'll recover quickly. As I was saying, it has all become common and boring, and I need a change of life beginning tonight, a return to the quiet of the countryside with intimates to think and write and feel the cool grass on my bare feet again. I need recharging, a rejuvenation to continue my art. So this is my farewell performance, dear Brenda, and a goodbye to all my fans, at least for now. There was so much more I could have given them, but critics like you wouldn't allow it, and I'm disappointed in that. Very disappointed."

Arlene's voice was shrill. "It has to be Drax; he was the only one in here with her! Butch, call the police. Norm, Joel, Cassidy, watch him close and jump him if he makes one move at Brenda! He must have a knife on him."

Brenda pressed back in her chair. In her peripheral vision she saw Joel leave his camera, Cassidy's hand on his holstered revolver as they began inching towards the set. Norm stood transfixed, chewing on his hands. The commercial break was forgotten, both cameras running.

The color was suddenly gone from Andrew's face, changing to grey in the lights, skin rippling around his cheekbones, and his voice was now husky. "One last trick for the cameras, Brenda, one last special effect for the fans," he growled.

The ripples in his cheeks rushed towards the nose and met explosively with a crackling sound. His forehead disappeared as a glistening muzzle thrust forward, part cat, part wolf, yellow eyes now huge and blazing, the prop fangs exploding into dust at the ends of three-inch canines glistening wetly. He lunged and grasped her throat with long fingers ending in sharp, curved nails before she could even think to cry out.

Joel and Cassidy charged the set as she finally let out a strangled cry, but Andrew only waved one hand and the two men were lifted into the air and slammed with great force into the far wall of the studio. Norm screamed, but stood by his camera, aiming it.

What had once been Andrew Drax snarled at the cameras. "Now *this* is magic realism, folks!" he growled, and then turned and tore out the entire left side of Brenda's neck with a single savage twisting bite.

It was strange how there was no pain, only numbness and sudden cold throughout her body. Brenda fell to the floor on her back, looking up at the ceiling while Arlene shouted in her ear, "Brenda? Brenda! What's *happening?*" She grasped her neck, felt life pulsing into the palm of her hand in great spurts. The creature that was Andrew Drax, mouth dripping with her blood, knelt beside her, face close. Behind him, studio doors banged open and there were outcries.

"Since our first interview, when I first smelled your delicious fear," said Drax, "I've desired you as much as I do Tasha. I will return for both of you when it is time, and we will have an eternity together, and then you will truly understand and savor the sweet taste of human terror."

"Get down on the floor, or I'll shoot!" someone shouted.

Andrew Drax raised his arms and changed again, and as the final bit of old life ebbed from Brenda's ruined neck she saw him disappear as a column of green mist into the air conditioning vent above her.

SKIRMISH AT HEKLARA

Blood-red light spilled on hot faces as the echelon of Drop Probes turned north on final approach. Giant Procirus rose to greet them, to warm the faces of the many who might die that day. The three-hundred troops inside the probes were young, hand-picked and just out of jump school. It was their first day of real combat, not the usual mop-up operation. Strong resistance was expected, and the sharp stench of fear filled their nostrils as they made a final weapons check. They joked nervously about snake odors, and made bets as to which squad would make it first to the airfield beyond Heklara. The reptilian invaders who had occupied the Terran colony of Torontos were now in retreat after a three year war. Payback time had finally arrived.

Velora Nett snapped a black magazine into her MAW-44, and released the safety. The assault module pulled back on her neck, and her spine was hurting. She let out a deep lungful of air with a whoosh, swallowed hard to keep down the contents of a pre-dawn breakfast and tried not to look at the others. *We're all scared shitless*, she thought. *Why can't we admit it?*

"Up and on! Two minutes to drop!" Colonel Teg Andrist walked down the center aisle as they stood up clumsily, turning to present modules for inspection. There was a quick inspection of thrusters and para-sail pack, a word of encouragement, a pat on the helmet. As a squad leader, Velora was first in line. With the others watching, Andrist turned her around to face him, put his hands on her shoulders. "Wish your dad was alive to see this. Kick some snake ass today, Corporal!"

"Yes sir!"

And then he continued down the line. "You are jump group one of the twenty-first Hestidian airborne division. You are the best there is!"

"Yes sir!" they all screamed.

"I know this as fact, because I have personally trained all of you. You are the Banchees, and today you will kill Kraa. Let me hear it!"

"Kraaaaaa!" they screamed in unison. For that instant, the fear was gone. In another instant, it would return.

"Load and lock!" Andrist stalked back towards the control room as thirty MAW-44 bolts slammed home. "Drop position—move!"

Clumsily they stood, leaning forward against the heavy weight of the modules on their backs, hunching over to carefully step down into the drop bay running the entire length of the probe. They sat down, legs stretched before them.

"Hook up!" Andrist opened the control room door and stood in the doorway, bracing himself. "Thirty seconds to drop!"

Velora plugged in her thruster, clutched her heavy weapon to her and remembered the look on her father's face the day she had graduated, the day he had come up to the platform, his uniform covered with battle ribbons, eyes glistening as he pinned the hawk and lightening bolts on her lapel. Her brother Tal, dear gentle Tal who should have been in her place, watched from the audience, came up afterwards to give her a kiss and a hug, and then disappeared into the crowd, away from his father's stern face. She had been given special applause, for she was only the third woman to graduate from jump school. Now she wondered if she was the only one left alive. She looked up at Colonel Andrist. *Someday*, she thought, *I will command a drop.*

"Visors down! And kill Kraa!"

The floor dropped beneath them and a shockwave of air hit their chests as thrusters came on. Velora swung to her right, taking her central place in the delta-wing formation dropping towards the valley below. They had come out at seven thousand feet, heading north. Low-lying hills were on either side of them and straight ahead the village of Heklara, now occupied by retreating Kraa survivors left to protect their last airfield beyond. She counted three Kraa Gull fighters and two S-10 Chugs before the concrete strip was obscured by the village, and then they were coming in low, taking forward fire as the lead unit in, followed by nine other drops. They were The First. Velora felt pride surge within her, even as thermite fire rose to meet their attack.

A human being next to her exploded, spraying Velora with blood and shredded tissue. She gasped, aimed her weapon from the hip and fired a burst towards the Kraa perimeter around the village. Dust swirled from the steel splinters of the Reaper rounds she fired and a reptilian face disappeared in gore. She hit the ground on the run as the thrusters shut down, pounded on the release catch twice before the heavy module popped off, suddenly feeling light and fast and emptying two magazines as she moved forward. The Kraa were falling back towards the colony village they had occupied, and a moment later she was chasing them, looking straight ahead, not noticing the spider-traps opening up around them on the hillsides, spilling forth the hundreds of Kraa hidden there. She didn't notice until Reapers and Red-Dots were tearing into her squad from all sides, bodies exploding like bombs or bursting into flame. Everywhere she turned there were Kraa, firing at close range. Everywhere she turned was carnage, bleeding corpses that were once human beings she was responsible for. The Kraa streamed own hillsides from every direction, screaming victory, tearing at torn bodies with sharp claws.

And Velora Nett ran for her life.

She sprinted towards her right, around the base of a hill, shredding two Kraa coming at her and running like she had never run before. In only seconds it was suddenly quiet, except for the pounding of her boots on hard ground. No gunfire, no screams of death, only silence, but when she stopped she heard the faint shrill victory cries of the Kraa and knew full well what they were doing to the wounded or any other survivors. She ran again, followed the line of hills until she could no longer hear the horrible sounds of the Kraa, and hid herself between three large boulders near a summit overlooking the village. Deep in shadow, she cried bitterly. Her comrades were dead—and she had run away.

* * * * * * *

Night came, blessing her with darkness. Velora ate a cracker, drank some water and listened for the slightest sound. At midnight she heard something, a scratching on rock and then breathing. She leveled her weapon downhill towards inky darkness, held her breath and watched something crawl towards her. A face. Human. She called out softly, "Over here, quick, in the rocks!"

A boy, younger than herself, smeared with blood and dirt, scrambled up to her and collapsed at her side. "Oh, is it good to find someone else out here. I thought I was all alone." Immediately, with the sound of his voice and his delicate face, he reminded Velora of her younger brother.

"Where did *you* come from? I thought everyone else was dead!"

"I'm radioman for drop four. We got caught right in the middle. About half of our unit pulled back and got away with the rest of the drops, but I was forward with my Corporal when the snakes started coming out of the ground all around us. They got the Corporal, and I ran like hell. Most of their fire seemed directed towards the first units. Is that where you were?"

"Drop one. I'm Nett. Velora. Corporal. Your radio still work?" She pointed to the mound on his back.

"Haven't used it yet. Think we should try it?"

"No, we'll wait until light. The village is just over the hill, and I want to see what's going on first. You got a name?"

"Private Avan Hansold, maam. I've heard about you. Your old man's a general, or something."

"Was a general, Gera Twenty-Third Skyhawks Division."
Survived the war only to die of a heart attack, she thought. *Just as well. Now he doesn't have to know his daughter ran from a fight and left people to die.*

"First ones in on Torontos, when the Kraa first invaded in full force. Boy that must have been something."

"Yeah. Look, we've got to move to the top of the hill and see what's going on. You have maps?"

The boy nodded. "And a recorder. Sure looks bare up there. No cover at all."

"We'll drag some brush up with us, enough to cover up with if a Gull comes over."

They left the rocks, and crawled on hands and knees to the top of the hill. There was no dried brush to be found, and they huddled in a shallow depression on the summit. It was totally exposed to view from above as they peered down towards the village. Velora scanned the visible and infrared spectrum with her binoculars, sweeping the valley. Below her green figures moved on the hillsides, popping into the ground and out of view. In the village two Chugs were moving into a street facing the valley, and a crude barricade had been restored there. Figures scurried around in the village square, and then suddenly came together like a herd of animals being driven. Velora moved in with the binoculars and saw a group of villagers being herded by four Kraa. She saw children there. "Oh, oh, they've got civilians rounded up. And the Kraa are going back into their spider traps again. Do they *really* think that can work a second time? What we need to do is call down some microwave and boil those hills."

"So give me a frequency," said Avan.

"No call now. I don't like those civvies being down there. Another attack and they'll all be killed for sure. But set it for thirty-five-fifty-five, and be ready."

"Yes, ma'am."

She looked at Avan over her shoulder. "I hate that word. Call me Vel. Look, we can clean those hills with a call, but I need to see what they're setting up in the village. We've got to get closer, maybe even into town. You with me for that?"

"Not too crazy about it, but you're the Corporal."

"Good. Best to move in now and get settled before sunrise. Let's see those maps."

Velora pointed with gloved fingers. "Here, here and here is where they've dug spider traps. We'll want to bracket all these hills. Write down the coordinates now, so you'll be ready."

Avan did as he was told, quickly yet carefully. Velora watched him work, struck again by how much he reminded her of her brother: quiet, thoughtful, contemplating a drawing of his, or lost in music and a dream world taking him away from a father who talked only about war. Sweet Tal, who was supposed to be the warrior, but couldn't be. And then the Kraal invasion of Torontos Colony had come, and there was a war for a daughter to fight.

It remained to be seen if Velora Nett could be the warrior her father had expected. At the moment, she was filled with doubt.

They crawled back to the base of the hill and circled towards the airfield, staying high enough to see the entire village. Small fires burned along the airfield, dimly lighting a line of Kraa shelters. Guards walked randomly around a trio of Gulls parked nearby, and two missile and Gatling platformed Chugs blocked the main street of the town. Velora made notes on everything and checked coordinates on Avan's maps before they moved on. They came to a shed at the edge of town, behind a darkened house that had shown lights earlier in the evening after the Kraa had herded the civilians into it. There had been muffled shots, and later the Kraa had left. Something bad had happened in that place, but it was close and so they hid in the shed until just before dawn, and then scuttled to the house in hopes of getting a better look at the streets. What they got was a look at another horror of war.

The stench hit them as they entered by the back door of the unlocked building. It intensified as they worked their way cautiously down a darkened hall, past a small kitchen heaped with debris and garbage. It stung their eyes as they entered a larger room at the front of the house. The room glowed dull red in the light of pre-dawn, and they saw the slaughter that had taken place earlier, the pile of civilian bodies broken in pieces and scattered around the room. There were men, women and children, Torontons, all of them third-wave humans with large, dark eyes engineered especially for the weakly lit planet of a red dwarf. They had come here for a new life and found death instead, their blood now covering the floor and walls and windows of the house.

Avan turned and threw up in one corner of the room. He wretched and wretched until nothing more would come up, and then wiped his mouth on his sleeve, ashamed, and came back to Velora at a window facing the street. "Doesn't this have any effect on you, or is it just all in a day's work?" he asked bitterly.

"Lucky all I've had to eat in twelve hours is a cracker. Besides, seeing this makes it easier to kill Kraa when the time comes."

"Yeah? Well, it doesn't help me much, but then I'm not in for life. You career people are hard asses."

Velora looked at him sharply. "You don't know shit, private. And what did you expect from the Kraa? They happen to fond of killing, and right now I feel the same way."

"Oh, Jesus," said Avan.

"What the hell did you get into this war for?"

"Nobody asked me. I was drafted."

"Oh. Tough deal. But you and your radio are important to me right now, and I want you sticking it out, okay?"

"I'm still here, aren't I?"

"Get over here by the window, but keep low. There's a Chug up the street can look right in here. Another one left of me, just sittin' there. We've got to get a message out about those spider traps, so start your recorder and set up the transmission for a half-second pulse."

Avan did as he was told. "If they've changed the entry code since yesterday, we're dead." He punched in the code letters, set the beeper to indicate a coming transmission, and turned to hand Velora the recorder. She talked into it for nearly a minute, giving the coordinates of the hills, the approximate number of Kraa hidden there, the placement of Chugs in the town, and the fact they had found slaughtered citizens.

They waited. The engine of the Chug up the street suddenly growled into life. Velora peered over a window sill. "They're loading up. Supplies coming out of a house across the street, carried by civilians. Only a few Kraa guards—whoa!" She ducked her head down into the gloom. "Almost saw me. Looked right over here for a second. I see four guards, maybe a dozen civvies."

The radio chirped. Avan checked the return code showing on the display, then jacked in the recorder and with the push of a button transmitted Velora's one minute message in a single half-second burst. In a few minutes there was another chirp as the return message arrived. Avan listened intently, Velora still watching the street. "Vel, I've got Colonel Andrist here. He says sit tight. They're comin' in at oh-six-hundred, and he's called in a microwave sweep from low orbit at that time."

"Okay, we stick it out here," said Velora. *And do what?* she thought. *How do I make up for running from a battle? Die?*

There was a sound from the kitchen in the back of the house, a rattling sound, and then a crunch, like someone stepping on broken glass. In the gloom of the hallway a shadow moved.

Velora swung the MAW-44 towards the hallway, pressing her back against a wall. "Avan, stay right where you are."

His eyes were the size of a credit coin.

The shadow came slowly down the hall and paused at the edge of the room. Large, liquid eyes gleamed dully in pre-dawn glow. A tiny girl stood there, barefoot, filthy dress brief enough to show dirty arms and pencil-legs. Her thumb was in her mouth and she looked straight at Velora, considering her for a moment, and then walked over to the far corner of the room to rummage around under a pile of broken bodies. She pushed and tugged at something, came up with a blond-haired doll covered with blood. She hugged it to herself, and looked at Velora again with huge eyes.

"Oh, my God," said Velora. "That must have been her mother."

The little girl started back towards the kitchen, but stopped when Velora beckoned to her. "Come here, darlin'. I'm a friend, and we won't hurt you. Do you want something good to eat? Here." Velora took a ration bar out of her pocket and held it out to the girl. The child hesitated only an instant, then walked boldly over to Velora and took the bar from her hand. Only at that instant did her thumb come out of her mouth; she tore the wrapper off with her teeth, and began to eat. Velora stroked her hair, smiling at Avan. "Tough little kid, a real survivor. How long you been in here, hon'?"

The child remained silent and the ration bar quickly disappeared. She stood there waiting for more, and Velora gave it to her. "Can you talk to me?"

Silently, the doll hugged to her breast, eyes never leaving Velora's face, the little girl wolfed down the second ration bar. Velora sat the child down on the floor next to her, and peeked out the window again. "Still loading. More guards, now. I think they're getting ready to move out."

She checked her watch. "Under an hour until the attack and all we can do is sit here."

"That's just fine with me," said Avan jovially. "All this draftee wants is to get home alive."

"And I don't? That's pretty stupid, private." Velora kept the tone of her voice amiable. "I think the only difference between us is commitment."

"Maybe. I don't have to prove anything to anybody in this war. I serve my time, keep my skin on and go home. You career people, this is your life, all this killing. I think it stinks."

Velora stared at him coldly. "You think it's all about killing, is that it? Well let me tell you, private, this is my first major combat mission and I'm just as scared as you are, but I'm never going to get ahead in any game if I'm dead. As far as proving myself, I didn't do very well at that when I ran away from the fight yesterday."

Avan's cynical smile vanished in a blink. "Run away? What were you supposed to do, stay there and die? That's not commitment, that's stupid. People were running for their lives all over the place."

"Not corporals," said Velora, looking at the floor.

"Oh, shit," said Avan. "I rest my case."

Velora sniffed disdainfully. "You remind me of my brother, the would-be artist. Nice, gentle guy who hates everything my father ever stood for, and isn't afraid to say so. He was the one who was supposed to be the soldier, not me. But he's not here, and I am, and whatever happens I'll do what I have to do. Got that?"

Seconds stretched to one horrible moment of stunned silence, and then Avan smiled at her sadly, hands playing with the controls on the radio. "Yeah, I've got it. Among my several weaknesses, I also have a big mouth. I'm here too, Vel. I just want to go home alive."

"Okay, then, we just stay here quietly until our people are in the street. There aren't many Kraa out there once the hills are cleaned, but if we're spotted it only takes one salvo from a Chug, and they'll take us home in a bottle. And we've got this little girl here. She understands everything we're saying, you know?" She looked down at the tiny child snuggled against her, a death-grip on the doll with one hand, the thumb of the other firmly locked in a speechless mouth. The pretty head had turned again towards the bloody remains in one corner of the room. Velora turned her around, hugged her tightly, looked into those sad, dark eyes and swallowed hard.

"God, Avan," she whispered, "she's only a baby."

Velora checked her watch. Only forty-five minutes until the microwave burn.

But from the instant she looked at the watch, it was only fifteen minutes until their own private war with the Kraa began.

* * * * * * *

In all the horror she had dozed, awakening with a start when Avan prodded her. He was right next to her under the window, whispering frantically into her ear. "Vel, wake up, there's screaming out in the street!"

She jumped to a crouch so quickly the child nearly fell over, crying out in surprise. It was the first sound she had made. Velora peered over the window-sill, saw a small group of civilians in a cluster in the middle of the street, surrounded by six, and armed Kraa. Women and two older children. The Kraa were poking them with their weapons, moving them across the street in a group and directly towards her hiding place. Down the street the crew of the idling Chug was climbing up onto the machine and dropping down inside it. Directly in front of her the engine of the previously silent Chug roared into life and a snake-like arm reached out to slam shut the entrance hatch. The vehicle lurched forward and rolled quickly down the street to her left.

The cluster of terrified civilians drew nearer and Velora could hear the pleading of the women in their rough, Toronto dialect; "Please, leave us here and save your own lives. Not the children! Please, not the children!" A Kraa growl that was a laugh answered their cries for mercy, and Velora's face flushed with the sudden realization of what was about to take place. This room in which they had hidden themselves would soon be a killing ground again.

"Avan, get to the kitchen and don't fire until I do. They're coming in the front, six of them and a bunch of civvies. Hurry!"

Avan duck-walked across body parts and a slippery floor, dragging the radio behind him. He disappeared down the hallway. Velora put the little girl in the corner by the window and backed up against her, the MAW-44 covering the front door. Close to her back she felt the child shudder and cling to her.

There were footsteps by the door, and hysterical screaming over the growls of the Kraa. The door burst open and the civilians piled in, shrieking at the sight of what awaited them. The guards pushed in behind, teeth flashing from thick, reptilian faces. Women and children stumbled to the far corner of the room, huddling there as the guards, backs turned to Velora, raised their weapons, but at that instant one of the children saw her and pointed. All eyes moved towards Velora's grim face and the weapon she held as she snapped it on auto and sprayed the room with splinters of death. Four of the Kraa went down on their faces in a pulpy mess, and a five foot section of wall disappeared in smoke. The fifth guard had stationed himself by the hallway, too close to the civvies for a clean shot, and now he was turning, bringing his weapon to bear on her. There was an explosion from the kitchen, and the Kraa's chest erupted in a fountain of blood and shredded tissue. Avan. First kill.

"Avan!"

"Yo!"

"Take them out back to the shed *now*." Velora jumped up to look outside, and stared straight into the face of the sixth Kraa guard who had remained outside. His claw was a blur, coming straight through the window and grabbing her by the throat, pulling her up on her toes as spots of colorful light danced before her eyes. She rammed the MAW muzzle up under his chin, and emptied the magazine into his nightmarish head.

"Out the back, out the back!" she screeched at the civilians, and then coughed, grabbing at her throat to feel where the guard had clawed her.

The little girl darted around her and threw herself into the arms of one of the women whom she apparently recognized, the woman sweeping her up with a tearful cry. Women and children stampeded down the hall and out the back door. Outside, the Chug that had been passing by had now stopped, was backing up across the street and turning towards her. No rotating turret, but it was quickly coming into position for a shot. Velora sprinted from the room and down the hall, slamming back the door as she exited and saw Avan herding the civvies into the nearby shed. "This way!" she called to him, and he ran to follow her as she moved away from the shed. They had gone only twenty yards when the house behind them erupted in a ball of fire and shattered into flying embers.

Reaper fire ripped the ground around them and Velora cried out as a splinter tore across her left cheek. Avan was right behind her when she went in the front door of a house and straight out the back, hidden temporarily from view by the advancing Chug. They entered the neighboring house from the back and crouched in a kitchen, Velora pulling the radio from Avan's back. "Tell them what's going on, and get help! In a minute we're outta here!"

Avan was sending frantically when she looked out the front window in time to see the house next door destroyed by flames in withering fire from the Chug, which then turned and headed straight towards her. It pulled up close, nearly on the porch of the building. "Thermite!" she screamed. "Lock and load, and get out of here!" She pulled a magazine of Red-Dot thermite cartridges from her belt and slapped it into the MAW. Leaped back to the kitchen, where Avan was struggling to load up the radio. "Leave it! Let's go!"

Avan followed her out the door. "She turned right, crept up alongside the building. The rumble of the Chug filled their heads. She turned over her shoulder and mouthed, "Get anybody?"

"Think so," Avan mouthed back.

Velora peered around the corner of the building, jerked back and yelled, "Follow me!"

The explosion was deafening as the Chug fired, but by then they were climbing up onto it, and the building they had left disappeared in flames. Velora stuck her MAW muzzle in a forward port, fired three times, and there was screaming inside the chug. "Get the hatch, get the hatch!" she yelled.

Avan scrambled to the top hatch as it came open, a claw outstretched. He pointed his MAW straight down and emptied the entire magazine of thermite cartridges into the living space of the Chug. Flame shot skyward, and the claw disappeared. Suddenly the surface of the machine was too hot to stand on, but as Avan clambered down he suddenly yelled as blood spattered his left leg below the hip. He fell heavily at Velora's feet.

"Oh shit, oh shit, oh shit!" he cried, rolling in the red dirt. A reaper had hit him from the side, well above the knee, at close range.

A Kraa came around the Chug, his eyes turned down to sight on Avan, and Velora shot him with a Red-Dot at point blank range, the heavy body flashing to ashes in seconds.

Flames from Kraa cinders licked at her boots as she stepped around the Chug and saw a wedge formation of infantry moving towards her from the airfield. She emptied the Red-Dot magazine at them, five of the heat-seeking thermite projectiles striking home, but still the line of shrieking creatures came on. One hundred yards away, then seventy, then fifty. She fired furiously, mindlessly, magazine after magazine, then scrabbled at her belt and found nothing there. Avan moaned as she tore his ammunition belt from him and grabbed up his MAW. By the time she aimed it, the nearest Kraa was only twenty yards away. She sprayed their ranks with Red-Dots and Reapers, weapon on full-automatic, the Kraa now stumbling over the bodies of their dead but still coming, screaming as when they had come at her from the hills. Save one round for yourself, she remembered.

But as she grabbed up her last magazine the ground around the Kraa erupted in a wall of dirt, pieces of shattered bodies scattering in all directions. Two D-7's swooped low overhead, spraying the street with their Gatlings, on course to the airfield and releasing their missiles a second later. Flames from exploding Gulls belched into the sky as the two-place fighters turned and came back to tear up the street one more time. Velora crouched behind the Chug. They passed her, veering sharply left and right over a burning Chug at the edge of the village. A cloud of steam surged up from the hills, punctuated with small jets she knew were microwaved Kraa exploding like boiling water balloons in their spider traps. Through the roiling steam she saw the APDP's coming in, dropping wave after wave of troops that raced towards her. Only then did she glance up the street, and, seeing no life there, got down on her knees beside Avan.

One leg and side were soaked in blood, and his face was

ashen-grey. He mumbled something incoherent and his eyes rolled around, not seeing her. "Avan, they're here, they're here! Hang on!" She slapped his face once gently, then a second time hard. "Don't you *dare* die on me now! Don't you DARE!"

* * * * * * *

Colonel Andrist looked up from a table heaped with paper as Velora entered his Quonset to salute him smartly. He returned the salute and smiled. "Good to see you alive, Corporal. For a minor operation, this thing turned into quite a mess that could have been avoided with some accurate reconnaissance. Still have all your parts?"

Velora took a deep breath, her intestines a tangled knot sending pain messages up every nerve in her body. "Sir—there's something I have to tell you, and it's not easy. But I have to do it, sir, with your permission." She clutched at her pants legs to keep her hands from shaking.

Andrist leaned back in his chair, made a teepee with his hands in front of his mouth. "Go on," he said.

"During the attack yesterday, when we were surrounded, and all the Kraa were coming at us from the hills, sir, I—I ran. I ran from the fight, sir. I have no excuse. It was—a reaction. I felt I had to get out of there, and I did.

Andrist chuckled. "Right into the enemy camp, from the sound of it. Bad thing for them." His smile faded as he saw the look on her face. "What's your point, Corporal?"

Velora was near tears. "I acted in a cowardly manner, sir. That's my point." *And that is the end of my career,* she thought.

Andrist sighed. "Tell me what happened. Everything."

And so she told him everything, from the moment she fled until the time she was fighting from behind a burned-out Chug, expecting to die.

"Now I want you to think about what you just said, and tell me if those were the acts of a coward."

"Sir, I—"

"They were not, Corporal. I had three hundred people in that attack yesterday, and the only reason any of them came back was because the squad leaders knew when to get the hell out of there, and be alive to fight today. That's just smart, Corporal. You stayed alive, and today you engaged the enemy on your own terms. And shot hell out of them. And saved lives. *That's* why I'm putting you in for Officers Training School just as soon as I can find the damn form in this mountain of paperwork. Expect your orders to be cut within a week. You have a lot to learn, but you will be one damn fine officer someday. Anything else?"

Velora stared in disbelief. "No, sir. Uh—thank you, sir."

"Good. That private who was with you is outside. I'll decorate the both of you when we get back in orbit." Andrist stood up, reached across the table and touched her bloody cheek. "Nice wound, there. Rub a little salt in it, should make an attractive scar. Let the troops know their officer has seen combat. Dismissed."

Velora turned to leave, still stunned as Andrist said softly, "If the General had seen you out there today, he would've bawled like a baby."

Avan was lying on a stretcher near the Quonset, attended by a medic. Velora rushed to him and fell to her knees, shouting at the medic, "Is he all right? Is he all right?"

The medic looked bored. "He's going' home. My guess is he's got a five-year limp ahead of him."

"There goes my dancing career," said Avan weakly. "Guess I'll be an architect instead. Hey, look who's here!"

Velora looked up; found herself surrounded by the group of Torontons they had saved from slaughter. The little girl was with them and stepped forward with a shy smile. "Her name is Myreika," said a woman, "and she wishes to thank you."

The little girl put her bloody arms around Velora's neck, and pressed against her.

"Oh, darlin', you're okay, you're okay." Velora hugged the child fiercely, looked down at Avan's grinning face.

"Tough guy," said Avan.

Velora reached down and squeezed his shoulder. "Yeah. And you, too."

SHADOW BELAY

Jenny Dunn was only a hundred feet down from the summit spire of Harrison's Pinnacle when things started going wrong. She was making an easy descent along a shallow vertical crack when the rope suddenly went slack as she leaned back to move her left foot off a small nubbin. Her right foot slipped off the rock and she crashed stiff-legged to a wide ledge eight feet below, sending a shock wave through her body that snapped her teeth together and neatly clipped off a small portion of her tongue.

"What the hell was *that* all about?" she asked aloud.

The rock didn't answer, but held her firmly. Her tongue felt swollen; she tasted blood, and gently sucked on it. The fall had taken her slightly off course. She would have to climb up from the ledge, and then make a traverse on narrow descending slabs to reach the familiar route she had used for the ascent. Between the traverse and the ground below was fifteen hundred feet of clear air, and the fall had wiped out her trust in the permanent anchor point near the summit. Below her was another ledge, wider than the one she was on, but there was no obvious route beyond it and the distance was marginally large for her rope. Sliding off the end of the rope would be a bad end to a highly successful day, but an even worse fate would be hanging help-lessly at the end of the rope, waiting to inflate the male egos of a mountain rescue team.

Jenny scowled at the passive rock, popped a piece of hard peppermint candy into her mouth and was sucking on it thoughtfully when she suddenly saw a new route. It would take her even further away from familiar territory, but looked solid and the exposure was less than the other alternatives she had to consider. Still, it was a new route, and there would be a greater chance for errors. *It's fish or cut bait time, Jen. You want to be a name climber? Now's the chance. Cap the solo ascent off with pioneering a new descent route on the same day and people will be talking about you around here for years.*

Jenny Dunn clipped in and then climbed up smoothly and spider-like towards her right, using small flakes for foot and finger holds. One move flowed smoothly into the next, athletic precision developed over years of hard work and dedication. The climbing machine was working well again, and wished for an audience. She set up a belay point at the base of a thumb-like spire with a wide, vertical crack reaching up from a flat shelf that circled out of view towards the sun. The shelf would start the route and, close-up, looked even more appealing.

She started forward to examine it more closely, but a sudden, sharp tug on her harness pulled her backwards. Off balance, she grasped frantically for hand holds on the steep rock and fell to her knees. Her slide stopped only a foot from where she had fallen, and she pressed her face against the rough rock, fingers burning as adrenalin pumped through her body. Her breath came in short rapid gasps and the moment of fear disgusted her. *You're hyperventilating, stupid! Stop it!*

She held her breath for several seconds as her heart began to pound more slowly. Fear changed to anger, she turned sharply to glare towards her belay point. The rock, and even the air, was silent. She pulled on the rope, straightened out a villainous snarl, re-tied it to her harness and popped another candy into her mouth, crushing it with one bite. She had begun to turn upwards again when there was a new sound that stopped her abruptly. Something was moving above her near the top of the crack.

At first it sounded like a small animal with tiny claws, scratching on sandpaper. She listened quietly, frozen to the rock, and swallowed hard. A shower of dirt came down the crack, followed by a grinding sound, the rubbing of rock against rock. Jenny began to back away towards her belay point, then froze again as the rock she gripped tightly trembled against her fingers, and something heavy came crashing down the crack, pushing a jet of dirt and skree ahead of it. Dust filled her nostrils, choking her. Three watermelon-size boulders belched from the crack and sailed in graceful parabolic trajectories towards the ground far below.

Jenny coughed twice, and then moved without hesitation while the crack continued to spew dirt and skree in a slow stream clattering down the wall below her. Throwing her coiled rope up over her head and down around one shoulder she wrenched her anchor point free and flattened herself under a protective overhang on the shelf. She lay there for several minutes, feeling the coolness of the place. *Everything is falling apart.* For the first time in her life, Jenny Dunn felt the near presence of panic, and realized that taking the route she had contemplated would have been her last act in life.

She had left the summit less than an hour before. The climb up had been her best effort yet, with flawless technique and supreme confidence in herself; the culmination of years of hard training under the watchful eyes and caustic advice of the predominantly male climbing community. She had been filled with exhilaration as she proudly dug out the summit register at the bottom of a small cairn, and signed in.

Jenny Dunn, Whitewater, Wisconsin
Solo ascent, route 5, August 7, 2010, 12:45 P.M.
Ascent time: 7 hours, from Granite Creek Meadow.
Let others now do what I have done today.

The statement might sound arrogant to someone, but Jenny didn't care.

But that had been an hour ago. Her problem now was to pioneer a new route down, but the anticipation of doing it was destined to be short-lived. She had crawled only a few yards along the shelf and around a sharp corner when she saw the first piton.

Jenny felt immediate disappointment. The route, at least this far, had been done before. She crawled up to the piton and pulled on it. The crack was bad, and the piton came out easily. Standard stuff, although people didn't use them a lot anymore, since they damaged the rock. But the letter E had been engraved just below the eye of the piece. *Owner's initial.* She clipped it to a carabiner on her sling and moved on along the shelf. *Still a chance the route hasn't been taken all the way down.* The shelf was now like a highway, wide enough for two people to crawl side-by-side, and she followed it for several yards out into the sunlight and back into the shade of a second overhang. She was brushing some skree off the shelf as she moved ahead, and it clattered on the rocks below. Mentally she timed the fall. Far enough to die.

She crawled out into the sunlight again and found a second piton hammered into the shelf itself. It was in deep, but came out after several sharp taps with her hammer. The letter E was there again, and her disappointment mounted. But there was no turning back at this point. Time had become a factor, and she felt a growing commitment to follow the route all the way. But what she saw ahead of her was not encouraging. The shelf was beginning to narrow, and was heavily covered with loose skree. Above it, the wall looked brown and rotten, full of holes and laced with large cracks partially filled with rocky debris. *Bad rock, and lousy for anchor points.*

The conservative part of her mind took immediate command. She thought about using the piton she had just pulled, but her hand responded by clipping the piece to her sling. It seemed like the right thing to do, but the sudden impulse felt strange to her. She placed two wired chocks on the wall, one low and one high, then threaded her rope through them and began to pick her way lightly across the shelf, balancing herself with one hand on the wall. Pieces of skree twisted and slid beneath her feet. *A bad place for my smooth-soled shoes*, she thought, but progressed cat-like for several yards and around another corner as the shelf narrowed steadily. The shelf began sloping downwards steeply. She paused, looked up sharply and jerked backwards a step. Three feet ahead of her, the shelf disappeared.

Beneath a high, fan-shaped overhang, a twelve-foot section of the shelf had broken away from the wall. Jenny cautiously peered over the edge. A tangled mass of rubble lay two hundred feet below on a plateau that widened in the direction she had been moving. *Too far for my rope.* She would either have to go all the way back, or climb up. But the rock looked so *very* rotten. She tested it several places with a piton. The rock crumbled into tiny fragments as she tried to hammer the piece in. It was a no-go. With mounting frustration she kicked loose skree off of the shelf and stamped one foot hard, then froze.

The shelf beneath her had moved downwards.

Her first instinct was to lunge away from the end of the shelf. The whole thing could go any second, taking her down with it. Her anchor point was several yards behind her. If the shelf went she could see herself swinging back and forth along the wall below, a long human pendulum, swaying for eternity with blood pooling in her legs and slow suffocation coming with the tight squeezing of her harness. A little like being crucified, she thought. She inched her way back along the shelf, feeling it move with each short step, and scraping off the skree in front of her as she progressed. Showers of skree crackled on the rocks below.

"Hey! Cut it out up there!"

Jenny froze in mid-step. The shout had come from directly below her. The voice was raspy, high-pitched and angry; it was a woman's voice. She glanced down and saw only boulders and skree in a jumbled heap. But there *was* something else, a narrow swath, like the shiny trail of an enormous snail, looping out into the boulder field and back again towards the wall below her. It gleamed in the late afternoon sun. She took another step and the shelf groaned softly, and there was a new shower of skree.

"Damn it, can't you hear me up there! Yell rock or something when you kick that stuff off. It's coming down here all over the place." The pitch of the voice had risen even higher.

Jenny swallowed hard, her throat dry, and felt shame at violating such a fundamental climbing rule. "Sorry, but I've got a hairy problem here, and I didn't know anybody was around." She looked down again, but couldn't see the wall directly below her.

"I can't see you," she called, her voice firmer now.

There was a liquid chuckle from below, then a deep gurgling cough that gave Jenny a queer feeling in her stomach.

"You bet you can't see me, kid, with all that crap you're kicking off. I'm hiding out for the duration. Wait awhile and you and that whole shelf will be down here with me." There was another chuckle.

"All of a sudden the rock turned rotten on me. I've got to get back to route five." Jenny took another short step on the shelf, putting her foot carefully on top of the skree cover. The shelf held steady.

"It's a long way back to route five, kiddo, and an even longer down climb after that. You'll be racing the sun after a while. Have a lamp with you?"

"Didn't think I'd need one," said Jenny, and she took another step. The shelf was definitely steady now. "I expected to be just about down by now. After that it's only an hour walk back to my camp." Another step, and then she stopped, curious about something the woman had said.

"You know route five?"

"I remember most of it pretty well. Been awhile, though." There was another liquid cough, muffled, below the shelf.

"You're a climber?" Jenny leaned out slowly over the edge of the shelf and looked down at the base of the wall. It was covered by dark shadows as the sun began its descent in the afternoon sky, and the glistening trail across the rocks had disappeared. The woman's voice came softly from the shadows far below, yet seemed close.

"*Was* a climber, and good at it too, but I got hurt bad—don't get around too good anymore. But I keep in touch with things." The woman's voice faltered as she spoke. Sadness, perhaps bitterness was there.

"You're Jenny Dunn, right?"

Jenny was startled by the sound of her own name. "Yes—but how do you know that?"

There was a pause, and another muffled cough before the answer came. "Heard the guys talking about you in camp last night. Knew you'd be up here today. You tried a solo on route five of Harrison's?"

Jenny felt her face flush with anger. "I didn't just try it."

"You made it?"

"Yes," said Jenny firmly, and she looked at her watch. It was time to end the conversation, and retrace her route back.

"Look, I've really got to—"

"I'm glad you made it, Jenny," the woman said quickly. "It's personal to me. I mean it's great that a woman did it first. I tried it myself a couple of years ago, and that's when I got hurt. I came down the route you're on now, but without a summit climb to talk about. You should feel great about today."

The woman sounded old and sick, Jenny thought. "Say," she called, "when you came down did you leave any hardware up here?" She peered over the shelf again. Down in the deepening shadows, something moved.

"Just a couple of pitons. I came down in kind of a hurry." Another chuckle. "You found them?"

"I found two pitons with the letter E engraved on them."

There was more movement, a dark mass in the shadows. Someone was watching her now.

"Thanks, Jen. They're mine. The E is for Ellen. I never thought I'd get them back, some little mementos of my last climb. Can you take them down to camp for me? I'll pick them up later. Appreciate it."

"Sure, Ellen, but I've got to move now or I'll never get back to camp." Jenny straightened up and then took two light steps back towards the anchor for her rope.

"Don't go back that way, Jenny," said Ellen. "You're nearly down now. All you have to do is get across that break in the shelf. Look beyond it—the way is clear all the way down."

Jenny stopped, and sighed. "The rock is rotten up here, Ellen. I wouldn't trust anything to hold me if the shelf went."

Ellen's voice came back strong and urgent. "You're being too conservative. Try more cracks. Some of them are good. A two-foot jump from the shelf to that overhang will give you good hand holds and you can hand-over-hand it across the break. Look ahead—see how the shelf slants down? It gets narrower, but goes all the way down to the plateau, and the rock gets better too. You can be back in camp in less than an hour."

"You *are* persuasive, Ellen," said Jenny. *But is she accurate?* She looked towards the overhang and beyond it. Past the break the shelf narrowed to boot width, but was clearly visible as it sloped down towards the plateau. It *was* a go.

"Trust me, Jenny. I know the route cold. One tricky traverse and it's quick back to camp. Nobody has done it since that shelf broke off. The guys say you're really good. It should be easy for you. I can belay you across the break and—"

Ellen's voice had risen with enthusiasm, but suddenly broke into a racking, gurgling series of cough

Jenny smiled at the absurdity of the suggestion. Even if her rope could reach the rocks below, which it couldn't, how safe would she feel being belayed by a sick, old woman who hid herself in the shadows and dreamed of climbing days long past?

"Look, Ellen, I really appreciate your advice. You're probably right, and I'm going to try it, but I don't think the idea of you belaying me is a very—"

"Oh I don't mean a physical belay, Jen," laughed Ellen, "but I can still talk you down safely with what I know. See that nubbin on the overhang? When you jump, aim your left hand for the nubbin. The overhang edge curls up to the right of it. It'll be like hanging from a high bar. Just aim for the edge of the overhang. It's flat beyond that." Her voice was enthusiastic, excited, like she was climbing again.

Jenny found two good cracks, placed wired chocks in them, and hooked up for the traverse. She found the nubbin on the overhang and focused on it. Why did she trust Ellen so much? It made no sense, but somehow she believed that behind the nubbin was a good hold and that the traverse would go as Ellen had said. She felt relaxed, and ready for the attack. And Ellen's voice came as a shout from below.

"Do it, Jenny!"

One short step, then two more in rapid succession, her knees flexed, and the shelf was beginning to move. Skree slipped beneath her feet. There was a groaning from the rock and she was weightless in air, her left arm thrust out towards the overhang, and her right arm moving up rapidly in support. The palms of her hands collided flat against the edge of the overhang, and she was squeezing down—hoping.

The hand holds were there.

"Right on, kid," said Ellen.

Two lateral swings and, filled with elation, Jenny stood on solid rock, pulling in her rope.

"Nice belay, Ellen," she called, smiling.

"Off belay, Jenny," said Ellen. "You did great."

For one short moment, they had climbed together.

Jenny coiled her rope, draped it over one shoulder and searched the shadows below. There was no movement, no sound.

"Ellen?" she asked softly.

Silence.

"It's safe to come out now, and I'd really like to see you. You helped me here, not just with advice, but with your confidence in me. I wouldn't have done that traverse without you being here. Ellen? I can toss your pitons down to you from here."

"Don't do that, Jenny," said the shadows at the base of the wall. "They'd get lost in all the debris down here. Just take them back to your camp for me." There was a muffled sound, then a cough.

Ellen was crying.

"Whatever you say, Ellen, but I'm grateful for your help. See you later." Jenny began stepping carefully along the narrow shelf. *What's the matter with her?*

"You don't want to see me Jenny. You wouldn't like it!" Anger and bitterness were there in the shadows.

Jenny frowned and began to pick up her pace downwards. *A little crazy, maybe?* Ellen called after her, the words spilling out and her voice rising until she was shouting.

"I'm sorry, Jenny. Watching you just brought back a lot of memories for me, that's all. I guess I'm—I'm just feeling sorry for myself. Can you understand that? You're a much better climber than I ever was, and you'll be the *best* someday. Can you hear me?"

Jenny's pace quickened further, and she smiled to herself. "I hear you Ellen, and thanks." *But did she see me reach the summit? Did she see me fall?*

"Be nice to my guys down there, Jenny. They'd like to meet you, but they think you're not interested in socializing. They're good guys, all of them, and they were hoping you'd make it today."

Jenny moved quickly now, and shouted over her shoulder, laughing, "I haven't had very good experiences with men, Ellen."

"Not *my* guys. There's no super-macho or condescension down there, just respect for you as a person and a climber. Give them a chance."

"Don't worry about it," Jenny shouted. "I owe you one. Gotta go now. See ya!" She plunged on at full speed with mixed feelings of exhilaration and sadness, as the sounds of Ellen's muffled subs and coughing faded into the distance.

Minutes later Jenny stepped down onto the plateau and after some boulder hopping found the couloirs leading to the meadows below. She hurried along in growing darkness, thinking only of cool water and hot food, and when she came out of the shadows at the edge of the meadows the sun was setting behind the jagged peaks above her and she was nearly running.

"Hey, night flyer—hold up a second!"

She looked up sharply to see a man descending a rocky slope towards her. Tall and sinewy, he bounced lightly from rock to rock, head down, his quick pace constant. *A climber*, she thought. She slowed her pace as he came alongside, and they walked together towards the brightly colored tents scattered like wildflowers around a creek flowing through the center of the meadow.

"I'm Bill Anderson, and you must be Jenny Dunn, the way you were moving just now," he said, and smiled broadly.

"Hi, Bill Anderson," and she forced a little smile of her own.

"Didn't expect to see you come down this way," he said. "The rock on this side of the mountain is real crud."

"Don't I know it," said Jenny. "I wouldn't want to do that route again."

"I bet," said Bill. "I did Brill's tower yesterday, and spent today recovering. Must be getting old." He laughed, and it was a nice sound.

They walked in silence for a while, then Bill suddenly said, "Don't keep me in suspense, Jenny. Did you make it?"

"Yes," she said, smiling to herself.

"All *right*," he drawled. "Everybody figured you had a good chance at it. I've tried to solo that bugger three times now. Hope you don't mind if some of us try to pick your brain about the last two pitches up there."

"I don't mind," said Jenny, enjoying the moment.

"You sure came down a weird route to reach that couloir. It must be a new one I haven't heard of."

"I followed a shelf all the way down to the plateau up there. You know the shelf with the big break in it?" She turned to look at him. He was studying the ground ahead.

"We all know about that place."

"I had a couple of hairy experiences, then things went pretty well until I got to that break," Jenny said, her eyes bright. "I had started to go back when I ran into an ex-climber named Ellen. She showed me how to get across the break, and the rest of the way was clear sailing. I found some of her—"

"Isn't it something the way a person can stay under your skin like that," said Bill, still looking at the ground. "I mean it's almost a religious thing. Ellen Harris sure could do it to people." He laughed softly, remembering something.

"Most of the guys up here were crazy about her. God did we get drunk after she died."

Jenny's heart froze. She couldn't breathe, but Bill didn't seem to notice.

"John and Alex took it the hardest. They were watching when that shelf just popped off and took Ellen down with it. She wasn't even roped up!"

Watch what you say, thought Jenny, and she struggled to breathe again.

"They got close enough to see Ellen was gone. It was pretty bad, I guess—the way she was smashed up. But things were really falling apart up there, and before they could get her out a big section of the wall under the shelf just sort of peeled away and buried her. Geez, she must be under a hundred tons of rock."

But none of this can be true. Jenny fought back a strangling sensation in her throat. "How can you be so sure she was dead and not just badly hurt?" Face grim, she looked at the ground, and Bill out a hand on her shoulder.

"We've thought about that, Jenny. No way—all smashed up—crushed, really, and under a mountain of rock. The rangers said it was useless to try to reach her. She didn't have any family, so they just left her there. We put up a little cairn, and the flowers are kept fresh by all of us. Only twenty-three years old. God, what a waste."

I talked to her. I heard her—

"They should have gotten her out!" said Jenny, and she pressed her lips together hard. Bill squeezed her shoulder, and then withdrew his hand, embarrassed.

"I wish they could have too. Then maybe John and Alex wouldn't have all those nightmares about Ellen dragging herself around up here, all mangled up like some kind of monster. They just about freaked out the first time they saw you up here. From a distance, and—well—even close up, you look a little like the Ellen we remember. Did you know her very well?"

Are you really up there, Ellen? "No—only for a little while." *Do I look like you?*

They reached the cluster of tents, Jenny's a few yards beyond the main group. It was nearly dark, and very quiet. Bill nodded towards the tents. "Climbing day for them tomorrow, but I'm going down then. How about you?"

"Sure," said Jenny, wiping her eyes with the back of one hand. "About eight o'clock?"

"Sounds good," said Bill, smiling again. "Hope this gloomy talk didn't wreak your evening after such a great day."

"No." Jenny smiled back. "It was good to talk about it"— *with one of Ellen's guys.* She started towards her tent, and Bill called after her.

"See you tomorrow then, and remember not to leave your stuff out tonight. We're having trouble with food and fuel thieves up here."

"Okay," said Jenny softly. *Is that you, Ellen?* She thought. She reached her tent, unpacked, and heated tea water on her little stove. The tea calmed her, and she sat in the darkness, munching a chocolate bar. Ellen's pitons, strung on a short yellow sling, were carefully stowed in the top of her rucksack. She sipped tea, and tried to remember her exhilaration at the summit. It was there briefly, and then escaped her. She felt so very tired. Her mind was a boulder field, jumbled without pattern, and streaked with dark shadows. Something was moving in those shadows.

Her tea cup fell to the ground, and she jerked upright, eyes half-closed. Thinking could wait until the morning. She yawned, crawled into the tent and pulled the rucksack in after her. Fumbling with boot laces, her eyes closed, she finally kicked the boots free and slid slowly into her sleeping bag. Darkness engulfed her, and she fell into a dream about climbing.

She was climbing with a young, faceless woman and they reached the summit, laughing, and the woman hid a smile behind her hands. They slid down the mountain and ran along a shelf like children playing, and then she was weightless, falling, and she looked up and rock was coming down on her, and darkness came suddenly. The woman was still with her, and didn't like the darkness, and she clawed at the rock with her fingers and screamed, "We're down here! Please get us out of here!" Then light was spilling down on Jenny's face, and she saw Bill reaching for her hand and he was lifting her out of the dark place. But something was pulling down on her legs, and she looked down, and she saw a monstrous thing clawing at her, eyes gleaming in what had once been a human face, coughing pink foam and pleading, "Jenny, please stay with me for a while." And she screamed back, "Where's Ellen? What have you done with Ellen?"

Jenny's eyes opened wide. The tent was bathed in sunlight, and it was warm. She looked at her watch. "Seven-forty-five. My God, I overslept." She rolled out of her un-zipped bag. The tent smelled foul, musty, and she crawled outside to put on her boots. Bill had already finished pulling down his tent, and he waved cheerfully to her. She waved back, bent over to lace her boots and saw the ground sparkling beneath her feet. All around her tent entrance, the ground sparkled like dew, like a trail she had seen before. Leaping to her feet she went to her tent, held her breath against the stench inside and pulled out her rucksack. Heart pounding, she opened the sack, looked inside and then closed it again quickly and smiled. Her climbing hardware was safe and sound.

Ellen's pitons, and the little yellow sling, were gone.

ARTIFACT

Bobby Harrison's naked body hit the icy water, and his breath exploded outwards in an avalanche of shimmering bubbles. He squeezed his eyes shut tightly, energy draining from every part of him as he clawed his way upwards. When his head broke the surface of the near-freezing water he was gasping for breath. The other boys were still running towards the little glacial lake, leaving a trail of clothing and rucksacks behind. Bobby swam rapidly towards the shore, trying to warn them.

"Better come in slow. The water's *freezing*."

He was too late. Columns of water erupted into the air, along with shrieks and howls as the icy lake claimed new victims.

Bobby ran from the water and spread himself on a flat rock to soak up heat from the afternoon sun. The other boys followed him quickly, laughing and shivering as they crashed through the clear water. Nate Larson, one of Bobby's cabin-mates, flopped down beside him.

"God, my toes have turned blue."

"Be glad it isn't your whole leg," said Bobby. "What held you guys up back there?"

Nate inspected his toes closely. "We were looking at the knife Keith found by the trail. It's all green and corroded." He turned and called to a boy who was bending over a rucksack, looking for something.

"Hey Keith, show Bobby the knife you found."

The boy straightened up, tall and sinewy, picked up the rucksack and walked over to join his cabin-mates. He sat down cross-legged, a first-aid kit in front of him, reached into his rucksack and handed the knife to Bobby.

"Be careful with that. It's like a razor; cut me when I pulled it out of the ground." He showed them a small cut on the palm of one hand, below the thumb. "Man did that hurt. I felt it all through me."

"Better watch for infection," said Bobby, gently turning the knife over in his hand. "Looks like this has been in the ground a long time."

Keith opened the first aid kit, grumbling to himself, and pulled out tape, gauze pads and a bottle of disinfectant.

What a find, thought bobby. A real artifact shaped like a carving knife and crusted green with patches of blue. The handle had eroded away, the edge of the seven-inch blade sharp and jagged.

"I think it's made out of copper," said Bobby. "Bet it's a fighting knife." He jabbed it towards Nate's chest. Nate yawned.

"Looks like a skinning knife to me. Better turn it in to the counselors."

"No way," said Keith, inspecting his bandaged hand. "They'd probably take it and tell me it's historical or something." He took the knife from Bobby, carefully wrapped it in an undershirt and pushed it down to the bottom of his rucksack. Envious eyes watched it disappear.

"I'll get my dad to make a handle for it, and then put it in with my arrowhead collection." Keith opened and closed his cut hand, carefully.

"Let's get going," said Nate, "or we'll be late for the ball game and you guys won't be able to show off for the girls." He struggled to pull socks over his wet feet. "You'd better have Hanna check that hand, Keith."

"Yes mother," said Keith.

The boys laughed.

The trail they took back to camp descended along a deep gorge choked with tall pine trees and small meadows filled with wildflowers. A fast-moving creek paralleled the trail and filled their ears with sound. At the edge of one meadow they saw a black bear ripping apart a decaying log in search of something edible. It was all great, thought Bobby, but in three days it would have to end. Back to the city, the heat, smoke and noise, and all the frantic people. In a year, though, he would be back again with the trees, clean air and cold water, finding even more quartz crystals to take home with him. Nate and Keith would be back, too, and they would share a cabin as they had done for the past four summers. Their common interests had drawn them together, Bobby's in geology, Keith's in archeology and Nate's in nature photography. And two of them waited impatiently as Nate took pictures of every new wildflower species he saw along the trail.

When the sun was still high they reached the sprawling campground. Cabins were scattered in clusters under tall firs. Nate talked excitedly during the entire trip, but Keith was strangely silent and constantly checked his bandaged hand, flexing his fingers. His hand hurt, seemed to pulsate along with his heart beat, and he felt curiously disengaged from everything around him. Bobby watched him carefully, but said nothing.

The baseball game had already started when they arrived. Bobby and Nate threw down their rucksacks and immediately joined the game, but Keith marched straight to the aid station. The camp nurse, Hanna Falk, looked up from a letter she was writing when he burst into the room.

"Hi, Keith. What's up?"

"Hurt my hand," mumbled Keith, lifting his arm to show her the injured part. He studied the floor in front of him.

"Let's take a look," said Hanna, smiling, and she took his hand gently in hers. Keith's gaze moved from the floor to the long tanned legs in front of him.

"It's just a little cut, not deep, and it looks clean. How'd you do it?" Hanna leaned over, trying to look into his eyes. Keith dared a glance back and swallowed hard.

She was beautiful.

"I found a piece of metal stuck in the ground near Blue Lake.

I think it was copper, sort of greenish." She was so close he could smell soap and perfume.

"Metal cuts can be bad, Keith," said Hanna. "There's dirt, germs, and—" her eyes widened at the suggestion, "Maybe even a Manitou."

Keith clenched his cut hand into a tight fist and stared at Hanna stone-faced.

Hanna laughed.

"If there's any redness or swelling by tomorrow, come and see me and I'll give you a tetanus booster. But it looks fine to me, and you did a good job taking care of it yourself. Okay?"

"I guess so" said Keith, adjusting the new bandage on his hand. He wanted to tell her it wasn't the cut that hurt. It was his entire hand. The pain was moving into his wrist, and he was a little frightened. He wanted to tell her about the strange stirrings he suddenly had being near her, but he said nothing and left the room quickly. Hanna's smile changed to a frown as she watched the slender boy stride away into the shadows of the tall trees.

* * * * * * *

High above the camp, Keith found a wide shelf jutting out from a rocky cliff overlooking the meadows and valley and he sprawled out on it. He had climbed rapidly, sweat pouring into his eyes, yet he felt increasing strength with each step. The pain in his hand had dulled to a throbbing ache that reached to his elbow and when he clenched his hand he felt a strength there he had never felt before. The muscles in his forearm stood out in high relief. His heart pounded from the effort of the climb, but there was something else, a kind of exhilaration. His senses seemed sharpened. The trees and flowers called to him with their fragrances and the murmur of wind against his rocky sanctuary drew him deep within himself.

There was a sudden brief odor of wet fur, and he looked down at the trees below. A deer was there, browsing quietly in thick underbrush near the edge of the meadow. He felt its caution and fear.

He was a part of all of it.

With the increasing awareness came confusion in his fifteen year old mind. The new feelings he had for Hanna were different. He had felt drawn to her, excited by her. How very strange, he thought. She was several years older than he. She had a boyfriend, Dan Adams, the swimming teacher. Late at night they walked among the trees, laughing, kissing, doing other things that excited the imaginations of the boys who followed them at a distance and strained their eyes to watch.

When Hanna mentioned the Manitou, Keith had been stunned. He knew about the Manitou, the good or evil spirits that filled the world. He thought of the knife, pulled it out of his rucksack and unwrapped it slowly, holding it out in front of him. Was not the Manitou only associated with living things? The knife was just a piece of sharp metal, green and old and corroded. There could be no spirit life there. But a knife could be used as an instrument of killing. He wondered if, under the green and blue corrosion, there was dried blood of a once living thing.

He remembered the pain when the knife had cut him, but there had been something else, something that burned like adrenalin and filled his entire body.

There was a shout from below. Someone was chasing a ball across the meadow, and the screams of the players came to him on the wind. Children, he thought. They play children's' games. They feel nothing for this land, and their society destroys it. His relation to them seemed subdued as he carefully rewrapped the knife.

Keith pulled on his rucksack, scrambled off of the shelf, and began the steep walk downhill through thick stands of firs. As he walked he sensed minute scurrying in the brush ahead, heard birds calling warnings to each other from the high tree tops, and he smiled to himself.

A voice crying in fear within him went unheard.

* * * * * * *

When the ballgame ended, Bobby hurried to his cabin to get a candy bar and store his rucksack. He found Keith sitting cross-legged and shirtless on a bed, staring straight ahead at a blank wall.

"Hey, man, we missed you at the game." He stuffed the rucksack under his bed and retrieved a candy bar from a shoe box there.

"Why?" asked Keith, unmoving.

"We missed your batting, man. We got slaughtered today."

"It's not important," said Keith.

"Well, excuse *me*," drawled Bobby. "I'm sure you have many more important things to do."

"I do," said Keith. Only his head moved as he turned to face Bobby. When Bobby looked back at him he thought of shark's eyes, and his mouth was suddenly dry.

"All right, it's none of my business anyway. You're going to campfire tonight though, right? This is the night Mister Voss dresses up like a medicine man and tells all those ghost stories." Bobby smiled in anticipation.

"Maybe," said Keith dreamily, and Bobby laughed.

"You on pain pills? How's your hand?"

"The hand is fine," said Keith softly.

"No swelling?" bobby started to touch the bandage. The hand was a blur of movement as it seized his wrist and began to squeeze.

"I said the hand is fine," said Keith, and his mouth curled up at the edges in a small suggestion of a smile.

Bobby gasped as the pain shot up his arm, and one knee buckled beneath him. Tears came to his eyes as he twisted free of the bone-crushing grip and jumped backwards.

"That did it, man," he shouted. "You want to be alone? Then be alone!" Bobby stalked out of the cabin, remembering how the veins on Keith's arm had bulged large and blue, and how Keith had never been able to beat him in arm wrestling.

Back in the cabin, Keith resumed his study of the blank wall. He searched his mind, trying to remember something, something he was supposed to do. His eyes focused on a spider crawling up the wall. A brother, or perhaps a sister, he thought, but the crawling one did not answer.

Keith sat quietly relaxed, waiting for a vision.

*   *   *   *   *   *   *

The food tasted terrible, something canned. Bobby didn't care, he wasn't hungry anyway. Something was terribly wrong with Keith, and he hadn't come to dinner. Bobby resolved to talk to the counselors about it in the morning. After the meal he wandered aimlessly along the edge of the meadow until it began to grow dark, and then hurried to the campfire area where men and boys were already piling up logs and branches for the large ceremonial fire. Nate soon joined him, fumbling to load a camera in near darkness, and there was a sudden blast of heat and odor of gasoline as the great pile of wood exploded into flames. The orange beacon brought people moth-like out of the darkness to huddle close together near the warmth. Images of their faces appeared and disappeared with the flickering of the flames. Bobby scanned the faces and finally saw Keith outside of the huddled circle of people, sitting cross-legged at the edge of the glow cast by the fire. At least he came, thought Bobby. It was a special night for all of them.

A slow drum-beat came out of the darkness, and the crowd was abruptly silent. Chanting followed it, a slow sad song, a song of tragedy and remorse. A shadow moved and then a tall figure was standing near the fire, his arms upraised. His face was painted white and yellow below the dead head of a black bear with mouth open and teeth gleaming in the firelight. A heavy robe reached to the ground.

"Spirits of the night, hear me!" cried the specter. "Protect all those within this circle, and I will tell them the tragedies and injustices of your earthly lives. Hear me, now!"

The stories began.

* * * * * * *

Keith sat at the edge of the firelight, but did not listen. The songs and the paint were wrong, and the robe was not used for the telling of stories. The very presence of the man was offensive, for his kind had destroyed both the land and a way of life that had existed for thousands of years. Still, the light of the fire and those sounds that penetrated beyond his consciousness stirred memories in him. He had been away and alone for such a long time, and his host was only a child. There was so little experience to draw from. He saw the one called Hanna sitting near the fire and nestled in the arms of her friend. There had been a girl, a girl with yellow hair and ivory skin that turned brown in the summer. There was a longing, an ache he could not define. Perhaps she had died. But he remembered the man, the drunken white man who had hung him from the branch of a tree and used his own knife to strip flesh from his face and body. And when he was finished with his butchery, he had fallen down on the knife in a drunken stupor and their blood had mingled together. He wanted to cry out with the memory of his vengeance. But it had not been by his own hand. And the girl, the one he longed for, seemed near.

At the edge of the darkness, Keith watched Hanna Falk dozing in the firelight, and smiled. The vision had come, and he now had a plan, a way to strike back for what had been done in his past.

If only the boy would stop fighting against him.

* * * * * * *

Story telling ended, the 'Medicine Man' returned to the darkness and people drifted away from the glowing remnants of the fire. Bobby wanted to talk to Keith, but Nate grabbed his arm excitedly.

"Hanna and Mister Adams are headed for the woods again. C'mon, let's go!

The boys motioned to Keith to follow them, and then fled into the darkness in frantic pursuit.

A part of Keith's mind watched them leave. It's just as well, he thought. I can prepare myself in peace for what's ahead, and with a boy as my instrument there is much risk, even an element of chance.

Keith stood up in the fading circle of light, walked to the remains of the fire and poked at the charred wood with a stick. He selected three small pieces of warm charcoal that crumbled at his touch; put the fragments in a metal cup left by the fire, then returned to the darkness and walked swiftly and lightly towards his cabin. A nearly full moon newly risen over tall trees lighted his way. It is a good sign, he thought, a good night for thinking, and a good night for hunting.

* * * * * * *

"I think we've lost them," whispered Bobby.

"How could we?" said Nate. "They were right ahead of us a minute ago."

"I don't know how, but they're gone. What do we do now?"

"Let's pay the girls in cabin five a visit," said Nate, and he held up his camera, grinning. "Maybe I can get some naked pictures?" The boys laughed as they crashed their way back along the dark trail.

Six feet from the trail Hanna Falk started to giggle, and Dan Adams hushed her. "Devils, all of them."

"Oh," cooed Hanna, "and what did *you* do when *you* were a freshman in camp?" She snuggled close, looking up at him in the darkness.

"Allow me to show you, madam," he said, and led her away to the soft cool place they frequented in the night.

* * * * * * *

The knife was ready. He had made a handle for it with wrappings of long leather boot laces and adhesive tape. The grip was spongy, but did not slip. He laid the knife beside him on the bed, crumbled pieces of charcoal into the metal cup and used a smooth pebble to grind them into a fine black powder. From a tube of glacial cream, he squeezed a short cylinder of snow-white goo into the bottom of the cup. He mixed it around with a finger, watching the mixture turn gray and then black, and repeated the procedure until the cup was partially filled with a flat black paste. He tried a sample of it on the back of one hand, and it pleased him. With the white glacial cream as a background, the mixture would be appropriate. The cup and the tube of glacial cream were placed on the floor beneath his bed, against a wall. He slid the knife carefully under his pillow, and then sat on his bed with legs crossed beneath him. A part deep within him was terrified, and feared the certain pain to come, but what he would do was demanded by the featureless lonely world he had existed in for so long. A new life would be brought forward with the coming day. With the pain would come joy.

There was a scream within him, and his consciousness flickered. Do not interfere, or I will kill this body. You will be gone, but I will still be here, he thought, and for the moment there was silence.

Keith slid off the bed, unscrewed the single bare light bulb on one wall and, in darkness, threw it far out into the trees. His mouth felt suddenly dry as he crawled back into bed. He pulled the sleeping bag up around his head, and waited.

* * * * * * *

The girls were waiting for them.

Nate had climbed the lower limb of a tree near the brightly lit cabin window and was struggling to fit a long lens on his camera when there was a shriek from the darkness.

"They're here! The tree in front of the window!"

Bobby turned to run as a barrage of water-filled balloons

erupted from the cabin window, and he heard Nate yell as balloons exploded against tree and flesh. Pumping his arms he fled into the darkness, a pounding close behind him.

"Hey, wait up," gasped Nate, pulling Bobby to a halt, and they listened to hysterical giggling coming from the brightly lit cabin.

They walked slowly, hearts pounding. "Man, what an ambush," said Nate. "I'm soaked." He brushed wet black hair out of his eyes. Bobby looked at him and laughed.

"Better you than me, buddy."

They neared their cabin. It was dark.

"Keith asleep already?" asked Nate. "That's weird."

"Weird is right," said Bobby, thinking of the day past. "Sounds like he left the radio on." He could hear faint music, singing or humming, changing pitch, and primitive. The sound stopped abruptly when they reached the cabin.

Bobby reached in the door less entrance, found the light switch and flipped it back and forth. Darkness. The hair stiffened on the back of his neck. Something was wrong.

"Come on, man, I'm freezing!" pleaded Nate.

They went inside, Nate stripping off wet clothes and grabbing a dirty towel from the top of his bed. He dried himself quickly and slid into his sleeping bag shivering. Bobby stood in the center of the room, eyes searching. Only his bed was illuminated by moonlight. The rest was near darkness, Keith's bed a motionless, featureless mound. He listened for the slightest sound from the dark corners of the room, then undressed and slid slowly into his bag. A strange alarm continued to sound in his head as he struggled to zip up the bag, but the moonlight on his face was somehow comforting. Exhausted, he closed his eyes. Some minutes later, as he was drifting into sleep, he thought he heard someone humming.

* * * * * * *

There was a muffled sound, and Bobby was suddenly awake,

eyes narrowed to slits and moonlight bathing his face. There was a creaking of boards, and then the sound of cloth ripping. Nate grumbled, half-asleep, "Leave me alone. Go back to bed."

The ripping sound intensified, and Nate's bed banged against the wall.

"God, what are you doing? Cut it out! Ow!"

Bobby's eyes opened wide and adrenalin surged through his body as Nate's head crashed hard against the wall.

"Nate!" cried Bobby, and he pulled hard on his sleeping bag zipper as he tried to sit up. The zipper jammed immediately and he pushed with his legs, squirming in a vain attempt to free himself from the bag. A dark figure stood over Nate's bed, slashing at it, and pieces of down were floating out the moonlit window.

His shoulders came free and he thrashed around on the bed, trying to free his arms. The figure came towards him out of the darkness, leaping up on his bed and straddling him so he couldn't move. Bobby stared up at a tear-stained death-mask face painted white with eyes, nose and mouth outlined in black.

"Keith!" he cried. "What did you do to Nate? What's wrong with you?"

"Bobby, watch out! He's got a knife!" screamed Nate.

Keith glared down at him, eyes wide and lips pressed tightly together. His entire body was shaking. He raised both arms, hands clasped, above him. Bobby struggled frantically, and saw the knife.

"No, Keith!" pleaded Bobby. "Wake up!"

Tears gushed from Keith's eyes and streamed down his painted face. His clasped hands shook above his head as if struggling against an invisible force holding them in place. Bobby squirmed beneath him, but could not escape any downward thrust of the knife. I don't want to die, he thought, "Please Keith, please stop!" he cried.

Keith's breath exploded in a wail, and his wild eyes closed. "I *won't*! I *can't*! Get *out* of me! I'll—I'll—"

Keith's hands came down with terrible force, Bobby's face

burning with the anticipation of death.

The ancient corroded blade slammed into the wooden frame of Bobby's bunk only inches from his sleeping bag, embedding itself half-way up to the hilt. Keith screamed, jerked the hilt to one side and there was a loud snap. Bobby recoiled from the two-inch remnant of shattered blade so near to his side.

The sounds of their crying and screaming brought people running to the cabin.

* * * * * * *

Two girls had been sneaking up to the cabin to dump water on the boys when they heard the commotion inside. One girl ran screaming to find Hanna, and Dan Adams followed them back. When they arrived at the cabin, Bobby and Keith were sitting outside on the porch and Nate was in the doorway, yelling at them.

"Damn it, Keith, you shredded my sleeping bag and you're going to buy me a new one!" Nate went back inside the cabin, mumbling to himself and rubbing the back of his head. "I hurt my head, too, and it's your fault."

Keith was crying, his face in his hands, and Bobby had an arm around his shoulders.

"That was a real nightmare, Keith. I thought you were going to kill us, and you wouldn't wake up."

"But I *was* awake!" sobbed Keith. He looked up at Hanna and Dan, tears smearing the black and white paint on his face. "I didn't want to hurt anybody. I didn't!"

Bobby then told them what had happened, while Keith sobbed pitifully, again holding his face in his hands.

"So much for old Indian tales and ghost stories around the campfire," said Dan. "It makes sleepwalkers dangerous." He smiled, but Hanna put a finger to her lips and shushed him.

"Does your hand still hurt?" asked Hanna. She stooped to check the cut on Keith's hand, rewrapping it carefully. "I don't see any redness."

"It doesn't hurt now," said Keith, "but that knife is dangerous, and it's stuck in Bobby's bunk."

They all went inside. Nate held up his shredded sleeping bag and glared at Keith.

"You can use my bag until I get you a new one," said Keith.

They crowded around Bobby's bunk. Keith got a rock from a windowsill. "Maybe I can pound it in or break it off again," he said. The jagged blade still protruded a couple of inches above the wood.

"Very old," said Dan, and reached out to touch the blade just as Keith moved closer with the rock in his hand.

Their shoulders touched.

"Ouch!' cried Dan and he stood up straight, his body filled with searing pain. As Hanna turned to him, he stamped one foot down hard and squeezed the injured hand tightly, forcing it to bleed. "Man, I felt that down to my toes!"

"Never again!" screamed Keith. He pounded the rock on the blade until it had disappeared beneath the wood of the bunk. "You're finished here. You'll never hurt anyone again." His body shook as Bobby and Nate stared at him, astonished.

Hanna took Dan's hand in hers, wiping away a trickle of blood with her handkerchief. He felt suddenly foolish, and was embarrassed by it. "Cut it on that damned knife," he said, looking down at his feet.

Hanna smiled faintly. "It's hardly anything," she said, then leaned down and kissed the tiny cut. "See? It's all better, now." And the look in her eyes made it seem so.

The boys finally calmed down and went back to bed, Nate in Keith's bag and Keith wrapped up in blankets for the night. It was late, the moon bright. Hanna and Dan sat out on the porch for just a moment. Dan turned to look at her and spoke with an impulse that came without conscious thought.

"I love you, Hanna," he said softly.

Hanna's eyes widened and she looked at him strangely, as if seeing him for the first time.

"You've never said that to me before," she whispered, leaning against him.

"There are a lot of things I haven't said to you before," and he held her tightly to him.

Head pressed to his chest, she heard the pounding of his heart, but could not know it pounded with joy.

TRAVEL REQUIRED

It seemed they were only a few minutes away from Central Park and the chaos of downtown Manhattan, but when the cab pulled up in front of a crumbling yellow building some twenty stories high Helen Trumbold's heart sank with disappointment. Because the driver had been brusque with her she gave him only a dollar tip and he left her standing on a badly cracked sidewalk, staring up at the sinister tower before her.

It was going to be another one of those days, she thought. Three failed job interviews in a week, and money short. Only the pretty ones got the secretarial jobs, especially when they had to travel with the boss, and the advertisement had specifically said travel was required. So why was the man who interviewed her over the phone so interested? After all, he had her resume and a recent photograph which Unemployment had sent over for him. She had seen the photograph and hated it, angry at the way she had lately let herself go. It was not that she didn't care anymore, but nothing she tried seemed to work. A frump is a frump, Helen, and that's you, she told herself. So why had this man requested a personal interview for a job she desperately wanted? It was her chance to get away from a tiny dingy apartment, traffic noises and screaming neighbors, a chance to see the world and be with interesting people. And why was the interview here, in this crumbling wreck of a building?

Helen marched boldly up the steps of the building and went inside. The foyer was dimly lit, empty of people or furniture of any kind, a rough unfinished concrete floor and thick columns bisecting the space. On the far side were three elevator doors made from polished copper shining dully in light filtering in from the street. Each door had a security access panel and there was no directory to be seen. Helen fumbled around in her purse and found the scrap of paper with the man's name and access code. Gerard Doreen, 51131. She punched in the code for the middle elevator door and stepped back to look at herself reflected from the polished metal. Frumpy.

The door to her left slid open; she peered around the corner and stepped inside. When the door didn't shut she punched the close button, feeling more secure in the brightly lit, enclosed space. The elevator rose slowly. She adjusted her hair, smoothed the skirt of her dark business suit and took several deep breaths to calm herself. The elevator came to a halt, the door immediately sliding open; she took another deep breath and stepped out directly into a softly lit, tastefully furnished office. A short, balding, middle-aged man in a neat blue suit was just emerging from another office beyond, and he smiled at her.

"Ah, right on time. You are Helen Trumbold?" The man put some papers on a desk and held out a hand to greet her. She watched his eyes move quickly over her, and waited for the *look* telling her what he saw was unacceptable. But instead, his smile broadened as he took her hand and led her to a plush chair in front of his desk. "Please sit. We have a moment before I send you upstairs for some tests. Tell me, are you willing to do any word processing on the job? Mister Pixl requires this on occasion, and I forgot to tell you on the telephone."

"Of course," she said primly. "I can type one hundred and ten words a minute with accuracy."

"Good. And one other thing we didn't discuss on the telephone, at least not completely. The position of Protocol Assistant demands extensive travel, keeping you out of town to the extent that maintaining an apartment here is a questionable expense. If you have anyone very—well, close to you, then you probably won't want to consider this position."

"That's not a problem. I don't have any attachments."

The man smiled. "Ah, then you don't have any necessary obligations in your life." He seemed relieved.

"Oh, I was married once," she quickly added, "but that was sometime ago." *Once upon a time someone wanted me, but then I got older*, she thought.

Doreen stood up. "Well, let's get you started. Mister Cox will give you some tests on the next floor up, turn right to room 430, and I'll be checking in on you from time to time." He pointed to a television monitor above his desk. "After that we'll have a little chat, and then you can meet Mister Pixl. If you find the tests to be unusual, please remember we are also testing your abilities to adapt, and that takes some imagination." His smile was mischievous as he guided her back to the elevator. "Good luck."

And so she went up to the next floor.

She stepped out into a darkened hallway, smooth marble walls curving left and right. Diffuse light came around the corner from the left. To the right she saw light coming from a doorway, and moved towards it. It was cold, and there was a strange stale odor in the air. She stopped once to listen. There was a chittering sound far down the hall behind her, and then it stopped. *God, I hope they don't have rats here.* She moved on, stepped up timidly to the doorway and looked inside.

A man was sitting behind his desk, staring at the opposite wall, hands folded neatly before him. He sat motionless, as if daydreaming, remaining that way when she knocked softly on the door jam. She checked the number above the door, and it was where she was supposed to be. She went inside and stood before the desk. "I'm Helen Trumbold. Mister Doreen sent me here to see Mister Cox for some interview tests."

"I am Mister Cox," said the man, facing her suddenly, and his voice flat and emotionless. "Please sit and relax before we begin." He gestured at a large table near his desk, on which were a word processor and two television monitors. When she moved to it the man's head did not turn, his hands returning to a folded position before him. "You have one moment to compose yourself. Do the best you can, and do not be concerned with the results. I'm here to help you in anyway I can, and to maximize your successes."

Helen suddenly realized she was talking to a mechanized mannequin, a kind of robot programmed to interview and give tests. But above his desk, a camera had turned to follow her when she moved. Others were watching this interview. "Thank you, Mister Cox," she said politely. At least a robot wouldn't give her that *look* she hated so much. She relaxed.

In the next half hour she whizzed through a typing test and two file formatting exercises, her confidence building. "Excellent," said Mister Cox, "and now some exercises in protocol. Please turn on the large monitor to your left, and use the mouse to move figures on the screen."

She used the mouse to move a square and a triangle back and forth on the screen before they suddenly vanished.

"Exercise one," said Mister Cox. "Please read carefully, and take all the time you need. When you are ready to continue, punch EXIT."

Helen rubbed her hands together. The palms were cool and moist. The monitor screen flashed, and she saw an array of little creatures like something out of a children's cartoon show: bugs, elves, tall gaunt beings clothed in capes and hoods, something that looked like a teddy bear she had once dearly loved, and a human. In the exercise, all these beings were representatives of various planets waiting to see the governor of a planet called Felant, an industrial center for heavy manufacturing in the local galaxy. Her task was to determine the order in which the governor would meet with these representatives without causing jealousies among them, and with an eye on maximizing poten-tial profit. It was a task she had done for Moffit and Nelson when she was younger, and before she had been turned in for a still younger model. She accessed data about each of the little crea-tures, having fun with the imagination of the exercise, feeling confident about her results when she punched EXIT only twenty minutes later.

The next task was similar to the first, only now the governor was giving a dinner party for his alien business associates, the same ones as before. The task was to place them properly at the table. Two unknowns were to be determined by selection: the race of the governor, who would sit at one end of the long table, and his protocol officer, who would sit at the other end. The machine instructed her to select SELF for the protocol officer. Okay, the officer is a human female. Now for the governor. She selected DEZIRLI, male, a species that looked like cats with large green eyes. Meat eaters, and dominated by males. In the end, the fact her governor was male was the biggest problem because one of the representatives came from a female-dominated world in which males were considered subservient. She seated this representative next to the protocol officer, another female who then proceeded to discuss business as if she were governor, but acting on directions of her superior.

Other problems were more easily solved, but took time wading through the myriad of data about each species, and her head was beginning to hurt. Finally she punched EXIT and sat back in her chair, stretching tired back muscles as subtly as she could.

A humming sound came from Mister Cox, and then a click.

"Excellent. You will be pleased to know only a few of our candidates have completed the exercises to this point."

A little knot formed in Helen's stomach. How many people were they interviewing? Surely one of them would be some young sweet thing, and she'd be out on the street again. Her head began to throb.

Another buzz from Mister Cox, and then, "Please remove your jacket, and stand in front of the mirrors to your right."

So now they wanted to take a *real* look at her. And why not? A protocol officer must be neat and pretty as well as charming, reflecting the good tastes of the boss. Where had she heard that before? So get it over with, Helen, and get out of here. She slid off her jacket and walked over to a set of three mirrors typical of a department store clothing section, glaring at her image there.

Dumpy shape wrinkled, a loose strand of hair, I'm a mess, she thought.

"Please place your toes on the white line and stand perfectly still for ten seconds," said Mister Cox.

She complied, wanting to close her eyes, painfully aware of the camera above the head of Mister Cox. She felt like a piece of spoiled meat on display.

"Thank you," said Mister Cox. "Now please remove the rest of your clothes."

"I BEG YOUR PARDON?" She jerked around, hands on hips, and glared straight at the camera. "I will not do that for any job!"

"Is there a problem?" said Mister Cox. "Others have—and, oh—I see—one moment please. Please resume standing as you were. We will proceed digitally. Again, remain in one position."

Now her head was splitting, and she wanted to flee from the room. But the part of her that desperately wanted a job, a sense of purpose in life, kept her from flight. She turned back to the mirrors, put her toes carefully at the white line as ordered, and prepared to endure whatever she had to except to remove her clothes and look at a naked body she loathed.

The room lights dimmed and the mirrors were suddenly black, her image there a sketch in red without detail, a bare outline. As she watched, the image turned round and round, changing every second, growing fatter, then slimmer, hair first cut short as she now had it, then becoming a billowing mass framing a thinned face. Even the clothes changed as she watched: a severe business suit, then a lacy blouse with full pleated skirt, something she never wore because it made her legs look like sticks. Next was a skin-tight body suit and then almost nothing at all. She gasped, and put a hand to her mouth. The image in the mirrors broke up into a sparkling red fog.

"Please remain motionless," said Mister Cox. "We're doing all of this in real time."

Helen put her arms to her side and resumed her position before the mirrors. Why does it always have to come down to how pretty you are? I had the looks before Carl left me; why do I have to keep up a charade the rest of my life? To please a man?

A figure shimmered in the mirror, a slender figure in a long sleeveless gown and hair piled high, standing in a regal pose. Helen swallowed hard to keep the tears from her eyes. She knew who the figure was, or was supposed to be, but in a moment, when the lights brightened, the reality would be there again, overweight and wrinkled, the gown and slender figure a fading dream. Why are they doing this to me? To see if I can cry?

"Well, that seems to be all for now," said Mister Cox, and the lights brightened in the room. The mirrors were ordinary again, but for an instant she had seen herself standing tall, chin up, gaze haughty yet serene. Princess of darkness, but now it was bright and she slouched once again.

"Are we finished here? I'd like to leave."

Mister Cox buzzed, head jerking towards her. "You must first return to Mister Doreen's office to complete the interview. Have a good day." He returned to his eyes straight ahead position, hands folded neatly before him.

The camera turned to follow her rapid exit from the room.

She walked quickly down the darkened hallway, head pounding, rummaging in her purse in search of an aspirin and finding none. She nearly fell down when her foot slipped on some floor moisture near the elevators. In slipping and catching herself she pulled a little muscle in her back, and now she was hurting all over. She punched the code for Doreen's floor into all three elevators, but only because she didn't know the code for street level and sudden escape from the building. Get the interview over, get out of here and find a nice little clerk's job on Wall Street where you don't have to meet people. Lunch in the park, alone. But it's better than being humiliated.

At least one elevator was nearing her floor. She waited in the darkness, rubbing the back of her neck with one hand, but when the elevators arrived two doors slid open at once, flooding the hallway with light. Head down, still rubbing her neck, she turned towards the left door. A loud squawk and rapid clicking sound froze her to the spot; she looked up and saw an appendage like a hairy fruit picker banging away at the access code panel inside the elevator. A huge head, multifaceted eyes and a beak for a mouth appeared for an instant to squawk at her again, and then the door banged shut, leaving her standing there with a hand at the back of her neck, her mouth hanging open. She held that position for moment, flushed hot, wondering if it was the headache or the stress of the interview. I've never hallucinated before, she thought. Or is it some other stupid test of my reactions?

She stepped into the other elevator and took it back down to Doreen's floor. He was waiting for her.

"Ah, come in, come in. Take a seat right here, please. And what did you think of our Mister Cox? A rather dull 'person', isn't he?" Doreen laughed, a nice natural laugh, she thought, and then he took his place behind a large desk.

"It's the first time I've been interviewed by a robot," said Helen. Her voice was strained, head hurting so fiercely now that little black spots danced before her eyes. She could imagine the lines appearing around her eyes and on her forehead. Pain lines, guaranteed to age.

The sight of the apparition in the elevator flashed through her mind, and she fought for control, clasping her hands together in her lap to keep them from shaking. Doreen leaned forward across his desk, looking concerned.

"Are you feeling ill?"

"No," she said too quickly. "It's nothing, really. I had a little fright upstairs, but it's nothing—nothing at all. *God, will you shut up! You're babbling!* She took a deep breath, letting it out slowly as Doreen settled back into his chair. He took a card out of a drawer and stared at it pensively, shaking his head slowly from side to side.

"These scores are really remarkable, Helen. I've never seen anything quite so close to perfection. Only one error, though the consequences might have been interesting to say the least. The Eridani you placed at your right hand should have gone at your left, because the entire race is left-handed, or should I say left-clawed?" Doreen chuckled at his little joke, eyes sparkling merrily.

"I'm sorry, I missed that," she said glumly. "The test was a little unusual."

Doreen laughed. "A test I designed myself, and the little alien characters were particularly fun to do."

You should have seen the big one I nearly ran into upstairs, she thought. Helen smiled faintly, squeezing her hands tightly together.

Doreen became serious, looking again at the card in his hand. "When I see scores like this and look at your experience I have to wonder why you've been out of work for so long. Can you give me some ideas about that?"

Her hands were suddenly two wet rags knotted together. "Well, I've been rather selective, trying for some good positions that would allow me to travel and see something more of the world. I've been in New York all my life, and—well, I just want to get around more and meet new people."

Doreen paused, then, "I'm thinking there might be more to it than that, Helen."

A flash of anger made her bold. "Yes, there is. I think the modern corporate executive thinks more about the appearance of his administrative assistant than of her abilities to do the job." There, it was out, and now *he* could give an answer.

Doreen leaned back in his chair, and made a little teepee with his hands. "It might surprise you to hear I agree with that, Helen, but it is a fact that neatness and good grooming are important in the business world. Look, I can identify with what you're indirectly saying. Three years ago I was in a position similar to yours, looking for a job, having difficulties finding a place that would accept me for my abilities rather than my corporate image, and it was very frustrating. But then I met R.E. Pixl and my whole life changed. He recognized my abilities and gave me the chance to use them, and in just three years I have become an executive in a major corporation with a future. And I'm expected to dress for the part."

"I don't have a problem with that," she said hurriedly. The interview seemed to be going downhill rapidly, and the black spots were dancing madly before her eyes.

"Good. It's like the digital hologram we checked you over with upstairs. You know—the mirrors. It's an electronic thing I play at a keyboard, giving me anything I can imagine."

"The thing your robot wanted me to take my clothes off for? You were watching, weren't you?"

Doreen actually blushed, trying to hide it with a hand. "I must take responsibility for that. So many cultures and customs, and I simply forgot how puritanical some of them can be. It's much easier to make digital reconstructions when the subject isn't dressed, and I had simply left it that way in the program. I'm sorry. And yes, I was watching. The images you saw were keyed in by me."

"They were interesting, although I really didn't know what was happening." She tried to sound indifferent, and came close.

"They were all you, or what you can choose to look like. I keep a hard copy of one I made of myself. If I lose another few pounds I'm going to look like my image in that hologram." Doreen smiled again, a warm friendly smile that seemed to relax her whenever she saw it. He wasn't really so short or portly as she had imagined from her first impression. A very neat man, quite professional yet warm personally. He stood up, leaned forward, fingertips on the desk top. "I think now it's time for you to meet Mister Pixl."

Doreen touched a button on a speaker phone to his right. "We're ready now, Mister Pixl. Can you spare us a few minutes?"

A hoarse voice answered, strangely distorted. "Yes I can. Bring her right in."

Doreen gestured to Helen to follow him into the next room. At the door he took her by the elbow, speaking in a whisper. "Time to meet the boss. He takes a little getting used to. He's very business-like, but fair, and extremely generous to his employees. Outside of me, you will be his closest associate here if you're offered the job. Okay?"

Helen nodded painfully, and Doreen pushed open the huge doors leading to the darkened office of R.E. Pixl, President.

Ahead of them was a black wall, glistening like clear plastic or glass, and on the wall was projected a huge image of a galaxy, thousands and thousands of stars showing individually as points of red, blue, yellow and white. "Oh," said Helen at the sight of it, for it was the most beautiful thing she had ever seen. Areas of the galaxy were outlined in red, green and blue, and a single yellow star out towards the galactic rim stood out brightly when compared to all the others. In front of the projection stood a massive desk, top bare except for a single computer work station radiating green light. A high backed chair in black leather was turned away from them when they entered. The walls were lined with computer terminals; all screens active, displays changing second by second. Helen barely glanced at them as she approached the desk, the sight of the galaxy holding her attention.

Doreen was close by her side. She whispered to him, "I've seen that picture before. It's the Andromeda galaxy."

He whispered back without looking at her. "No, Helen, that is *our* galaxy, and the bright yellow star you see up there is our sun."

She started to say something, but then the chair was turning towards them, light from the computer terminal on the desk illuminating the tall gaunt figure sitting there. Helen made an audible gasp, and Doreen squeezed her arm reassuringly.

The figure in the chair was anything but human.

Huge black eyes looked at her from a triangular face with two vertical slits for a nose and a tiny, almost circular mouth. The head was massive, crowned with a pair of earphones from which a tube curved around the face and to the mouth. The figure leaned forward and placed a small box on the desk, then eased back into the chair. Helen got a glimpse of a slender hand with long fingers and an opposing thumb. Doreen's hand was lightly around her arm; she reached over and clutched it firmly, struggling to control herself.

"Helen," said Doreen, "I'd like to introduce you to R.E. Pixl, our president."

The galaxy spun in a blur of color. Helen's knees sagged, and Doreen's grip tightened on her arm.

"How nice to meet you, Mister Pixl," she said, and her voice was steady.

Pixl nodded his massive head, and pointed to a chair. "Please sit," he said. "I do understand your surprise, Ms. Trumbold."

The sound of Pixl's voice seemed to come from the little box on his desk. Helen sat down in a plush chair, Doreen hovering over her. Pixl sat quietly, fingers drumming slowly on the desk top, and she immediately had the feeling he understood what was happening to her, understood her distress in observing something beyond her wildest imagination. She pushed herself up in the chair, swallowed hard and forced a smile. "I've had several surprises today, Mister Pixl, but I think—no, I'm sure I'm ready to answer any questions you have about my qualifications." She combed a strand of hair back from her forehead with one hand and took a deep breath.

The small mouth moved and Helen was reminded of the chittering sound she had heard before, but then a louder voice came forth from the little box on the desk. "Of course, Ms. Trumbold. My only function in this interview is to tell you something about the company."

Pixl stood up, dwarfing his visitors. He stepped up to the wall projection, a black robed figure against the light of the galaxy, and pointed out various features.

"The little box is a translator," whispered Doreen into her ear.

"As Doreen has told you, Ms. Trumbold, this is your galaxy and this is your star. The star of the parent company is over here, a journey of a thousand years by light, so you see this is also *my* galaxy. Within the blue and yellow sectors I have thus far established one hundred and fifty outreach centers, and now we're moving into the red sector closer in towards the galactic core. My business, Ms. Trumbold, is trading, anything and everything. My current interest on your planet happens to be in heavy and exotic metals, and helium. Business is good; the galactic demand is high for these products." Pixl put a hand on one hip and glanced at her, looking for a reaction. What she saw before her was not an alien, but a chief executive officer. She nodded, showing he had her attention.

"Everyplace I go I take on ten partners, but only one of these joins me in my travels. On your planet, Mister Doreen is that one, and he is in immediate need of an administrative assistant to handle our protocol problems as well as contract language in many different cultures. That person must be highly adaptable, able to deal with a variety of races, only some of which are humanoid, and be willing to travel extensively. I note that you have not run from this room in fear, and you have not even mentioned your brief contact with one of our associates upstairs."

"Trizyrl is still shaking," said Doreen, grinning at her. "He has never seen a human female up so close."

Helen looked at Doreen, and then back at Pixl. Suddenly she was a little angry. "I didn't tell Mister Doreen about it, because I thought he would question my sanity. It really was quite a shock for me."

"I'm sure it was, as it was for Trizyrl, but you adapted to it, and that is important. The person for this job must be very flexible, but in return I will show that person a hundred new cultures and half a galaxy. Really, now, I must get back to work, and Doreen can answer any questions you have. Please excuse me." Pixl sat down in his chair. The interview had clearly come to an end, but he extended a long hand to her.

Helen went to his desk and shook his hand. "Thank you for your time, Mister Pixl. You have been very kind to see me during your busy day." His hand was cold and dry, the grip fragile. Pixl nodded once, and then turned to the computer console and began working. Doreen guided her out of the room.

"This has been an unusual day for me," she said.

"I'm sure it has. I can still recall my own experience; it was frightening, but still fantasies come true for me. I wouldn't leave it for anything, now. Do you have any questions?"

"The distances you travel seem incredible."

"Well, we do travel several months a year, but I see what you mean. I don't understand the details, but to put it into Mister Pixl's words, 'the shortest distance between two points is a singularity'. It always delights him to say that."

"Do you have any more questions about me?" she asked.

"No, I think we have everything we need. Will you be home this evening for a phone call? I need to move ahead on this pretty quickly, so one way or another you should know my decision this evening." His face was serious, more so than she had seen before.

"Yes, I'll be home." *Where else would I be?*

Now he smiled again. "Good, then I'll be in touch." He took her by the elbow, guiding her few steps to the elevator. "I'll call a cab for you right away."

The elevator door opened. Helen smiled, held out her hand and he took it firmly. "Nice to meet you, Helen," he said.

"Thank you, Mister Doreen, for everything." The elevator door closed, and at first she had a good feeling. But then, during the brief descent, she thought about the exam error she'd made, her prudish response to the robot Cox and her knees sagging in Pixl's office.

When she reached street level, Helen felt miserable again, and the headache was still there. It was enough for today; home to relax, then another job search tomorrow. The entire day had been unreal, including the rapid appearance of a cab that took her back to her apartment. She plodded wearily upstairs to the second floor, breathing in the odors of curry and hot peppers and something burned. She let herself in and turned on the dim light. Home sweet home.

She kicked off her shoes, plopped into an overstuffed chair by the unmade bed and stared at the picture of her deceased mother on the dresser across from her. The room was small, with a kitchenette in one corner. A single window looked out at the brick walls of a neighboring building blocking any sunlight or warmth, so it was always cold and gloomy inside. She paid for steam heat, but only occasionally got any and spent a lot of her leisure time in bed. The walls were bare and she shared a bathroom down the hall with three other tenants on her floor. It was a dreary place, but it was all she could now afford. And so she sat there, looking at the kindly face in the picture, wondering at the waking nightmare her day had been and knowing she could never tell anyone about it. It's bad enough to be plain, single and out of work; another thing to be crazy, she thought. Momma, what would you think if your daughter said she wanted to be a dinner hostess for six-foot cockroaches?

She thought about the horror in the elevator, and Pixl's long fingers drumming on the desk, and the serious look on Doreen's face at the end of her interview. Executive or not, that man had warmth, and she decided she liked him. But the whole scenario was still beyond her imagination: traveling in interstellar space, business with bug-people and hopping around the galaxy like fleas? If you wanted travel, Helen, this is the ultimate in it.

Her head still throbbed, and she closed her eyes to relax. Wait for the call, he'd said, but she knew what the answer would be. Sorry, Helen, but you're just not quite right for the position. We've found someone younger, someone willing to take off her clothes for Mister Cox, and besides that you made an error on the examination that could have started a war. Also, Mister Trizyrl doesn't like your look; it's offensive to all his senses and he is an important client of ours. You really must do something about your appearance, you know. You're so plain, drab and dumpy. How could you imagine we would ever have considered you for—?

Her world was shattered to blackness with the ring of a telephone in the hallway just outside her door. She heaved herself from the chair, glanced out the window to see that it was now dark. She jerked the door open and grabbed for the telephone, nearly taking it out of the hands of neighbor Luís García, who glared at her and mumbled something in Spanish. There was no time to be nervous or apprehensive, but she knew who the call was for and who would be on the other end of the line. *Get it over with*, she thought.

"Hello?"

"Helen! Gerard Doreen here. I'm glad I caught you at home. Do you have a minute to talk now?'

"Oh yes. You said you'd call tonight." Her heart was pounding.

"Well, I made a couple more calls and talked it over with Mister Pixl, Helen, and we'd like to offer you the position with a starting date as soon as possible. Certainly no later than two days from now, because we ship out then. If you can give me an answer right now that will be great, but if you want some time you'll have to get back to me by tomorrow morning. What do you think?"

She had been holding her breath, unbelieving. It couldn't be possible; she was still back in the chair, sound asleep.

"Helen, are you there?"

"Oh, I'm sorry. This is really a surprise, Mister Doreen; I wasn't at all sure of an offer, and so I haven't given it much thought. I don't think I can really give you a good answer right now, but I have your number, and—"

"Call me by tomorrow morning, Helen. Please. We really think you're the best we've seen, and I know you'll love the experience. I can show you a hundred worlds you've never dreamed of, Helen. Isn't that what you want?"

"Yes, of course it is. It's just that the whole thing is like a kind of dream, and I'm having trouble believing it. Can you understand that?"

Certainly I can, Helen. It hasn't been that long since I had the same experience. The difference is I know what lies ahead, the things you can look forward to. There's nothing on this planet to compare with it. Look, I've got a messenger on the way with something you can keep even if you turn us down. That some-thing is from me, Helen, and it's personal. I want you to look at it, and think about it before you call me back Okay?" the cadence of his speech had slowed, his voice now softer.

"All right. I'll call you back tomorrow morning"

"Anytime. Call me anytime, Helen. I won't be disturbed by it"

She went back into her room, locked the door behind her and paced nervously for an hour before undressing and slipping into bed Her mind seemed a jumble, her logic constipated. You wanted a job and now you've got it and now you don't want it. Why? Working with creatures out of a monster movie and a boss to match? Something about Doreen, who sounds so eager for me to take the position? She looked at the picture on her bureau. Oh mother, why did you have to leave me so soon? If only you were here to talk to, but then you'd probably not believe anything I said.

She dozed, falling into a dream of a banquet with herself at one head of the table, Pixl glowering at her from the other end. Around her were bizarre creatures, mouths slavering, antennae waving frantically, their conversation a jumble of chitterlings and shrieks, and then the one nearest her put a three-fingered claw on her forearm.

She awoke groaning and sweating, jerking herself upright in the bed. She needed a glass of water, got up to get it and stopped. An envelope lay on the floor where it had been pushed underneath the door. She retrieved it. On the front were only her name and address, and then she remembered. Doreen was sending something to her. So soon. She opened it up, expecting to find a letter or contract, but what she found there made her gasp. A picture, flat yet three dimensional, lay in her hands. When she bent the picture in handling it, the figure there seemed to move, rotating so she could see front and back. It was a picture of an image she had seen in the mirrors, a woman in a long white, sleeveless gown, a picture of herself as Doreen had visualized with his computer. She turned it over; on the back was a scrawl in black ink. "If you decide not to accept the offer, this is still yours. This is the real Helen, and I hope you'll believe in her." It was signed 'Gerard Doreen', with a flourish.

She sat down on the bed, staring at the picture for a long time. The face was radiant, the figure slim. It wasn't her, and yet it was. Doreen had simply modified her true image in the mirrors: new clothes and hair style, a little digital carving of excess flesh here and there. But there was more. The look on the face was self-confidant, haughty, almost regal. She remembered the days when she had felt like that, when she was younger, the days when she was in demand, the days before Carl had left her.

It struck her then that it had all changed when Carl had left her. Change of life, he'd said. It was a frantic escape from a life that was stifling him, a desire to be free. Oh, so that was why he'd taken up with a girl half his age? The girl had been carrying his child even then, yet he'd said over and over again he had no desire for children, despite her own pleadings. It was then she'd decided it was all her fault he was leaving. She was old, undesirable, a pathetic bore without a future. And for seven years she had believed it, dressing a part, acting a part, ruining her own life because of something a man had done to her.

She looked again at the picture—and saw herself there.

García peeked from his doorway while she was dialing the telephone, but her withering glare made him dart back inside again. Doreen answered on the first ring. "This is Helen," she said. "I've decided to accept your offer, Mister Doreen; I'd be foolish not to accept such an opportunity. Would you be able to help me with some last minute arrangements? I'm going to give up the apartment here."

"Oh, Helen, I'm so please, so very pleased. Yes, of course, I'll do whatever you ask. How about an early start over breakfast in the morning, say seven-thirty? I'll bring your contract along."

That sounded just fine to Helen.

* * * * * * *

She stood before the wall-sized screen gazing at a mammoth red star, prominences arching out far from the surface and falling back in a splash of ions. In the foreground a green planet with scattered white clouds floated lazily. They had made two jumps, but had been traveling at sub-light speed now for nearly a month.

The door behind her slid open and Doreen glided into the room, a plastic drinking bottle in each hand. He touched down lightly beside her, held out her volume of bluish liquid and she took it with a smile.

"All out of champagne," he said, "but this is even better. Sip it slowly so it can linger on the palate a while." He held up his bottle in a toast. "The adventure begins."

The two bottles came together soundlessly before the red sun.

"Thank you for the chance, Mister Doreen," she said sweetly.

"Oh please, Helen," he said, "please call me Gerard."

ABOUT THE AUTHOR

JAMES C. GLASS is a retired physics and astronomy professor and dean who now spends his time writing, painting, and traveling. He made his first story sale in 1988 and was the Grand Prize Winner of Writers of the Future in 1991. Since then he has sold seven novels and three short story collections, and over fifty short stories to magazines such as *Aboriginal S.F.*, *Analog*, and *Talebones*. Jim writes science fiction, fantasy, and dark fantasy. He now divides his time between Spokane, Washington and Desert Hot Springs, California with wife Gail, who is a costumer and healing dancer. There are five grown children and eleven grandchildren scattered around the country. Jim also paints mountain, desert, and red rock scenics in oils and pastels, and is often heard playing didgeridoo and Native American flute. For more details, please see his web site at:

www.sff.net/people/jglass/

CPSIA information can be obtained at www.ICGtesting.com
Printed in the USA
LVOW041110030312

271323LV00002B/4/P

VOYAGES IN
MIND AND SPACE

Here are six long stories of mystery, fantasy, and science fiction to entertain you, and a rare poem by the author.

A woman and her daughter discover there is more to death than biology, a young student bullied at school finds power in a poster, and a hog-farmer begins a journey to his destiny in a rainstorm. A grandson finds himself in danger for suspecting that his grandmother is doing a "bad thing" in her basement. A creature from mythology is reunited with her lover from a distant past, and an astronaut dreams of a love unbounded by space or time. Great reading from a master storyteller!

Borgo Press Books by JAMES C. GLASS

VOYAGES IN MIND AND SPACE

STORIES OF MYSTERY AND FANTASY

JAMES C. GLASS

James C. Glass (signature)

THE BORGO PRESS

MMXII

VOYAGES IN MIND AND SPACE

FIRST EDITION

Published by Wildside Press LLC

www.wildsidebooks.com

DEDICATION

For the writers, editors, and readers who have encouraged me over the years. Thank you very much for the support.

CONTENTS

FOREWORD

Here is the second set of stories rewritten specifically for this volume and appearing in print for the first time. The mix is a bit different from that of "Touches of Wonder and Terror." There is a poem, two novelettes, and a couple of psychodramas for your consideration. The poem "Night Demon" was inspired by the fondness my wife and I had for the TV series *Beauty and the Beast*. "Moon-Man" sold to *Eldritch Tales*, "Following the Rain" went to *Owlflight*, but neither appeared in print before the magazines folded. "Social Security" was sent to a couple of mystery magazines and lay forgotten in my files for many years until now. The rest of the stories were near-misses in the magazine market, and I have used useful comments by editors such as Kris Rusch, A. J. Budrys, and Dean Wesley Smith to do the rewrites. Some rewrites have been extensive. "Cold Sleep" in its present form is thirty percent shorter than the previous draft. And, in response to comments on "The Depths of Love" by Kris Rusch, the entire story has been changed.

Rewriting the stories in this volume has been an educational experience for me. Rewriting is necessary, but difficult. In the heat of publishing efforts, a piece can often be sent out too quickly before an author can see what work remains to be done. On the other hand, it's possible to rewrite a story to the point where no life is left in it. A balance must be found, and I have tried to do it here. I would appreciate reader comments on these stories. Please send them to my web site at www.sff.net/people/ jglass/ and, if nothing else, at least let me know which stories

were your favorites.

My hope, of course, is that you enjoy all of them.

RAINBOW LADY

A practitioner of The Field arrived in morning mist with showers of gold and red leaves stirred by wind streaming down from the summits of Three Sisters. The small Oregon town was not yet awake, did not see her sudden appearance, a flash of bright colors in thick fog at the end of the main street. She followed the wind down the center of the street past the gas station and pharmacy, a café where lights newly glowed from upstairs windows. Her heavy coat was striped in rainbow colors, and she carried a small black satchel in one hand. She walked straight to the little shop she had rented by mail, and hung out her sign as the sun appeared over the mountains to the east.

"Ellen Barstead, Energy Practitioner and Quantum Healer," said the sign.

Within a day she was the talk of the town: an attractive, middle-aged woman, pleasant and well-spoken, likely some new-age practitioner who had come for the tranquility and tourist trade of a mountain town. Children who first saw her called her the Rainbow Lady. She did her grocery shopping and greeted her new neighbors in a friendly way, but was rarely seen outside after that first day. In her shop, she sat near the window where people could see her, and seemed to be lost in a meditative state for much of the time. Other times she watched the street carefully, perhaps waiting for a client to arrive.

And quite soon, when the wind was again blowing swirls of colorful leaves down the center of the street, someone did come to see her.

* * * * * * *

Nina Cole had always dreamed vividly in color, and in her dream the walls and ceiling were painted gold, and light flashed from a thousand facets in the crystal chandeliers hanging above her. Mark whirled her around the floor in a fast waltz and Nina tilted her head back, laughing. They had never actually danced here, but she remembered the place, a grand ballroom in Spokane's Davenport Hotel where they had once spent a night of delicious luxury before Angie was born. Mark whirled her to the rhythm of music unheard, kissed her neck and murmured, "I love you, wife," and she kissed him back hard on the lips, but the intensity and warmth of the kiss broke something inside her and the light went away.

She awoke in the darkness of the bedroom, and the bed was empty beside her. Mark was still dead, Angie recovering from the terrible accident that had nearly killed both of them, the drunken man responsible for it imprisoned for the next twenty years of his young life. Tears gushed as Nina sobbed into a clutched pillow. Her breath came in little hiccups and her cheek was wet against the pillowcase. She cried until she heard the click of a door latch, and sat up abruptly in the bed.

Angie stood in the doorway, pressing a stuffed turtle named Oscar to her chest. The eight-year-old's jammies were decorated with running bears, and reflected light from outside made her eyes seem huge in the darkened room.

"I'm sorry, honey, did I wake you up?" Nina sniffled, and held out her arms towards the child.

Angie was silent, but ran to the bed, climbed up onto it and crawled into Nina's arms. She reached up and touched her mother's wet face.

"I had another dream about daddy," said Nina. "It made me sad. I miss him so much, and I know you do too."

Angie hugged her turtle, and closed her eyes.

"We'll talk about it when you're ready; there's no hurry, but you'll feel better when you talk about it." Nina hugged Angie

tightly to her, and the child made a sad sound in her throat.

In minutes Angie was asleep again. Nina carried her to the other bedroom and tucked her in with Oscar. The wheelchair stood in a corner, unused for the past seven months. Physically Angie was whole again, but something remained broken inside her, a mental thing. She had cried in the hospital when they treated her broken bones, had called for her mommy and daddy, but since the day she'd learned her father was dead she hadn't spoken a single word.

Her imaginary playmate had come later.

Nina watched her daughter sleep and then left the room, closing the door softly behind her. She returned to her own half-empty bed and cried softly into her pillow before finally falling asleep. And if there were new dreams to make her feel sad, she didn't remember them.

* * * * * * *

"I'm sorry, Nina, but there's nothing more I can do. I'm not a psychiatrist," said Doctor Branson. "The x-rays are clear. She's perfectly mended. The rest of it has to be psychosomatic. In time it should go away. Be patient."

"I know she can talk. I hear her talking to somebody in her room sometimes, but when I go in there she's alone, and when I ask her about it she won't say anything. Could she be angry at me about something?"

"You're stretching, Nina. This has nothing to do with you. Angie has lost her father, and misses him. It's common for people to find comfort in speaking to a dead parent or loved one. It can be healing, as long as it doesn't become obsessive."

Nina shook her head. "It's not her father, but an imaginary playmate. When she's alone outside, swinging or in the sandbox or twirling around like she's dancing, I see her chattering away, and when I get close it's just gloomy silence. It's getting worse. We had our interview for a private school last week, and she was catatonic for it. They won't take her when she's like this."

"There's a child psychologist in Bend I can refer you to," said Branson.

Nina's eyes brimmed with tears. "She doesn't need a psychologist, she needs her father, and I can't be that for her."

Branson nodded his head, sighed, and thought for a moment. "There is something you might try locally, though my colleagues would not be happy with me if they knew I suggested it. A new-age healer recently opened an office here. You know: auras, chakras, energy balancing, that sort of thing. Reminds me a bit of Native American shamanism. I'm a professional skeptic, but I've seen it work, especially when there was no obvious physical disorder in the patient. You might give it a try. Her office is just down the street, where the old candy store used to be."

Nina sighed. "That's all you can suggest?"

Branson shrugged his shoulders. "I'm out of ideas. It's either that, or wait for time to heal things. She's a healthy little girl, Nina."

"If things get worse I'll remind you that you said that," said Nina, and Branson only smiled.

Angie was waiting for her in the outer office, perched on a chair and frowning. Nina took her hand and led her outside. "The doctor says you're fine, honey. He says you'll talk to me when you're ready to. We're going to see a lady who might help you with that."

Angie scowled at her, but didn't pull back.

"I'm not trying to rush you, hon, but if I don't do this now I won't do it at all."

The walk was short, and a door opened as they reached it. A tall woman stood there, white hair, handsome, a rainbow of colors in blouse and skirt. "Come in, come in. Your doctor just called."

They entered a place with comfortable chairs and couches. The room smelled like lavender. Soft music and the tinkle of chimes came from somewhere, and water tumbled from a desktop fountain. "I'm Ellen Barstead, and you must be Nina," said the woman, and extended a hand. When Nina took it she

felt a liquid warmth flow from fingers to wrist and up her arm. She started to introduce her daughter, but Ellen was already leaning over to look closely at her.

"Hello Angie. You'll always be welcome here." It was said softly, but seemed to echo from a distant wall in the room. Angie looked up at Ellen with full moon eyes.

They sat. Ellen gave Nina a brochure describing the work she did, and asked about the problems Nina was having. It was uncomfortable at first with Angie sitting right there, but the child seemed mesmerized by Ellen and kept staring at her. Nina talked about the accident, the long period of physical healing, the longer period of complete silence and an imaginary friend. She was surprised when Ellen reached over and put a warm hand on hers.

"And how is mom doing? You've lost something too."

"I'm working through it," said Nina, her vision blurring.

"Dreams?"

"Yes."

"Vivid dreams? They can be healing or hurtful, depending on how you construct them. The Field can be used for good or bad."

"I don't understand."

"The Field is everywhere," said Ellen, "and we use it without thought. A vaster source of energy and information cannot be imagined. It can produce tiny forces, drive miniscule chemical reactions or accelerate the expansion rate of the entire universe."

Nina glanced at the brochure in her hand. "The vacuum state?"

"Some call it that. We see it so indirectly, a kind of flickering disorder beneath our reality, but connected to us. Many of us believe everything that has ever existed, or will exist, anywhere in the universe, is stored as information in The Field and can be retrieved from it. Some believe we come from The Field, and will return to it when we die. Death is only a change in form."

"I'm sorry," said Nina, "but I'm just not a believer in this sort of thing. I've never been a religious person."

"This isn't about religion, and you don't have to believe in The Field to use it. A part of you is using it now, and knows what to do. You're both sensitives, I could feel that right away. All you need to do is worry less, love each other and yourselves, and your healing will proceed nicely. Angie is actually making good progress at this point, but now her mother needs to begin healing."

Nina's face flushed. "That's it, then? No meditations or mantras or the holding of hands? And how much do I owe you for this consultation?"

"There's no charge for this interview," said Ellen, "and I will include your case in my own meditations."

"Well thanks for that, anyway." Nina stood up and took Angie's hand in hers. "Come on, hon, there's nothing more for us here."

"You're disappointed," said Ellen.

"Yes, I am, but this isn't the first time I've hurt myself by having expectations that were too high. I'll get over it."

Angie pulled back a bit, seemed hesitant to leave, and kept looking back at Ellen. And as they reached the door, Ellen said, "Say hi to Betina for me, Angie."

Outside, Nina looked down at Angie, and squeezed her hand. "Who's Betina?" she asked.

Angie's face was a portrait of pure astonishment, and for the first time in over a year she was smiling.

* * * * * * *

Nina awoke sobbing, and it was late morning. Sunlight streamed in from the window. The alarm had gone off and run down, and she hadn't heard it, but it seemed she'd been wide awake only moments before. Mark had been sitting on the edge of the bed, holding her hand; she could feel his warmth and smell his familiar musk, and it had been so real, not like a dream at all. "Hold me," she'd said to him, and he looked sad.

"I want to, but I can't, not the way you want me to. I love you,

Nina, I'll always love you, but we can't go on this way. There are things we need to talk about."

"What's so important to talk about?" she asked, and felt, not imagined, the squeeze of his fingers on her hand.

"About letting go, darling. You have to let me go."

The shock had awakened her with a gush of tears, and she sat bolt upright, hearing a sound, a voice. It was Angie talking to herself or someone else in the other bedroom. Nina slipped out of bed, put on a robe and opened her bedroom door slowly without a sound. Angie's bedroom door was ajar, and the child was still chattering away. Nina crept up to the door and listened, one part of her cautious, the other joyous at the sound of Angie's voice.

"Mom won't believe anything she says, now. It won't work," said Angie.

Nina peeked in along the partially open door and saw Angie sitting on the edge of her bed, facing the door. She gestured with her hands, looked to her right as if talking to someone sitting there with her.

"Well, you're real to me, sort of. I wish you wouldn't fade in and out like that. Why can't you be solid so mom can see you too?"

There was a pause, Angie listening, and then, "I don't know what energy is. Missus Barstead talked about that Field thing, but I don't understand that either. I'm not as old as you. If mom could see she wouldn't think I'm lying, and I could talk to her again."

It was only a tiny touch, a lean too close, a wave of hair touching the edge of the door. The door moved, and creaked. Angie looked up in fright. "Oh," she said.

Nina pushed the door open, and stepped into the room. "Sorry, but I've been listening. Are you talking to your friend?" she asked, and held her breath.

Angie's expression went from surprise to fear, and suddenly to defiance. "Yes," she said.

"I can't see her," said Nina.

"I know. You don't have the right resonance, she says. You don't overlap, like I don't overlap with daddy." Angie's eyes suddenly glistened.

Nina's heart thumped hard. "What's your friend's name?"

"Betina."

Another shock. "Is she right there beside you?"

"Yes."

"Hello, Betina. I'm sorry I can't see you. And I don't understand what's going on." A tear ran down Nina's cheek, and she sniffled.

"She's sorry too," said Angie, near tears. She turned and shouted, "Well, can't you at least try?"

Nina stepped forward, held out her arms and Angie rushed into her embrace.

"I'm not lying, mom."

"I believe you, honey. Why did you say what you said about daddy?"

"He talks to you and touches you. When I see him in my dreams I'm a little girl, not even in school yet. It's all just memories."

"It's all in dreams, Angie."

"No—it's not. You want to believe that."

"What else—" she started to say, but then the air at the edge of Angie's bed seemed to shimmer, and for one instant a figure was there, sitting on the edge of the bed, no more than a silhouette. Nina gasped. Angie jerked her head around to look towards the bed, but as quickly as the apparition had appeared, it was gone.

"Did you see that, mom?"

"Yes."

"Maybe it was enough, Betina. Thanks for trying. Oh, bye."

Angie looked up at her mother. "She's gone now. It was hard for her to do that."

Nina hugged her daughter tightly. "It's so good to have you talking to me again. You're all I have left to love."

"What's happening to us, mom?"

"I don't know, but I wish it would stop."

They hugged for a long time after that.

* * * * * * *

The call was unexpected, and came in early afternoon before Angie had arrived home from school.

"Nina? This is Ellen, just checking in to see how things are going for you."

"Some strange things have been happening." Nina told her about the dream with Mark the previous week, and the apparition on Angie's bed.

"That's really quite good," said Ellen. "The memory of The Field is holographic, and you have to establish a resonance with it to retrieve information. When I said you were a sensitive I was more correct than I thought. I'm so glad Angie is talking to you again."

"I don't understand. Mark talked to me; it wasn't like a memory. Was I making it all up?"

"He is a living entity, Nina, but not in our world. His world is without time, and limitless. He has much to learn and explore, but you must allow him to do it. You have to break the resonance that binds him to you."

Nina felt sudden anger. "And how am I supposed to do that?"

"By saying goodbye to him, and getting on with your life. Could you and Angie come by my office this evening? There's someone you both need to meet, and I think it's time for closure in your case."

"I don't think so," said Nina. "I admit I've experienced some strange things, but the explanation still seems to be new-age nonsense to me. If it were true, everyone would be experiencing it and it would be headline news. An overactive imagination due to stress is a much simpler explanation. It's nothing personal, you understand? I think you believe what you say, and you're genuinely trying to help us, but it's not the right path for me."

"I won't try to force you, Nina, but it's important we meet

tonight. We should all be together to solve this. Think about it, talk to Angie, and get back to me before this evening, one way or the other."

"Fair enough," said Nina, "but it won't change anything." And she broke the connection to Ellen.

Angie came home from school an hour later, and Nina told her about the phone call.

"We should go, mom."

"No. I've had enough of this, and I don't want to be talked into believing it again. It's just confusing me."

"Please, mom."

"No!" Nina turned away from Angie, went to her bedroom and closed the door behind her. She heard sobbing beyond the door, sat down angrily on the edge of the bed and put her face in her hands. Tears came with her anger, and she spit out her words to the empty room.

"Why can't everyone just leave us alone, and let us do our grieving in peace? Why us? This is all so unfair."

A cool breeze moved the curtains by the window, and fell on her face, bringing with it a sweet odor that made her heart ache. She felt something touch her shoulder, and she started to turn around, but then there was a soft voice, saying, "Don't. You won't see me this time. My God, wife, you are the most stubborn woman I've ever known. Why can't you, for once, just do what you're told to do?"

The bedroom door flew open, and Angie was standing there, her eyes huge and her arms reaching out.

"Daddy!" she shrieked, and took a step into the room.

"Hi sweetie. I'm supposed to see you tonight, if your mother will let it happen."

Nina jerked around to look behind her, but nobody was there.

"Daddy," said Angie softly. "He's gone. He's GONE!" She burst into tears and ran from the room. A door slammed shut.

Nina sat there for a moment, stunned, then went to the telephone and placed a call to Ellen Barstead.

* * * * * * *

It was dusk, and the street lights were just coming on when they arrived at Ellen's office. It had been humid that day, and the lights were hazy with mist as ground fog began to form.

Ellen was wearing her colorful blouse and skirt, and her little black satchel was sitting on the floor near the door. She sat down with them at a table lit by a single candle at its center, and folded her hands around a crystal bowl in front of her. "Well, let's get started, then, and get you on your way."

"We're not having a séance, are we?" asked Nina warily.

Ellen laughed. "All that has ever been or imagined, past, present or future, is in The Field, Nina. My function is to open channels for you to The Field, but you have done some of that on your own. I know you don't believe this. I just want you to put aside your disbelief for a moment and experience something others want for you and Angie."

"Others?"

"The people in this town, this universe, your husband, everyone who is with him now or in the future, the group awareness that makes up The Field. It's so rare to find people as sensitive as you and Angie, Nina. But we can only help if you'll let us. I want you to relax, both of you, and close your eyes. We're going to dream together. Listen to the tone, and let yourself fall away from it."

"Are you trying to hypnotize us?" asked Angie.

"Just relax. You're both safe here."

Ellen's voice seemed distant, and Nina felt a tingling on her face and neck as if fine hairs were standing up there. There was a pleasant feeling in her fingers and toes, a wave of pleasure starting in her chest and sweeping down her legs.

"You've arrived. Open your eyes when you're ready." The words were muffled, barely audible.

Nina opened her eyes. She was still at the table, Angie beside her, the child's eyes closed. But the room was gone. In every direction, up and down, sidewise, was a shimmering curtain

of rainbow colors, and they were floating there, yet beneath her Nina could feel something solid.

Angie opened her eyes, and gasped. "Where are we?"

"I don't know. It's some kind of illusion." Nina took Angie's hand in hers; it was solid, and warm.

"It's actually a representation," said a familiar voice.

Mark seemed to materialize out of a curtain of red and blue, walked up to them and smiled.

"Daddy," said Angie, and reached for him, but her hands passed right through him as if he were an illusion.

"Ohhh," she said, and sat down hard on her chair.

"I'm sorry, sweetie. I want to touch you too, both of you, but it isn't possible here. Ellen has made a special resonance for us so we can all see each other at the same time, and talk. It's like a window, Angie, but no energy or matter can pass through it."

"I miss you so much," said Angie.

"Me too," said Mark. "My little girl is beautiful."

Angie made a whimpering sound. Nina squeezed Angie's hand, remained mute, but now Mark looked at her.

"Hello, wife," he said, and Nina smiled. "I think you know why we're here."

"You're going to say goodbye," said Nina, and a strange feeling of calmness washed over her.

"Yes. For a while, at least. In the end we're all together, but for now you might say I'm being reassigned. I'm moving on to another place, a world unimaginably far from yours. I won't remember you clearly for a while, but you won't be alone, Nina. Something and someone wonderful is coming for you. It's all here in The Field, and I've seen it. It makes it easier for me to leave."

Tears came. "I don't see it, Mark," said Nina, and Angie started to cry.

"Angie, my baby, I am so proud of who you are and what you will become. The day will arrive when we recognize each other again, and then we can share memories. I wish you could see what I see. It's all so beautiful."

Angie sobbed, and Nina put an arm around her. Mark leaned over to look closely at them. There was no scent that Nina could detect, only an image.

"I'll always love both of you. Remember me when you can. Angie, you have a friend here who wants to meet you. I met her father, and now he and I are friends. But now I have to go. Please thank Ellen for this; she has arranged everything. Love you."

"Goodbye," said Nina. Mark's image faded and was gone, and all that remained were shimmering curtains of color and a sobbing child in her arms. She closed her eyes.

And opened them again at a table in a darkened room illuminated by a single candle. Ellen was not there. In her place was a blond girl around Angie's age, dressed in jeans and a denim jacket. She seemed startled, looked first at Nina and then Angie.

"Betina!" screamed Angie. The two girls leaped from their chairs and clung to each other, crying and talking so fast Nina couldn't understand anything.

Ellen came out of the darkness, took Nina by the elbow and led her away from the girls. "Betina lost her daddy too," she said softly. "She just said goodbye to him. The girl lives in Salem, and it's not so far from here. Her mother brought her in, and they're staying at the motel. Mom's name is Anne. Get to know her, let the girls be friends in the flesh. It'll be good for all of you."

"I thought she was imaginary. I saw—" said Nina.

"—Oh Nina, you can't intellectualize everything. There are just too many levels of reality that can't be seen by the human eye. Walk with me." Ellen picked up her satchel by the door, and Nina suddenly noticed the woman had put on her colorful coat.

"You girls stay here. We're going for a walk," said Ellen, but Angie and Betina barely glanced at her. Still talking excitedly and clutching to each other, they were nose to nose.

There was a damp cold in the street, and fog had moved in, creating fuzzy halos around the street lights.

"Where are we going?" asked Nina.

"I'm going away," said Ellen. "Make sure the door is locked after the girls finish their reunion, and take Betina back to the motel. You'll like Anne. The two of you have a lot in common."

"Why are you leaving? You just got here."

"The job is done, three cases in one, this time. I feel good about it."

"How do we get in touch with you?"

"You don't. You're on your own now. You have everything you need, both of you."

"But where are you going? The bus quit running an hour ago."

"I'm being picked up. It's just a short walk from here."

Ellen stopped, put down her satchel and grasped Nina by both arms, smiling. "This is goodbye, Nina, but I'll think of you. It's the strength of your emotions that makes your talent so strong. You have more to look forward to than you can imagine. Say goodbye to Angie and Betina for me. They're going to be life-long friends, you know."

Ellen picked up her satchel again. "Wait here. I have to go alone."

Why? thought Nina. "Thank you, Ellen, for everything. I wish you could stay longer."

"Me too," said Ellen. She gave Nina a wry smile, turned, and walked up the street towards the brow of a hill where swirling fog glowed between two street lights. And when she reached the top of the hill, her figure blurred by the fog, there was a sudden, colorful flash, and Ellen was gone.

Perhaps, thought Nina later, it was only the fog that had obscured her departure so suddenly from view.

NIGHT DEMON

(Vincent's Song)

I am the Moon-Man, imprisoned yet free.
Do not expect any mercy from me.

Blood I will take, until there is none,
so you and your victims will be buried as one.

Moon-Man, Moon-Man, violent and strong,
sustained in new life to make right the wrong.

Your victim cries out as your knife plunges down,
but Moon-Man is on you without even a sound.

Your throat disappears in a mouthful of gore,
and your murderous heart will not beat anymore.

Moon-Man, Moon-Man, prowling the night,
killing the wrong and defending the right.

She screams when you grab her, she struggles and moans,
but I am there quickly to make you atone.

She shrieks in her fright, not of you, but of me,
as I splatter your organs to help set her free.

Moon-Man, Moon-Man, protecting the dear,
but aching inside for the beauty so near.

She calls to me sweetly and then once again,
but still I must flee her because of the pain.

Her voice it reminds me of a departed one dear,
who once came to love me in spite of her fear.

The one who is with me, in the face of our son,
the sound of his laughter, the good things he's done.

So I wander the streets, a dark creature of night,
destroying the wrong and defending the right.

Moon-Man, Moon-Man, passionate and free,
locked in the bonds of an old memory.

MOON-MAN

Billy Corkill had been in his new school only two days when the gang caught up to him. He was standing on the corner, waiting for the North Long Beach bus to take him back home after a pretty good day. He had purchased a kosher pickle at Norby's, nice and sour, wrapped in a paper napkin. Every kid on the corner had one. It was the thing to do after school, and he had just taken his first juicy bite when three kids sauntered out of the alley next to Norby's and locked onto him like heat-seeking missiles. Tough kids he'd already been warned about. The slime of Garfield junior high society: Luther Fragen, tall, skinny, pocked-marked face, Erwin Monk, small, wiry, weasel eyes, and Chovy Willis, obedient follower of the other two, fat, and a little slow. They came up to him in step, like a firing squad, and the other kids scattered before them like mist, leaving Billy by himself. The three made a semicircle between Billy and the street, and pressed in close. Erwin took a switchblade from his pocket, flicked it open and tested the edge with a thumb, smiling.

"Hey, East L.A., what 'cha doin'? We been lookin' for ya all over the place." Luther's face was close, his breath smelling of cigarettes. Billy looked at the switchblade and swallowed hard.

"What do you want with *me*?"

"Want to meet the new kid. We hear East L.A. are tough. You don't look so tough." Luther's eyes were serpent black. He fondled Billy's collar. "Nice clothes. Momma dresses you good. Got any money?"

"No. I spent it all on the pickle. Look, I don't want any trouble with you guys, and my bus is coming."

"No money with those nice clothes? What *do* you have?" Luther sighed.

"Just my bus ticket." It was brand new, and had cost his mother fifty dollars. Only three fares had been punched on it.

"Then we'll have to settle for that," said Luther. "Hand it over."

Erwin raised the switchblade so Billy could see it better. The bus pulled up to the corner and the other kids scrambled onto it, one girl saying something to the driver and pointing towards Billy. The driver just sat there, keeping the door open.

Billy fumbled in his pocket and pulled out the bus ticket. "How am I supposed to get home?" His voice quivered with both fear and anger.

"Oh, we'll take care of that," said Luther, and Chovy giggled. Luther grabbed the ticket and tore off one corner. "There you go." He handed the tiny piece back to Billy. "You be cool, now, and don't cry about it. You say anything to anybody and we'll get you good."

He heard them laugh at his back as he got on the bus and handed the ticket nubbin to the driver. "It's all they left me," he said, near tears. The driver took it, shook his head and slammed the door shut. The bus was nearly full and Billy had to walk clear to the back past silent, sad faces, eyes avoiding his. He was thankful that nobody laughed, but that night was the worst part, when he explained to his mother how he'd lost the bus ticket, dropping it somewhere. She didn't scream or yell or hit, she just cried. On a clerk's salary, fifty dollars was a lot of money. He had never been so irresponsible, she said, even in the hard times. They had lived in squalor for ten years while the Long Beach house was being paid off by renters' money, and now they were in it, and now this. How could he do this to her?

Billy fled to his room, locked the door behind him, hot with shame and humiliation, and threw himself on his bed to scratch and tear at the pillow. He would pay her back from his paper

route earnings over time, of course, and she would forgive him as she always did. They had stuck together like glue since his father had run off. But how could he pay back the shame for allowing himself to be robbed in front of the other kids? He turned over on his back and stared at the huge poster on one wall, the figure in black, studded leather, hairy face with golden eyes and fangs exposed in a roar of challenge, metal claws reaching. Moon-Man, the crime-fighting werewolf of L.A. His hero, from the comics piled neatly in one corner of the room. He went to a closet and got the jacket he had saved for two years to obtain, put it on and looked at himself in a bureau mirror. Inserted the fangs, made for him for free by his best friend and fellow fan Lynn back in East L.A. where he had left him forever.

He looked in the mirror and saw a tall, skinny kid wearing heavy leather, and teeth that could punch holes in pop cans. Incomplete. He rummaged in a drawer, found the envelope he kept hidden there from his mother and counted the money in it. With the comics, and paying back his mother, another year of saving for the rest of the outfit. He returned the jacket to the closet, the fangs to a vial kept beneath his socks in a bureau drawer, and lay on the bed until dark, staring at the poster. That night, in Billy's dreams, Moon-Man came to him and told him what he should do.

* * * * * * *

Billy met George Silver in the middle of his first semester at Garfield. George was a huge kid, a hulk with brute face and lumberjack hands even Luther and his gang didn't mess with, although it was said he had once run with them. He seemed a nice, gentle guy to Billy, but George had a reading problem, and so when he was called on to read out loud before the English class it was a cause for amusement for everyone. Except Billy. George read slowly, haltingly, mouthing every syllable until kids were rolling their eyes at each other, so when he came to the word 'pick' and it came out 'prick' everyone screamed in

laughter.

George slammed the book to the floor, snapping its spine. "You sons o' bitches!" he roared, and stormed out of the room. Missus Hobsen glared at the class, then hurried from the room to find George. The class settled down except for Luther, sitting in the back row near Billy. He just kept laughing and laughing, until Billy frowned at him and caught his eye.

That was a mistake.

Luther's laughter stopped like a plug to his brain had been pulled. "Who you lookin' at, faggot?" he snarled, then jumped from his chair, took four big steps over to Billy and slapped him hard across the face. The slap was like a pistol shot in the deathly silence of the room, and no heads turned. Luther resumed his seat as Billy struggled to breathe, holding his face in his hands to hide the tears, saying nothing when Missus Hobsen returned to reprimand the class for their rudeness.

After class, Billy walked past George as the big kid was opening his locker, and stopped abruptly. There, on the inside locker door, was a poster of Moon-Man! He pointed at it and grinned. "Hey, I've got a big one like that in my room. You a fan?"

"Sort of," said George, not looking at him.

"I've got all the comics clear from number one."

"Yeah?" George rummaged in his junk-filled locker, looking for something. Found it, a small paper bag that looked like lunch.

"I got the jacket and the fangs, too. Still saving for the other stuff. How about you?"

"Can't afford it," said George. "My old man takes all my change and drinks up most of it. What I keep, we eat on. I gotta go to lunch, now." George slammed the locker door and started to walk away, but Billy kept up with him.

"Maybe you could come over sometime and read some comics with me."

"I don't read so good. You just saw that, right?" George still didn't look at him, and mashed the bag in one big hand.

"Oh, you'll get better at it with practice. Lots of people have

trouble reading. Look, I'll read some to you and then you try if you want to. I live just down the street, and maybe after school—"

"I work after school, and the old man won't let me go anywhere after. I hafta clean up after him." George stopped suddenly and glared down at Billy. "What do you want from me anyway?"

Billy couldn't look at him. "I just want to read some comics with someone, is all. I—I don't have any friends here yet."

George seemed to soften. "You're the new guy. Heard you had a run-in with the school creeps. Lookin' for protection?"

"No!" said Billy. "I'll take care of that by myself."

"Pure mean, all of them. Stay away from them or put up a good fight once so they won't be so quick to bother you again. They got the whole school buffaloed."

"But not you," said Billy. "I heard."

George smiled. "Broke Luther's nose when he called me stupid once too often. They haven't called me that since."

"But you're *not* stupid; you just need some reading practice. Look, I can bring in the comics and we can read during lunch. Just the two of us. That's all I want."

George thought for moment. "Okay, but not on the school grounds. You know that little park behind the ball diamond?"

Billy nodded.

"I'll meet you there at eleven tomorrow." George turned, and walked away.

And that was the start of their friendship.

They spent every lunchtime together from that day on. They sat shoulder to shoulder on a bench in the little park hidden from the school by tall trees and thick brush, and read a different comic each day. At first Billy did all the reading, pointing at the words while George watched closely, knitting his brow in concentration. Billy's mother had taught him the same way at age four, cuddling him in her lap with the funnies or a picture book, teaching him words and phrases before he had even learned his alphabet. And so now he taught George. Pretty soon

George was reading out loud the pages they had just finished and over the weeks it came quicker and quicker until George was reading to Billy with a satisfying, growling imitation of the voice of Moon-Man. They took parts, each reading the words of a character or two and lunch hour became a time of total fantasy for both of them. George's confidence grew, along with their friendship.

Billy managed to avoid Luther and his gang for a while, but there came a time early in his second semester at Garfield when they gave him no choice. The school jazz band was giving a noon-hour concert on the quad around the flag pole and kids were scattered on the grass, eating their lunches. Billy and George arrived separately from the park and as Billy tried to move closer he stepped squarely on a peanut-butter and jelly sandwich Luther had deliberately placed in his way. Squish. The next moment was a blur. Luther shouted a curse and grabbed Billy, pinning his arms, dragging him to the periphery of the crowd. "Fagot, fagot!" he screamed. "You did that on purpose!" Erwin and Chovy were right with him, darting away from Billy's kicks. "We're gonna can you!"

He was dragged to a trash can half-filled with garbage and Chovy finally got a hold of his feet. They slammed Billy head-down into the garbage can, his mouth filling with paper and something sour as the kids screamed, "Fight, fight!" but made no move to interfere. They pounded his head into the garbage again and again, and then suddenly there was a series of popping sounds, bone striking bone, and his legs were free. The garbage can tipped over with Billy still in it and he scrambled out sputtering and retching onto the grass.

Chovy was in front of him on the ground, holding his stomach and gasping for breath. Erwin lay flat on his back, crucified to mother earth, out cold, and Luther was struggling to stand, eyes rolling, his face covered with blood. In the midst of them stood the colossus named George, arms relaxed at his sides, fists still clenched and bloodied. "You all right, Billy?" he said gently.

"I guess so," said Billy, wiping banana from his face. "Geez,

it stinks in there." A kid wearing a letterman's jacket bent over to help him up. Kids were all around him, looking terrified, and then the school principle, Mister Kaufman, a former linebacker for U.C.L.A., burst through the throng like an angry tank. He pointed at Luther, Erwin, and Chovy.

"Okay, that's it for you three! I saw the whole thing, and there'll be no more of it! You're outta here as of now! Get off the school grounds immediately and don't come back until you're invited! I'm calling your parents, and checking you into Langsten for five weeks!"

The crowd murmured. Langsten was the disciplinary school across town where all the bad kids went. It was rumored the teachers there were all former Red Berets. Erwin, of course, didn't hear Mister Kaufman, and Chovy responded by throwing up the remains of a cheese sandwich onto the grass. Luther struggled to his feet, swaying, his face a demonic mask of blood and destroyed cartilage. He reached into his pocket and Mister Kaufman charged up to him, spitting words into his face. "You pull a knife on me, boy, and I'll break both your arms. That's a promise!"

Luther staggered away, hand in pocket, fixing his crazy eyes on Billy and George. "You're dead meat, both of you! I'll kill you! I *will* kill you!" The crowd parted for his exit.

"You name the time and place, asshole," growled George.

"Shut up, George," said Mister Kaufman, "and go get your hands repaired. The rest of you, break it up! You ought to be ashamed for standing by while this happened!"

And that was the end of the jazz concert on the quad.

It was *not* the end of Chovy, or Erwin, or of Luther Fragen.

Alone in his room that night, Billy pondered Luther's threat. What would he do if the maniac came at him with a knife? And those crazy eyes. He could be killed only because George had defended him. He lay on his bed with a crawling feeling in his stomach, a new comic as yet unopened on his legs, looking at the big poster on the wall: fierce eyes, sharp and horrible claws. *If only I could be like you. Luther would run like a deer.* The

figure in the poster stared balefully back at him in the gloom, absorbing him. In the shadows it seemed as if a cynical smile flickered on those thin lips. *It begins deep inside, with quiet courage and determination. The aggressor has the advantage until his prey becomes dangerous to him. The aggressor can know fear.*

Billy sighed, opened the comic and read it quickly from cover to cover, then sat up in disbelief, reading the last page over and over. The prices of the year-end sale were *half* of what they usually were. Carefully, he cut out the savings coupon and the order form and filled it out, his hand shaking. The following morning he took all but five dollars of his savings, purchased a money order at a supermarket, and mailed in his order. Four weeks delivery time. Four whole weeks to wait while Luther healed his face and nourished his hatred.

And it was three weeks later when the gang made its move.

* * * * * * *

George and Billy were reading in the park when the gang of three came crashing through the bushes near their bench. George jumped up, head lowered like a bull, muscles bunched. Billy stood ground beside him, fists clenched, feeling frail and small, but the gang didn't draw near or make any threatening gestures. Just stood there, faces somber. Luther stepped forward, nose flattened and twisted strangely to one side, eyes black and unreadable. He pointed at George. "You said name the time and the place, and I'm here to do it. Just you and me, stupid, right here at this bench at ten o'clock Saturday night. And bring a knife."

"You've got it," growled George, "but leave Billy out of things."

Luther's eyes never left George's face, and he snorted with contempt. "I got no business with the faggot. Just you and me, stupid. You don't show up, your house burns down the same night. Be here." Luther turned, and the others followed him

through the bushes without a backward glance.

"You can beat Luther," said Billy, relieved.

"Yeah, but the others will be here too. You can count on it."

"Then don't come, George. Meet him on your own terms."

George shook his head. "Can't do that, Billy. A deal is a deal."

"That's stupid," said Billy, then looked at George's face and hated himself for saying it. He put a hand on George's shoulder. "I'm sorry, George. It's just that I don't want you hurt over something you did for me."

George looked away. "It's not that, Billy. This thing between Luther and me goes way back. You're just an excuse to him."

"But I *am* involved," said Billy fiercely. "I'm involved because you're my friend."

George looked at him and swallowed hard. "Best friend I've ever had, Billy. Never thought I'd say that to anyone. What you've done for me you've done right here on this bench, and I don't want you getting cut up here Saturday night. It's my fight. Got it?"

Billy's mouth was dry and he shivered with frustration. "I'll—I'll think about it."

"You do that," said George, and then he turned and bulled his way out through the bushes, leaving Billy with his face in his hands, a half-read comic opened on the bench before him.

George didn't come to school the next day, or the one after that. Billy's lunches on those two days tasted foul, the comics left unread. He paced the little park, searched the brush for places to hide, imagining himself there ready to spring like Moon-Man onto the unsuspecting gang, tearing and shredding with fang and claw. *I've never had a real fight in my life. What good would I be?* And he remembered his relief when Luther had said he wanted George, and not him. *You're a wimp, Billy Corkill. Go home to your comic books. Leave it alone.*

In his room on Friday night he put on the heavy leather jacket, inserted his fangs and retrieved a baseball bat from the closet. He posed in front of the mirror, trying every way he could think of to look menacing, then threw down the bat in disgust.

Maybe I could make them all laugh themselves to death. He threw himself on the bed and fell asleep with the poster image of Moon-Man scowling at him.

The package arrived for him the following morning.

His mother was out shopping with his grandmother, and would be late. There was a pizza for him in the freezer. When he picked up the mail the package was there inside the front screen door. He threw the rest of the mail on a table and rushed to his room, tearing at the package with both hands. The claws were made from light aluminum, a kid's toy, but sharp. He strapped them to his hands, tested them on the package wrapping, felt something stir within him at the sight of the jagged slashes in the light paper. In minutes he was in full costume, posing before the mirror. Better, but still no menace, nothing to frighten three tough kids with knives. He studied the poster, realizing suddenly the first thing he had looked at was the horrible, golden eyes. The menace was in the eyes, windows to the savage beast-spirit inside. *It begins within, with courage and determination. The aggressor can know fear. Yes, I see that, now.* Billy lay costumed on his bed all afternoon and evening, without eating, staring at the eyes of Moon-Man and calling up the memories of his humiliation. *You're smiling at me, I can see it even in shadow. You know what I'm doing. You've told me what I must do. If only you could give me a sign.*

The image in the poster shimmered in dim light, eyes glowing, one claw growing larger as if reaching out for him. Within the gloom there came a low, threatening growl, startling him. Billy Corkill cleared his throat, and growled again.

His mother was due back at eleven. Billy locked his door, as usual, knowing his mother would think him asleep. He climbed out of his window, and left it ajar. It was ten o'clock when he left the house.

He reached the alley through the gate in his back-yard and followed it to within a block of the school. There was a dance at the gymnasium that night, and kids were everywhere on the streets. But the alley branched right to another, ending at a near

empty parking lot across a darkened street from the twelve-foot chain-link fence at the edge of the park. He had climbed it before, but never with claws for hands. He took a deep breath as a car filled with screaming kids roared by, then ran in a crouch across the street and leapt up onto the fence, claws hooking it. In seconds he was over the top, breathing hard with excitement and fear. The clearing was only yards away, and he could hear voices. Sweat broke out in tiny beads on his forehead, the jacket suddenly heavy and hot. His legs disobeyed his command to hide and moved him silently forward between the bamboo and scrub trees until he saw a bright light. Through the brush he saw a gas lantern sitting on the bench, light flickering on and off as figures moved in front of it.

The three of them were circling George, knives open and thrust forward. George's hands were out from his sides, palms up. "Come on, Luther. Just our hands. Just you and me. Let's see how tough you really are."

Luther laughed. "I'm not here to prove anything. I want you dead." He lunged, slashing low. George looked soundlessly down at the red slash in his tee-shirt, then hopped to one side as Erwin lunged at him from behind, narrowly missing a straight thrust.

Billy grabbed at the brush, shredding leaves and sprigs.

"What was that?" said Luther, startled, then pointing with his knife. "You got that wimp back there ready to run for the cops? Chovy, check it out. If it's who I think it is, drag him out here and we'll carve him a new face."

Chovy smiled and sauntered straight towards Billy, tossing his switchblade from hand to hand. The fat kid was only a yard away when Erwin lunged again at George and stabbed him in the side. George screamed and dropped to one knee. Perhaps it was Chovy coming for him, or the sound of the scream, or the sight of a helpless friend that did it, providing the excuse for something dark within him to come out, something that had always been there, but suppressed by a gentler soul. He would never know for sure.

But Billy Corkill exploded in a mindless rage.

The growl scalded his throat, and even as he erupted from the brush the fat kid was backing away before him, eyes wide. He feinted with the knife and Billy slashed at it, tearing flesh, the knife dropping to the grass. He slashed four times with both hands, Chovy's shirt disappearing in bloody shards, then hacked him on one ear, hooked him, pulled back hard. The scream turned his blood into hot lava, and he shrieked with delight. Chovy staggered to his left and stumbled from the clearing, crashing blindly on and on into the brush.

Now Erwin was coming at him in a crouch, waving his knife in great sweeps. Billy saw the instant of recognition in his eyes, the surprise but lack of fear as the blade swept upwards, ringing against a claw, and then he had the forearm in his hands, wrenching it to his mouth and biting down so hard his head vibrated as the fangs struck bone. Erwin's scream deafened him, the kid dropping to both knees before sprawling in the grass in a dead faint.

He advanced on Luther with a low growl, felt hot blood dripping from his mouth and chin. George looked up from one knee, holding his side with a hand. "Billy," he said weakly. "Jesus— Billy." Luther took one step forward, then started backing up, holding the knife out as if to ward off some kind of evil spirit. Billy stalked him, bloodied claws outstretched, backing him up to the bench and moving within arms reach. He looked in Luther's eyes and saw everything he wanted to see there. "Make your move, asshole," he growled.

Half bent over the bench, Luther's thrust was feeble. Billy parried it with one claw and slashed him rapidly across the face three times before the kid rolled over the bench and ran screaming into the brush.

"Billy!" cried George, sitting down on the grass, one side of his tee-shirt stained crimson. "Billy, you should see your face! Is it really you?"

"No," growled Billy, leaning over to check his friend's wound, "it's really the Moon-Man."

* * * * * * *

Erwin Monk never made it back to school. Sometime during the summer he got hold of some bad dope and was now a resident vegetable at Long Beach Memorial. Chovy Willis would finish out school at Langsten, where the good special education program there would get him ready to be on his own. It was Luther Fragen who showed up at Garfield in fall semester, ready to start ninth grade, and everyone was surprised. His face was streaked with long scars that would mostly disappear before the year was over, and it was said that the whole gang of three had had their collective clocks cleaned by some drug-pushing associates of theirs. But Luther had done well at Langsten, under the Gestapo teaching methods there, even scoring high on intelligence tests. Word was he was college material, and everyone was astonished by the news. He was changed in other ways as well. He was quiet, now, even subdued, and the anger had gone from his eyes. Still, there was anxiety on that first day of English class when Luther was sitting forlornly alone in the back row and Billy Corkill walked in and took a seat right next to him. Luther sat rigid in his chair, staring straight ahead as Mister Harkness came in to begin the class.

Billy leaned over and touched Luther on the arm, lifting his hand when the boy recoiled from him. "Hey," he said softly, "no more bad times for either of us. A new beginning, huh?"

While Luther looked him straight in the eyes, Billy smiled, and waited patiently.

"Okay," mumbled Luther.

"We're going to start with a reading by a student of mine from summer school to show what the summer reading program can do for you if you take advantage of it," said Mister Harkness. "You all know George Silver from last year, and *The Tale of Two Cities* you finished up then. I've asked George to read the last page of the book to you. George?"

George arose shyly and went to the front of the class, the kids slouching a little, preparing to be embarrassed for him again.

But when he read this time the words flowed freely and clearly, without a hitch, his voice rising and falling with the emotion of the final execution speech of the protagonist. When he finished, there was stunned silence in the classroom.

"I've never heard it read better, George," said Mister Harkness, and on that cue the entire classroom full of smiling kids exploded in applause, Billy slapping his hands together until they hurt.

"I owe a lot of it to a comic book and friend," shouted George above the din.

Billy laughed, looked over at Luther and saw that he was reluctantly applauding with the rest of them.

FOLLOWING THE RAIN

Homer Ewing twisted the steering wheel of the bouncing truck and squinted hard, trying to find the muddy road ahead of him. The rain was torrential now, roaring in his ears; corroded rubber on the weakly flopping windshield wipers did little to help his vision in the weak glare of the headlights. *I wouldn't even be here if some Jew hadn't hit a guy and tied up all the highway traffic*, he thought.

A road sign flashed by on his right: ELLINGSTON—ONE MILE. Lot of good that would do him; the whole town had been abandoned two years ago. It was a falling down ghost town now, and the road through it was in even worse shape. Officially, his shortcut was closed, and now Homer Ewing cursed himself for ignoring the road barrier back at the highway. But that had been before the rain.

It was his last thought before the collision.

Homer strained to find that single rut guiding him on the road. Rain and fog swirled violently ahead of him, but strangely there was no wind, and then the truck lurched suddenly from side to side and the cab was filled with light. He had a brief glimpse of a gravel road in full sunlight and he started to turn the wheel. The nose of the truck rose in a jerk, then slammed down hard, banging Homer's mouth against the wheel and one knee against the steering column.

The truck stalled, then roared into life again.

Homer tasted blood in his mouth. The motor was running at high speed, screaming in his ears. Windshield wipers squeaked

back and forth on the suddenly dry glass before him. He leaned forward to shut off the engine, and felt the warmth of sunlight on his face. Ahead of him was a grove of Aspen, swaying gently in a soft breeze, leaves covered with dew sparkling in morning sunshine. Homer swallowed hard and looked at his watch. It was eleven-thirty-five, at night.

He stared incredulously ahead for a moment, but it was starting to warm up in the cab and his heavy yellow rain slicker made it seem even hotter. He pushed the door open slowly and stepped out, feeling the truck swaying beneath him. A quick glance showed the front tires bobbing a foot off the ground, front axle buried in a flower-covered embankment. He had missed a sharp curve in the road, and driven off it; the truck was hopelessly mired in the embankment. He walked to the back of the truck, felt water spray on his face, and heard the sound of rain. He looked up at flickering blackness spewing droplets, and then it was gone and he was staring at a well kept gravel road winding its way through sunlit meadows and tall Aspens again. Homer leaned on the truck gate, the sound of his heart pounding in his ears.

He watched the road closely, but there was no more flickering darkness, or sound, or sprays of water on his face. Just the road, trees, sunshine, and a harsh call from a crow somewhere behind him. He considered alternatives, as his heart-beat returned to normal. Could he have been knocked unconscious, and just awakened? No, the sun was too low for the time his watch was telling him. The watch *could* have stopped at collision, and just started again. That was it. But his mouth was still bleeding, and his knee hurt like hell. Fresh pain; he was thankful, at least, for that. When you have pain you know you're alive.

Don't you?

The fact remained that night or day, alive or dead, the truck was stuck, and back at his ranch there were a lot of hungry hogs and chickens to feed. Homer draped his rain slicker over one arm and started off down the freshly graded road towards the ghost town, then eight more miles to Hadley, and back to the

ranch. The warm sun felt good on his leg, and after a while he lengthened his stride. But at first he kept his eyes fixed straight ahead, trying to ignore the disturbing messages from his peripheral vision.

The scenery around him seemed to be changing, flickering, like the darkness and the rain on his face. Hills covered with thick stands of trees faded, only to be there again, then a flat plane, and rocks. Once there was a rumbling sound, startling him, and the smell of rotten eggs for just an instant. A part of his mind told him to ignore all of it, and then he saw the sign.

WELCOME TO ELLINGSTON—POPULATION 365.

The sign was new, and freshly painted. The three bullet holes in it even looked fresh. And when Homer saw the buildings, fear clutched at him.

Ahead of him the gravel road was lined on both sides by white wooden buildings, fresh looking, shining in the morning sun. He passed a bar: Jake's Palace. The sign in the window said it was closed. The grocery store next to it was also closed, but the windows were clean, showing off a carefully arranged display of canned goods. Drug store, law office, mercantile, and what looked like a warehouse, all were closed. Like Sunday in a small town, he thought, but it wasn't Sunday.

It was Thursday.

There was a gas station on the far edge of town, and Homer quickened his pace when he saw it: old-fashioned gas pumps with cylindrical glass tops showing pink liquid inside, and three cars were parked alongside them. Old cars, all classics. A thirty-four Ford two-door with an open rumble seat held his gaze the longest. A pretty penny somebody paid for that, he thought. The old Buick was nice, too. A few yards from the pumps was a ramshackle garage, doors open, with another old car up on the lifts, and a radio inside was blaring a big band tune. The deteriorating garage contrasted starkly with the freshly painted restaurant attached to it: white, like the rest of town, long rectangular

windows, and four steps leading up to a screen door. Lights were on inside, and faces peered out at him through the windows. Old, weathered faces and peaked caps, farmers watching him with the curiosity expected in a small town. A sign was painted on the front wall, red on white: ROSA'S GAS'N EATS. A small sign hung in one window: OFFICE. Homer stepped up to the door with a sense of relief. There were people here to help him get the truck unstuck and going again. The hogs had to be fed soon. He went inside.

Several heads turned to stare at him as he entered. He nodded to them, and they turned back to quiet conversations over empty plates and cups of steaming coffee. The restaurant was long and narrow: oil cloth-covered tables along the windows, and a counter bordered by a row of vinyl-covered stools with no back rests. The air was thick with odors of grease and coffee and potatoes frying on a grill. Homer suddenly realized he was hungry. He sat down on a stool just as swinging doors leading to a kitchen burst open and a short, heavily built woman with enormous breasts rushed out, carrying a metal tray heaped with dishes of food. She glanced at Homer with small black eyes, then screamed back at the kitchen.

"Ernie! Customer!"

She hurried to a far corner of the room, where three men smiled up at her, and one called out, "Hey Ernie! Rosa wants you!" There was laughter at the tables.

"I want you too, Rosa," said another, and there was more laughter.

"Oh shut up Frank," said the sweating woman. "I know what you want me for, and you're not getting' any." The faces at the tables were beaming, now, as she walked back to the kitchen with an empty tray. When she looked at Homer, there was a smile on her chubby face. "Just a sec," she said, then pushed her way into the kitchen.

"ERNIE!"

Somewhere in the kitchen a chair slammed up against a wall. "Jesus Christ! Break my ear-drums why don't you!" The kitchen

doors swung open and a short beefy man emerged, wiping his hands on a towel, and accompanied by a warm, sour-smelling breeze. He was a very hairy man, wearing a tee shirt, and on one massive upper arm was a heart-shaped tattoo circumscribing a name: Rosa. He looked from side to side, saw Homer, then walked over to him with a sheepish grin.

"Sorry. A man can't even have breakfast in his own place. What can I get you?"

"I had an accident," said Homer, "down the road, by a sharp curve." He pointed towards the other end of town. "Wonder if I could get some help to get my truck going again?"

The man looked at Homer closely, wiping his hands slowly on a towel. "You okay?" he asked. "There's blood on your mouth."

"Banged it on the steering wheel. I'm all right. The truck isn't damaged or anything, but the front axle is hung up on an embankment, and I'll need help to pull it off."

"Sure," said Ernie, "in a little bit. How'd it happen?"

"I don't know," sighed Homer, feeling relieved but suddenly a little foolish and confused. "I must have been knocked out. I mean, first it was dark and raining, and then morning sunshine. But I don't remember being knocked out. I just don't know." Homer shook his head, knowing how confused it all sounded. And he didn't dare say anything about Ellingston being a ghost-town. They'd think he was a nut.

"How about a cup of coffee?" said Ernie, looking concerned.

"Thanks. Maybe a doughnut, too. Any kind will do. But I've got to get going pretty quick. I've got a hog operation down by Hadley, and the animals are probably getting pretty hungry by now. Don't want them tearing up the place." He smiled as Ernie pushed a cup of coffee over the counter to him.

"Don't get down to Hadley much. Didn't know there were any ranches around there."

"Haven't been for very long. All of us moved in about the same time, in the middle sixties. Been at it for ten years, now."

"Oh," said Ernie.

Ernie put a plate heaped with large glazed doughnuts in front

of Homer. "Take your pick," he said.

Homer was startled when Rosa slid her ample body onto the stool next to his, and smiled at him shyly. Ernie seemed nervous about something, wringing his hands on the towel, then he held one big hand out across the counter and nodded towards the woman.

"I'm Ernie Bucholtz. This here is my wife Rosa; some people just call her Rose."

Homer shook the big hand; the handshake was firm, but moist. "Homer Ewing," he said, then took another bite out of the doughnut.

"Hi Homer," chirped the woman. "You married?"

Homer saw Ernie give her an angry glance. "Nope. I'm a confirmed bachelor. Bucholtz," he said, "now that's a German name."

"Yes."

"Good people, the Germans. The way they built their country up again after the war is a tribute to their character. Real backbone. We could use more of it in this country, and put the commies in their place."

"I guess we haven't seen that yet," said Rosa, looking at her husband.

Homer warmed to his favorite topic of conversation. "God, the way this country has gone downhill since the second world war. No guts at all, little countries pushing us around, the Russians taking over one place after another, and all we do is sit and stare. Before you know it, they'll be teaching Russian in our schools. We oughta nuke the whole bunch of them before they decide to do it to us. Won't do it, though. No guts."

He shoved the remaining piece of doughnut into his mouth, and licked his fingertips clean. "Sure, the president has been talking tough lately about this Chinese thing, but take my word, if China invades India, we'll just sit back and watch. That's all we ever do." Homer wiped his hands on a napkin, then pulled some coins out of his pocket and put three quarters and a half dollar piece on the counter.

"That should cover it," he said. "I've really got to get going, now."

Ernie pushed the quarters back, picked up the half dollar and studied it carefully on both sides. He handed it to the woman and she looked at it for a while before putting it back on the counter. "Nice-looking man," she said.

"Pretty good president, too," said Homer, wondering why Ernie didn't pick up the quarters, "before that commie Oswald shot him. John F. really had the country going someplace for a spell. Castro was probably behind the assassination, but we didn't do anything about that either."

Ernie took the coin to an old mechanical cash register, rang up the sale, then came back and put the change in front of Homer, who stared at it incredulously. Thirty-five cents: three shiny mercury dimes, and a slightly worn war nickel, all silver.

"You can't be serious," said Homer, feeling sudden greed. He handled the coins, inspecting the dates and mint marks. "This stuff is worth around twenty bucks now."

Ernie shrugged his shoulders and looked nervously at Rosa. "Fifteen cents for coffee and a doughnut. That's your change for a half."

"That's crazy," said Homer, then jumped when Rosa put a tiny, soft hand on his shoulder.

"Homer, there's something you have to know. Ernie and I will try to explain it to you, and it will be hard for you to believe it at first, but please try."

"What are you talking about?" Homer shrugged his shoulder, irritated by the touch of a woman, and her hand dropped away from him.

"I wish Ledoux were here," said Ernie. "He can explain things real good, and I know you'd believe him."

"He'll be here soon," said Rosa. "He always comes in when the storm is this close. But Homer needs an explanation right now, Ernie, before he runs out of here and tries to reach his truck."

"Right," said Ernie. "It's not safe outside now, Homer. We

have to stay inside for awhile because there's a sort of storm going on out there, and you could get lost and never find your way back, and I'd hate to be responsible for that. Just stay with us a while, and then some of the boys and I will help you get your truck going again, and get you back home. I promise your animals will get fed on time, if you just don't try to go outside now."

Homer Ewing said nothing, but remembered the water blowing out of a black void onto his sunlit face, and then a ghost town that wasn't a ghost town, and hills flickering in and out of view, and a rainstorm that stopped as if someone had thrown a switch.

Rosa patted his shoulder, then rubbed it. "Poor man. This must seem like a nightmare to you. But I think you know something strange is going on outside. Don't you?"

Homer nodded his head slowly.

"I thought so. Well, we'll try to tell you what's going on, but first answer one question for me."

Homer nodded his head again.

"What year is it, Homer?" asked Rosa.

"Year? Why it's nineteen seventy-five. There's nothing wrong with my mind, you know."

"Things were heating up," said Ernie, and Rosa gave him an angry look. "Sorry," he said, then poured another cup of coffee for Homer without looking up from the counter.

"Homer," said Rosa, patting his shoulder for emphasis, "Where you are, right now, it's nineteen forty-five."

Homer stared at her for a moment, then tried a knowing smile.

"Nineteen forty-five," said Ernie.

The smile faded.

"We got news about the new bombs, the atomic bombs dropped on Japan, just a few weeks ago. The war is expected to be over any day now." Rosa suddenly looked at her husband; his eyes were moist, and he rubbed one hand on the back of his neck.

"And Germany is a pile of stones and dead people," said Ernie.

Rosa leaned over and whispered to Homer as she reached out a hand to her husband. "He still has people in Germany. We haven't heard from any of them in over a year." Ernie took her hand in his, held it for an instant, then went back into the kitchen, momentarily leaving them alone at the counter.

"He's so worried, but he doesn't say much about it." Rosa looked at Homer sadly, then she was again alert, and urgent. "But you must believe us; here and now is nineteen forty-five. That accident you had this morning, near the curve on the road, everything you remember, is exactly the way it happened. You ran into a kind of time storm. I don't understand exactly what it is, even after Mister Ledoux explaining it to me several times. He's from the future, Homer, even the future for your time. I hope he comes today; he always comes over when there's a storm, and he's a teacher. He can make you understand. But please don't leave now. If you get caught in the storm, you might go far into the past or future, and never find your way back, and Ledoux says that could really mess up the flow of time, even change history." She looked pleadingly at her husband, who had returned from the kitchen and stood quietly listening.

"I didn't even finish the seventh grade," said Rosa.

"Ledoux explained it to me, too," said Ernie. "Something about turbulence, and stresses building up in some kind of space, and different causally related times getting mixed together at the same place, and if you wait a while the same turbulence comes by, and if you know what to look for you can walk back and forth between any times there are in the storm. We've been living with them for five years now. Don't know why they started, and neither does Ledoux. They're just here. They start out on the edge of the valley we're in, near where you crashed, and then move in as the day goes on. That's when it gets dangerous, and everybody stays inside. Hills disappear, and you see deserts and sometimes volcanoes. Saw a mammoth once, for just a minute. You know, those old elephants? Just

stood there, over by those trees, staring at us." Ernie pointed to a grove of trees just a hundred yards from the restaurant. The trees swayed in a light breeze, the hills beyond brown, clear and motionless. Homer watched them closely for a moment, waiting for something to happen.

"The storm is usually in those hills by this time of day," said Rosa. "That's where Mister Ledoux comes through. All of a sudden the hills sort of fade out, and there are really tall, green buildings, like a big city somewhere, and then they're gone, and here comes Ledoux walking down the hill to spend an afternoon with us. Real matter-of-fact about it all. In the evening he goes back to the hills, and we see the buildings again, and then he's gone. I've lost track of how many times he's been here."

"Comes over to stuff himself with Rosa's cooking," said Ernie, smiling. "always takes an apple pie back with him."

"Poor man says most of the food he gets in his own time is synthetic. Sounds awful." Rosa wrinkled her nose in disgust.

Homer looked back and forth, first at Rosa, then Ernie, a dazed expression on his face, wanting to believe, nearly believing, but stunned by it all. Ernie poured another cup of coffee for him; he sipped it a couple of times, then asked a question to nobody in particular.

"How am I going to get home?"

"I don't really know," said Ernie. "Like Ledoux does it, I guess. Aside from him, you're the only person from another time we've run into. Oh, there was that Bradley kid from our own town, but he doesn't really count. Got drunk one afternoon, and followed Ledoux back into his time. Popped back almost the instant he had gone through. Poof-poof, sort of. But Ledoux said the kid spent hours with him, and he showed him all around. Bradley didn't like it there, said nothing was green except the buildings, all the land sort of brown and dead looking. I guess they can't grow anything there, but Ledoux said they're trying it indoors now, with chemicals. Sounds crazy, doesn't it?"

Rosa just shook her head, not understanding any of it.

"Ledoux says in a single storm only a few hours are mixed

together, and these eddies, he calls them, can hang around for as long as a few days. When you leave, you pick a marker, a cloud or something that won't repeat exactly in time, and when you want to come back you look for that marker in all the boiling scenery. When you see the marker, you get into the storm fast, and—well—poof-poof!"

"You'd never get me to try it," said Rosa firmly.

"But that's how Ledoux is always so sure of getting back to his own time. It works for him," Ernie added.

Homer thought of the rain storm, and the black shimmering void suspended in air, rain blowing out of the blackness and into his face. "I have a marker," he said, and smiled.

"We'll get you home somehow, Homer," said Ernie, stretching his neck to look at something over Homer's shoulder. A stool made a squeaking protest as Rosa turned to follow Ernie's gaze.

"The storm is here," she said softly.

Homer turned around quickly, squinting through the polished windows and not seeing anything at first. But as he watched, the hill tops seemed to change colors, oranges and shades of red, then fading to light brown, and the sky was no longer blue but a murky yellow, like dust or heavy smoke, and then the hills were gone and there was a flat plain and a sudden burst of steam from its depths. The plain dissolved in boiling dust rising to meet yellow, turbulent clouds descending from the sky, forming a wall that rolled towards the restaurant like a giant surrealistic wave, threatening them, then suddenly stopping as portals opened across its length. Sunlight streamed through in rays of gold and red. Something green flashed by a rapidly growing hole in the boiling cloud mass and Homer focused on it as the plain again appeared, just behind the grove of trees so very close to him.

And then he saw the city.

Emerald green buildings flickered, allowed a steady view for only an instant, rising high into the turbulent sky from bases obscured by the roiling cloud. Shining surfaces reflected the dull red orb of a setting sun.

"It's so beautiful," said Rosa, and then she pointed excitedly. "I think he's here. See?" She smiled at Ernie, then slid off the groaning stool and went to the window for a closer look, pointing again. "The little brown cloud just to the left of the trees. There he is!"

Homer squinted hard and saw a human figure emerge from the base of the boiling cloud directly below the now flickering image of an emerald metropolis. It was a tall, slender man, long strides bringing him down the hill. He was dressed in white from top to bottom, and carried a large bag with one hand. He walked jauntily, with a springy step, then waved one long arm over his head. Rosa waved back from the window, and two men at the tables were also waving. They watched with apprehension as the man skirted one edge of a steaming crevasse that appeared suddenly and faded from view. He crossed the road and quickened his step as he approached the restaurant, the big bag swinging in one hand. Rosa's face was a picture of delight, and Ernie leaned over to whisper to Homer.

"Wife kinda has a crush on this guy. He really is a charmer. But he has his time, and I have mine, right?" He gave Homer a wicked grin, and nudged him with an elbow as the door flew open and Robert Ledoux entered the restaurant.

"Rosa!" he shouted, put his bag on the floor and held out his arms. The woman let out a squeal, rushed to him with an embrace that made him grunt and then laugh. He waved to everyone in the restaurant, kissed Rosa on the hairnet covering her tangled mass of hair, then held her out in front of him. "I have something for you," he said, "from my wife."

"I was hoping she would come over with you this time," said Rosa.

"I bet," said Ernie, and she turned to glare at him.

"Ernie, you big bear, your Rosa is safe with me!" Ernie grinned mischievously back at the man. "No, I couldn't talk her into it this time either, but I'll get her over one of these days. She wanted you to have these, partly to pay you back for all the real food I've eaten here." He picked up the bag and handed it to

Rosa, who looked inside with disbelief.

"Tomatoes?"

"Have you ever seen anything like it?" said Ledoux. "Hydroponically grown, and firm all the way through. We can grow our own food!" The man was ecstatic, blue eyes sparkling. Sharp features, high cheekbones and a large nose, Homer noted. French name—French nose.

"They're *huge!*" said Rosa, and she pulled one tomato out of the bag. It was the size of a small cantaloupe, and she looked at it with awe as she carried the bag back into the kitchen.

Robert Ledoux slid easily onto a stool next to Homer and pumped Ernie's hand vigorously. "How are you, old man?" he said smiling, and turned quickly to glance at the stranger seated next to him.

"We're getting by," said Ernie. "Can't get much meat or gas, but the war is nearly over now."

"Ah yes, the war," Ledoux nodded. "The second big one."

"Right. Say, we've got another visitor here you should meet. Comes from nineteen-seventy-five and got caught in the storm this morning. Only visitor we've ever had from another time, besides you, that is." Ernie nodded his head in Homer's direction.

"Mister Ledoux, this is Homer."

The friendly face turned towards him, and they shook hands. Homer was curious about the man's clothes: white, head-to-foot, long sleeves and a skin-tight hood pulled over his head, showing only his face. *Looks like he's ready for scuba diving,* thought Homer.

"Interesting suit you're wearing," he said, and Ledoux laughed.

"Purely functional, believe me. It's uncomfortable as hell, but lead impregnated, and it keeps my whole body dosage down when I go outside." He looked closely at Homer. "You see, there was another big war after the second one."

Homer felt a sudden tightening in his stomach, and he took a deep breath. "Where in the future do you come from, Mister

Ledoux?"

"Two thousand and fifteen," said the man.

Homer's stomach was a tangled knot; he swallowed hard and felt his face flush. Ledoux was watching him for a reaction, smiling with his secret knowledge. He leaned over, and tapped Homer on the knee.

"Tell me, Homer, what's your last name?"

"Ewing. I'm Homer Ewing."

"Oh—my—God," said Ledoux, turning towards the counter. "Had a feeling. A name like Homer just isn't that common. Can I have some coffee, Ernie?"

"Sure." Ernie picked up a cup and poured coffee into it. "Do you know Homer from somewhere?"

"Can't say, Ernie." He sipped, eyes twinkling with amusement.

"*Do* you know me?" said Homer.

"Of course I do, Homer. I just met you." He slapped him in on the back, grinning, then turned back to his coffee. "Who would ever guess it started this way? Guess it's true about storm portals being causally related." His chuckle echoed in the half-empty cup. "My, my."

Homer felt a growing irritation, and his narrowing eyes showed it. Ledoux's smile faded. "Ernie? See if Rosa can fix me up a sunrise omelet with one of those tomatoes, will you? And maybe a mound of hash browns. Homer and I are gonna have a little talk over in the corner."

"Sure, Mister Ledoux," said Ernie. "You'll tell him about the war, won't you?"

"Something like that," said the man. Ernie smiled faintly at both of them, then went back into the kitchen to find his wife. Ledoux motioned Homer to follow him to a corner table by the windows. They sat in silence for a moment, sipping their coffee and watching the shimmering landscape outside. The boulders and the plain were there again, for the moment, but the turbulence had moved back up on the side of the hills and the landscape of nineteen-forty-five was slowly returning at the edge of

the valley.

"I've probably got a couple of hours here before I go back, unless I spend another day eating Rosa's cooking." It was a light remark, thought Homer, to ease the tension between them. "Where did you hit the storm?"

"On the road the other side of town, by a curve about a mile out. My truck is stuck right at the spot."

"When you try to go back, do you know what to look for?"

"Yep. There was a black hole, sort of, with rain blowing out of it. I was in a rain storm when I crashed."

"Sounds like a good bearing. I don't think you need to worry much about getting back, if you move quick. But now there's something else I have to tell you about, and I have to do it right the first time."

"You *do* know me from the future," said Homer, a little relieved.

"I know *of* you, Homer. We won't meet again after today, and I won't say more about that. You have to understand that anything I say to you can affect your actions when you return to your time, and it's a very critical time, Homer. Dreadfully critical. I know my history, I teach it, I try to teach our kids not to make the same stupid mistakes their ancestors made. What I tell you can change history, just by changing a man in any way, and as much as I'd like to change what happened in the past, I don't want to go back up in those boiling clouds this afternoon to find my family, or even my city, gone. Things are kind of tough there, but we're making progress, and it's sort of pioneer days all over again. I like that, Homer. Do you understand?"

"Yes, I think so."

"So I'll tell you what I think you should know, and you keep it all to yourself, and let your instincts tell you what to do." Ledoux was nearly whispering, now.

"Agreed," said Homer firmly, but with a little fear of this man who knew *of* him from the future. At the same time, it excited him.

"There's going to be a nuclear war in your time. Oh, it's

not going to kill off most of humanity, but it's going to be bad enough. It'll start with a Chinese invasion of India."

"And we'll watch it happen," said Homer, with a frown.

"Wrong. The retaliation will be immediate. The United States was more closely allied with India than anyone knew, Homer. Many agreements were never made public until after the war. My analysis is we hoped when we'd pumped enough technology into India they could exert sufficient pressure to bring down the Chinese system economically. But the Chinese understood what was going on, and then the invasion."

"But it wasn't an all out nuclear war?"

"It was a farce, Homer. Half the first wave of missiles on both sides never left the ground. Nothing worked right. In China, more buffalo were blown up than cities. Manhattan was burned a little, but New Jersey was heavily damaged when the smoke cleared."

Homer swallowed hard. "What about here?"

Ledoux looked down at his coffee cup. "Los Angeles had some light damage, but one small missile, with typical Chinese precision, hit just this side of Bakersfield."

"Oh," said Homer.

"I live in the New Bakersfield, a real metropolis in my time. Most of the people all the way up the valley moved there because they couldn't farm anymore. The soil was sterilized. We're trying hydroponics now, and you saw some of our results."

"How about Rosa and Ernie, and the others here?"

"I told them about the war, and they know when to leave, and they'll keep it to themselves. That's the way it happened; this town was deserted when the war started."

"Yes, it was," said Homer, and Ledoux smiled.

"Of course you would know that. I forgot the year you're from."

Ernie approached the table cautiously, then cleared his throat to let the whispering men know he was coming. They said nothing when he served the omelet to Ledoux, and filled their coffee cups. As he left, Homer winked at him.

"Nice people," said Ledoux. "they'll end up in the south-central United States, and things will be a little tough for a while, but then it'll get better."

"But what about me?" Homer knew immediately he shouldn't have asked that.

"Can't say, Homer," and again a slight smile as Ledoux took a big bite of egg and tomato. "But I *can* tell you this; the war could have been a lot worse than it was, but something stopped it quick." He chewed his food slowly, relishing it, gesturing with his fork and talking between swallows. Homer sipped, and listened.

"There was a fringe group in San Antonio, Texas call People for Peace. They were mostly communists, run by a laborer named Diego Riverra, and not taken seriously by anybody. But about a year before the war, Diego was thrown out, along with some others, and the group was taken over by right-wingers. They still called themselves People for Peace, but were militant as hell: combat drills in the woods, nationalistic propaganda, and all that good stuff. Attractive, though, and their member-ship went up fast, almost overnight. They were a strange mix: communists and fascists, whites and blacks, Jews, and even a couple of Arabs. People marveled they didn't turn their guns on each other. But what the public saw was only the tip of the iceberg; the group was really a small part of an international organization funded by industrialists whose empires would collapse in a world war with nuclear weapons. They knew a war was coming soon, and poured money into a desperate plan to stop it."

"But there *was* a war," said Homer.

"Very limited, compared to what could have happened. The plan worked, but not perfectly, and that's the way history says it has to be."

"I'll have to sell my ranch and livestock," said Homer.

"Not for the reason you think," said Ledoux. "I wish I could give you details. There were kidnappings and assassinations at the highest levels on both sides by People for Peace and others.

Both sides capitulated almost immediately after the war had begun. And when you sold your ranch you moved to Texas."

"Why?" asked Homer.

"Can't say. I hope I haven't said too much already. Just think about it, and remember that I've heard your name in my time I never imagined I could be involved in this way"

Homer shook his head "Maybe I do know what you're trying to tell me, but how fast do I have to get out?"

Ledoux just shook his head. "Homer, I've told you everything I can."

Ledoux sat up straight and smiled. "What do you say we get Ernie and Rosa over here? They're probably feeling a little left out right now, and Rosa looks a bit scared by all this whispering we've been doing."

Homer turned around, saw Rosa frowning at him, and with a sudden compulsion he smiled at her. The chubby face brightened, and she waved at him timidly. At that instant, the personality of Robert Ledoux changed again.

"I'm not leaving here without my apple pie," he shouted indignantly. Rosa laughed, picked up a whole pie, and showed it to him from afar.

"Ah," said Ledoux, "that's the one. Let's eat it over here, all of us."

Ernie got some forks and small plates, and they joined the two men at the table, Rosa cutting the pie into four enormous pieces, and beaming as the men devoured it greedily.

The four of them sat there the rest of the afternoon, just talking, mostly small things, and Homer felt like he'd known them all for years. He felt comfortable. Perhaps it was because he was suddenly comfortable with himself. His political views had always been unpopular at home. Neo-nazi, people called him. But was that really *all* bad? Certainly he was a nationalist, and a militant, but thousands or even millions of people dead in a war that accomplished nothing? It didn't make sense. Something had to be done, and soon, something more important than the raising of hogs.

Ledoux tried explaining the time storm to them again, drawing diagrams on napkins and gesturing a lot with his hands. Something about one-dimensional brane slippage in a four-dimensional world, with time doing the slipping. Homer did a lot of reading at home: military history, tactics, weapons, and biography. But in science, his knowledge was describable by a single word: nothing. The conversation switched to hydroponic farming, and the progress Ledoux's people had made in feeding themselves real food. Rosa offered him some seeds to take back with him, but he said no you'll need all those seeds to make more seeds for later, and everyone around the table understood what he meant.

They didn't talk about the war.

It was mid-afternoon, and tree shadows had just begun their eastern crawl along the ground when Ledoux began looking nervously out the window towards boiling scenery half-way up slopes of the hills. He searched for a flash of green, a tower reaching into the sky. Homer understood a very special thing had happened this day, a communication that could change history, alter the future, the life of Robert Ledoux. When he returned home, would it still be there? Would it be gone because of something he had said or neglected to say? The man had taken an awesome chance, confident in his knowledge of the history he was now so much a part of. Homer was feeling a bond with this man, knowing they must both leave soon to play their respective parts in the drama of the past—of the future. Rosa went to the counter and brought back a fresh pie for Ledoux to take with him. He kissed her on the cheek, and she closed her eyes when he did that. Ernie just smiled. Friends.

"I'd better go now," said Robert Ledoux, looking at Homer. "You take care of yourselves, all of you." He got up from the table, leaned over it and shook hands with Homer. "I'll know soon," he said, and Homer nodded.

Rosa followed him to the door. "I want to see your wife with you next time," she said, "and more of those tomatoes."

Ledoux chuckled. "Anything you want, Rosa."

"I'll walk you up the hill," said Ernie, and the screen door banged shut, leaving Rosa standing there alone and trembling a little.

The two men crossed the road, passed the grove of trees, and started up shallow slopes towards the turbulent specter above them. Rosa watched them for a while, then walked over to Homer and looked down at him with dark eyes. "Isn't he a nice man?" she said softly.

Homer gazed out the window. "You and Ernie are nice people, too," he said.

There was a sniffling sound. "My, my," said Rosa, "hasn't this been a lovely day?" And then she hurried back to the kitchen.

Homer watched the figures of the men growing smaller, nearing the edge of the time storm and then walking along it towards his left. He watched for green towers thrust into a yellow sky and reflecting a red sun, and saw only a boiling mass of brownish mist. But the men on the hill had seen something, had stopped, standing with their backs to him and waving their arms, then Ledoux rushed into the mist and was gone. Ernie waited for moment, then hurried down the hill, nearly running, sprinting past the trees and across the road and pulling his apron off as he pushed open the screen door.

"Now we've got to get you home," he said, totally out of breath. "Rosa! Homer has to leave now!" He went over to a table to talk with three men; they glanced back at Homer, then got up quickly and nodded to him as they went out the door.

"Wait a minute!" came a shriek from the kitchen.

Ernie pulled a ring of keys from the cash register drawer and grabbed a leather jacket off a wall hook, narrowly avoiding a collision as the kitchen doors swung open and Rosa rushed out with another apple pie. She put it in front of Homer, smiling at its perfection. "For your trip," she said.

"I don't know what to say. It's—it's very nice of you—", but Ernie was pulling on his arm.

"He thanks you, Rosa. We've *got* to get going, and the boys are waiting in the truck."

Rosa looked distraught. "Everything's happening so fast!"

Ernie dragged his visitor towards the door, Homer precariously balancing apple pie and rain slicker on one arm, and Rosa watched them leave without a further word. Homer looked back once, raised his head in a silent good-bye, and saw tears well up into her black eyes.

They piled into a battered green pickup truck, coils of chain and the three other men from the restaurant sitting in a heap by the gate. Odors of apple pie quickly filled the cab. One grinding scream from the gear box, and the truck lurched forward onto the gravel road and sped through the little town, into the countryside. It was not a long drive, and the rode in silence, the men in the back looking anxiously from side to side as the scenery flickered around them. But one thing was clear; the storm was receding fast, and Ernie drove with the accelerator pedal pushed flat on the floor. They neared the curve where Homer had crashed. Crossing the road was a roiling mist in greens and blues, and just for an instant a flash of something black. Homer's heart pounded with excitement and anticipation. Somewhere in that roiling mass was his way home.

And then they saw the truck.

It was exactly where he had crashed, front axle still hung up on the embankment, only now the vehicle was covered with a thick layer of red dust. "Thing was clean when I left it this morning," said Homer.

"God knows where it's been since then," said Ernie, slowing to a stop a few yards away. He leaned out the window and shouted.

"Alf!"

"Yo!" said someone.

"I'm stopping here till things calm down a bit. We'll use the black chain and those two Aspens across the road."

There were voices in the back of the truck, and the clinking of chains being moved. Ernie leaned back in his seat, then looked over towards Homer staring at the sight ahead.

"Scared?"

"Yeah, I guess so."

"No need to worry; Ledoux said you'd make it back all right."

"How does he know that?"

"Beats me. He saw his wife today."

"What?"

"When he started back, up in the hills."

"I couldn't even see the city."

"Oh it was there sure enough. Real clear, through a big hole near ground level. That's where we saw her. She was calling to Ledoux, asking him to come back. We waved to her, but I guess she couldn't see us. Ledoux had a big smile on his face, and he said it was Ellen, right where and when he'd left her too scared to come over with him. Then he said tell Homer to follow his instincts, and not to worry about getting home. Right after that they both disappeared."

Homer felt a weight lifted from his chest; he exhaled a blast of air with relief.

"I guess you understand all that?" said Ernie.

"No."

"Don't suppose you can tell me what you and Ledoux were whispering about today?"

"Can't say, Ernie," said Homer.

They waited in the truck for over an hour before the storm retreated just beyond the curve and seemed to steady. A flash of blackness was there, then again, and a burst of rain drops splattered against the back of Homer's truck, leaving little craters in the thick layer of red dust.

"That's it!" said Homer, opening the door. "The rain storm I was in."

Ernie slowly opened the door and stepped out. "No hurry," he said. "It'll get steadier in a while."

The men attached a chain to the undercarriage of Homer's truck, stretching it taut and wrapping it firmly around two closely spaced trees on the other side of the road. With two of them holding the chain in place around the trees, the other three pushed hard against the center of the tightly stretched line of

steel. With a groaning sound, the truck popped off the embankment and rolled to a stop in the center of the road. Homer got in, fumbling with his keys and holding his breath as he turned on the ignition. The engine turned over and over, coughed twice, then started with a roar. He gunned the engine loudly as the other men cheered, then backed up and drove forward until the truck was only a couple of yards from where he had seen the black portal into his own time, and home. A long burst of rain fell against his windshield; he turned on the wipers, and left them on, suppressing a sudden urge to drive forward, and then the rain stopped and he was looking at swirling mist again. Ernie came up to the open window beside Homer and handed him an apple pie.

"Forgot this," he grinned. "Rosa would never forgive me if you left without it." He stepped back, studying the truck. "Nice machine," he said. "Think I'll get me one of these someday."

"I'm sure you will," said Homer. "And thanks, Ernie, you and Rosa, for everything."

"Nothing," said Ernie, shielding his face with one arm against a new burst of rain. "Be ready, in gear, Homer!" he shouted. "I'll tell you when!"

Homer nodded as the rain stopped again, but now the black void was always there, flickering in intensity, beckoning him forward, and his hands felt cold on the steering wheel as he gunned the engine and peered out past the slowly flopping windshield wipers. Then the windshield turned black, rain coming in the window onto his shoulder, and Ernie screamed.

"Go, Homer!"

The truck lurched forward, spewing back gravel. There was a teeth rattling shudder from side-to-side, and rain was pounding the roof, roaring in his ears, and ahead was only inky blackness. "Idiot!" Homer shouted out loud. "You forgot the lights!" The rear of the truck swerved as he turned on the lights, saw two muddy ruts in the road and steered into them, closed the window and began fishtailing his way down the old road back to the highway. When he reached the pavement, exhausted, he

stopped for a moment, using his pocket knife to cut the apple pie into four large pieces, then pulled out onto the empty highway and headed for home. By the time he reached his ranch, an hour later, he had eaten the entire pie.

* * * * * * *

The citizens of Hadley wondered about the sudden disappearance of Homer Ewing, though they didn't miss him. A strange man, they thought: argumentative, right-wing red neck, certainly no fan of the human race, and a loner. He had suddenly put his ranch and livestock up for sale at half what they were worth, and the bank, smelling an incredible opportunity, bought him out immediately. Bank president Rodney Erhardt was still bragging about that deal, and people were tired of hearing about it. The man just bailed out, it seemed, and within a week after the sale he was gone, leaving a forwarding address in San Antonio, Texas. But what puzzled them the most was news Don Seifert brought back with him a few months later. Don owned the general store in Hadley, and vacationed in Mexico each summer, passing through San Antonio on his way back. He looked up Homer Ewing, and couldn't believe what he found. Homer was working with a bunch of communists! No, not possible, they all said. Yes, he had put all his money into an organization called People for Peace, and was some kind of officer in it. Homer Ewing for peace? They laughed at that one; that hawk wanted to nuke everyone. Maybe, said Seifert, but there were rumors the peace people had Para-military groups training in secret camps outside the city. All very hush-hush. Well, they all agreed, that sounded more to Homer's liking.

They forgot about Homer Ewing, and read their newspapers. The dispute between China and India was really heating up, and China was threatening invasion. One thing Homer had said was probably true. The United States would just sit back, and watch it happen.

SOCIAL SECURITY

Clara Peterson was in the basement when the doorbell rang. The work had been tiring, and she held her back as she shuffled up the stairs, an unlit cigarette dangling from her lips. The wet cement on her hands was getting hard, and she washed it off in the kitchen sink as the doorbell rang angrily again.

"Wait a minute, will you? I'm coming." Her slippers made sucking sounds as she went leisurely to the door. It was probably a renter, answering her ad. Hanna had vacated the room early; there could be double rent for nearly three weeks. Hanna wouldn't mind, not now. She was beyond that.

The bell rang again as she reached the lace-curtained door and saw the tall, angular shadow outside. Clara looked at the shadow, and put her hand on the doorknob.

"Who is it, please?"

A male voice answered.

"I'd like to see the room you have for rent."

"Sorry. I only rent to older women. You'll have to go someplace else." Disappointed, she turned away from the door.

"Please, there isn't anyplace else. I just got a job at the foundry, and I don't have a car. I can walk to work from here."

Clara sighed, and opened the door.

He was just a boy.

"I only rent to retired ladies, young man. There are other rooms available in the neighborhood."

"Not now. I've been looking for two days, and everything's taken. Couldn't I take the room temporarily, until I find some-

thing else? I'm quiet, and I don't smoke or drink."

Clara laughed, the cigarette dangling from her mouth, hands on her hips. "Well, I do," she said. Nice looking kid, she thought. Clean, slender, and peach fuzz.

"How old are you?"

"Nineteen."

"Kinda young to be out on your own, aren't you? Where are your folks?"

"Fresno. And I'm old enough to take care of myself. Please, just for a month or two until I can find someplace else. I start work tomorrow."

"You got money?"

"Enough to get started."

"It's two-fifty a month, with meals, and you keep to your room. There's washer and dryer on the back porch. No visitors, no phone calls."

"Sounds fine."

"Okay, come on in and take a look."

His smile made her shudder; it was warm, and open, reminding her of someone she had tried hard to forget. It hurt— for a moment. She showed him the room: small, clean, with bed, bureau, and a writing desk. There was a closet, and view of a backyard overgrown with weeds, thick underbrush around two large apple trees that never bore fruit.

"Looks good," he said, smiling again. "Can I have it?"

Clara wanted to say no, but something wouldn't let her. There was an attraction for the boy, a familiarity she was feeling without understanding it.

"Payment is in advance. You can move in today. What's your name?"

"John Doyle," he said, pulled out twenties and tens from his wallet and handed them to her. "My stuff is at the foundry, but I can be back here in an hour. Thank you, Missus—"

"The name is Clara Peterson, John. And dinner is at six."

The boy rushed excitedly from the house, and Clara watched him walk briskly down the street, swinging his arms, full of life

and youth. She lit her cigarette, one of the twenty she ordinarily allowed herself each day. She wondered if she had done the right thing. John's presence triggered memories from long ago: a husband, a son, both gone. Painful memories. So much time had passed. She sat down in a chair, smoked three cigarettes in a row while she thought about the long lonely years and her fight to survive. The Good Lord was still testing her, she decided.

She made a stew, cooked it slowly all afternoon and into early evening. John returned with a box of books and a suitcase, spending the day silently in his room. At six o'clock she knocked softly on the door and called him to dinner. They ate in silence for a while, John quickly devouring a plate heaped with stew and looking expectant, so she served him another. Strange, she thought, how the sight of the boy eating her food pleasured her so much.

When he was finished eating, John leaned back in his chair and sighed. "That was good. I haven't eaten so much in a long time."

Clare smiled, her meal only half-finished. She had been watching the boy. "You'll have to eat properly to be a working man. What do you do at the foundry?"

"Aluminum casting. It's recycled can metal, mostly. I make fifty-pound bars out of it. I really want to be a machinist, but it'll be a few months before they let me start on any of the machines."

"You like to work with your hands?"

"Yes. I like to make things."

Clara picked at her food with a fork. "I had a son who liked to do that sort of thing, but he's gone now. Left me many years ago."

John looked at her seriously, a question in his eyes.

"Dead," she said.

"I'm sorry," said John. And then he suddenly remembered something, pulled a crumpled envelope from his hip pocket and pushed it across the table.

"This must belong to your previous tenant. I found it on a top shelf in the closet, pushed clear back against the wall."

Clara took the envelope; the name Hanna Vogel was printed neatly on the front, in pencil. It was not sealed.

"There's money in it," said John.

The paper money was in various denominations. Sixty-five dollars. Clara replaced the money, licked the envelope flap and sealed it. "Thank you, John," she said. "You're very honest, and I'll make sure Hanna gets this. I have her forwarding address."

"She must have forgotten it was up there," said John.

"Probably. She's old, and her health is failing. I think she's had a couple of little strokes. Her family became concerned and asked her to live with them in San Francisco. She's there now, and I'll send the money along to her."

"Sure," said John, smiling again and standing up. "I'm going to my room now. Have to be at work before eight o'clock."

"How about breakfast at seven?"

"That's fine. Good night, Missus Peterson."

"Clara," she said, and looked up at him. "Good night, John."

She was still smiling to herself when he closed the door to his room. She washed the dishes quickly, retrieved a bottle of red wine from the refrigerator and went to her own room at the back of the house, closing the door behind her. She put the bottle on a night stand, sat on the edge of the bed and stared for a moment at the envelope marked Hanna Vogel. She opened it, took out the money and put it in a night stand drawer, then tore the envelope into small pieces and dropped them into a waste basket.

The wine bottle opened with a pop, and she left it to breathe while she dressed for bed. She filled a water glass with wine before slipping beneath the blankets to read her bible in the dim light of a lamp. She read and drank, then took a framed picture of a man and a boy out of the night stand drawer and stared at it for a long time. When she turned off the lamp there were tears in her eyes and the wine bottle was empty.

Warm in his room, John lay on top of the covers and read a paperback book until his eyes refused to focus. He turned off the light and stared into darkness for a moment before sleep came, wondering how a feeble old woman could get up on a

chair or ladder to hide money on a high closet shelf, and why she would do that.

* * * * * * *

They developed a routine. Breakfast was at seven; John came promptly to the table, smelling of after-shave lotion and soap, and eagerly ate her cooking. He talked about his work, Clara listening silently, sipping coffee and eating little because the wine of the previous evening always upset her stomach in the morning. She gave him some space to store food in the refrigerator, and he made his own lunch for the day, carrying it to the foundry in a metal lunch pail and looking like a working man. While he was gone, Clara cleaned the house and spent an hour with paperwork at the writing desk in her room before going down in the basement.

The remodeling went slowly; concrete and plaster work was finished for the moment, and she painted one wall in light yellow, a little each day. In the afternoon she shuffled to the store four blocks away to get her exercise, buying a newspaper and the day's groceries and returning painfully home to retrieve her mail and work at the desk again before starting to cook dinner for herself and John. Cooking was once more a pleasure for her; the boy was so hungry in the evening, and he was so skinny. She tried new things from a cookbook unused for years, and watched him eat while she picked at her own food. She listened to his excited talk about the day, and the machines he would be learning to operate. He never mentioned the money he had found in his room, or whether he should find another place to live. He seemed comfortable where he was, and Clara left it that way. But the evenings were still lonely, after John had closed his door, and Clara lived with her wine and her bible, and a picture from the past.

* * * * * * *

Behind the closed door of his room, John Peterson began to write in a new diary, starting with the day he had moved in. "I met Grandma today. She had a room for rent, and I took it. I was going to tell her who I am, but chickened out at the last minute and gave her a false name. I'm John Doyle to her. I get my meals here, and she's a good cook. I think she's a nice lady, not at all like dad said. She still drinks a lot; there's wine bottles all over the place. I don't know how she affords it. I found some money an old lady had left behind in my room when she moved out. Sixty-five dollars. I think it's strange an old person would leave that much money behind, but Grandma said Hanna—that's the old woman's name—is kind of feeble, and she'll return the money to her. She tells me she had a son, but he's dead now. Probably she's trying to believe that. I'll wait a while before telling dad I'm with Grandma. I don't think he'll like it."

* * * * * * *

The trouble began on a rainy day, when Clara asked John to do the shopping for her. She had awakened in the morning with ankles and legs horribly swollen, knowing it was from too much smoking and drinking, and that she was letting things get out of hand again. Too much thinking about the past. At breakfast, she shuffled slowly around the kitchen, grimacing with pain, and John looked at her worriedly.

"Are you sick, Clara?"

"A little gout, John. It comes with age."

"You should be in bed; you can hardly walk."

"I know, I know." She collapsed in a chair, sipping coffee and breathing hard. The pain surged into her upper legs, bringing tears to her eyes.

"I'll do the dishes before I go to work. Why don't you stay in bed today? I can pick up some pot pies or something on the way home, and do the cooking tonight. You need to rest."

"That's good of you, John. You're right, I have to take better care of myself, now that you're here. I'll make a list of groceries

we need, and you get what you want for tonight. I should be better by tomorrow."

"I'm glad to do it, Clara. You've been waiting on me; now I can do something for you." John smiled and began clearing dishes from the table. Clara smiled back at him warmly. It was so nice to be cared for. She hadn't known that feeling—ever.

She gave him some money and hobbled painfully back to bed, escaping into a sound sleep the moment her head was on the pillow. She was beyond exhaustion, sleeping the entire day and into early evening, waking only briefly when dreams of a man and boy became too intense. The boy in the dreams was her son, but she couldn't remember the face of the man. When she finally awoke it was getting dark, and the pain in her legs was gone. There were rattling sounds in the kitchen; John was fixing dinner for her.

"I feel much better," she said at the table, and John served her a pot pie in an aluminum tin.

"You should eat more."

"I know. I just don't feel like it most of the time. And I know I drink too much."

John said nothing, eating slowly.

"Too many memories, John. An old person can have too many bad memories. You make mistakes in life, and look back at what you did, and wish it could be changed, but it can't, and so you live with it. It's very hard to be old and alone."

"You're not alone," said John softly.

"No, I'm not. It's good to have you here, John. Someone to talk to."

"You had older ladies living here before."

"Yes, but that was different. They were so old, and kept to themselves most of the time. They ate almost nothing, and I guess I've gotten into that habit, too. And when they talked, it was only to complain about something: the weather, or the food, or the cigarette smoke, or family abandoning them. Never anything nice to say."

"You don't have any family?"

"No, all dead, for a long time, now. Maybe I should have gotten married again, but my first marriage wasn't good, and I guess I was always a little cool towards men after that. I had my chances; I was pretty in those days."

"I believe that," said John.

"How about you? You seem so young to be out on your own."

"Dad and I agreed I should start making my own way. He had to do it when he was eighteen. He's a mechanic; I thought about doing it, but I like working with lathes best, so I'm going to be a machinist."

"What does your mother think about your leaving home?"

"She died several years ago. Dad's alone, now. I had an older sister, too, but she died in a car crash the night she graduated from high school."

"I'm so sorry."

"Me, too. She'd been drinking. Dad took it pretty hard; he said if I ever drank while I was living at home, he'd break my neck. I can understand that. It was tough for him to let me leave; he still misses mom a lot, and now his kids are gone. So I know about loneliness."

"And so do I," said Clara. "But you work, and survive. It gets even tougher when you're old, living on room rent and a little Social Security. But you survive."

"Oh, I forgot," said John. "Your check arrived today."

"What?"

"Your Social Security check. I picked up the mail on my way in tonight. It's in the front room. There's a check for Hanna Vogel, too, and some other ladies."

"I'll have to complain at the post office again about forwarding the mail. They're *so* slow."

"I'll clean up, now," said John.

"Thank you, John. I'm still pretty tired; I think I'll go back to bed. See you in the morning."

"Goodnight, Clara," said John, thinking how old his grandmother suddenly looked, worrying about something more than that but wanting to put his arms around her. A moment later he

heard her room door close, then washed a few dirty dishes and went to his own room. He noticed she had taken the mail and the checks with her. Feeling a sudden need for privacy, John Peterson locked the door to his room that night, and wrote his concerns in his diary.

In her room, Clara sat at the desk and removed the checks from their envelopes. She carefully endorsed them with a practiced hand, first her own, then Hanna's, Carolyn's and Margaret's. Sweat glistened on her forehead as she concentrated, writing slowly with different pens and filling out deposit slips to four different banks. The writing styles were so different; she paused occasionally to practice on a sheet of typing paper before signing a check, talking softly to herself.

She put the checks and deposit slips in her purse, then opened her door silently and padded into the kitchen for a bottle of wine and a glass. For a while she paced nervously back and forth in front of the desk, gulping wine and mumbling an inaudible prayer to herself. Her legs were aching again when she finally went to bed, a little drunk, still mumbling to herself. She fell asleep with the nightstand light on and a half-consumed cigarette smoldering in an ash-tray.

* * * * * * *

John Peterson lay on his bed, heard the refrigerator door close and the quiet footsteps back to Clara's room. He wanted to knock on her door and tell her who he was, but he hesitated. Why? There was something about her, cold, perhaps detached from reality. He remembered his father talking about her drunken withdrawal from the real world, and her violent rages that led to the divorce, and how he never wanted John to contact her. "No-telling what that crazy will do," he'd said. But John had found her, and he liked her. She seemed pleased he was there. Still, something was wrong. First the money in the bedroom closet, and now four checks, only one of them for his grandmother. The other women were likely her previous tenants; he

was certain about Hanna Vogel. Why would their social security checks still be coming to an old address? Old people needed those payments regularly, and on time, unless they had other income or family helping them—or if they were dead. The last thought horrified him, and he dismissed it immediately. Such a thing could not be true.

John again wrote his concerns in the diary, pausing to think, listening to the creaking floor as Clara paced back and forth like a caged animal in her room. The sound frightened him a little; something was going on he didn't understand, something his grandmother was doing. Her family was dead, she said. And a few feet away, her grandson lay on his bed, worrying about her.

* * * * * * *

They ate breakfast in silence the following morning, deep in private thoughts, not looking at each other. John made his lunch, then left for work without saying a word. The silence weighed heavily on Clara, but she felt unable to speak until he was gone. When she heard the door close behind him, she spoke aloud to the empty house.

"Why do you torture me so? Haven't I taken care of myself all these years? I'm responsible, now, done everything you said. Why bring John into this? He's a nice boy. I don't want to hurt him. Not like Hanna. She was nosy, and mean. You took the others from me, and then there was no rent money. I did nothing wrong, and you said I must take care of myself."

She repeated the prayer again, eyes filling with tears as bitterness returned. She broke a self-inflicted taboo about morning drinking and drank two large glasses of wine. Calmness returned. Fortified, she spent the morning grocery shopping for the weekend, changing buses several times to make deposits at four different banks, then stopping at a liquor store to order two cases of German vintage for delivery that day. In the afternoon, she worked in the basement, painting.

That evening, Clara had to call John to dinner twice. When

he answered her second call, she had a disquieting feeling his voice had come from her room, and when he came to the kitchen he gave her a sheepish grin.

"Had to go to the bathroom," he said.

They ate in silence for a moment before John spoke again. "Sorry about this morning. Being so quiet, I mean. I slept lousy last night."

"Are you sick, John?"

"No, nothing like that. Just a lot of things on my mind. The job—and everything."

"You should get out more. Find some friends. You've been here three weeks, now, and you haven't been out anywhere. That's not healthy for a young man. Tomorrow is Saturday. What are you going to do with it? Sit around and read?"

"I have to watch my money; I'll need to buy some tools soon."

"So take a long walk in the sunshine. Go to the park. Meet a nice girl somewhere."

John smiled. "Girls cost money."

"Not the right ones; at least, not at first. That comes later."

They laughed.

"I could help you," he said.

"I don't need any help around here."

"In the basement, I mean. Whatever you're doing down there."

Clara looked at him, momentarily startled, knowing he could see it in her eyes. "Just some light refinishing and painting, John. I'm nearly finished, anyway, and it stinks down there. Get some fresh air tomorrow."

"You want to come along?"

"The way I hobble along I'd just hold you up. Cramp your style. I have plenty to keep me busy this weekend."

"Okay, I'll look around town tomorrow. Tonight I read," he said, getting up from the table, "after I do the dishes."

"You're spoiling me."

"Somebody should."

Clara bit her lip, holding back the tears.

Late that night, John Peterson wrote in his diary. "The more I get to know grandma, the more I like her. She's had a tough life, and seems so alone. But I still think something funny is going on with her and those social security checks. And tonight, when I offered to help her in the basement, she looked like I'd shot her. I saw a picture tonight of grandpa, and dad when he was a little boy. Dad has the same picture back home. It was on a nightstand in grandma's room, lying face up next to an empty wine bottle. I wish she wouldn't drink so much. It changes her."

Clara read her bible until John had fallen asleep, then said her prayers softly to herself. Her last prayer was a simple request. "Lord, the door can't be locked. Please don't let John go down into the basement."

In the morning, she found him there.

* * * * * * *

Clara was doing something in the basement, something she couldn't or wouldn't tell him about. He had to find out what it was. After breakfast, John padded softly down the stairs into the darkness, feeling guilty and clandestine. Something brushed his forehead; he grabbed at it and pulled, and the light from a bare bulb flooded the room.

There was nothing there.

Four blank walls, freshly painted.

Paint cans were scattered on the floor, and a used brush, hard as a knife blade. He found a cardboard box in one corner, and rummaged through it. Old dresses, and a hat with black lace. Old women's clothes. He wondered if they were Clara's.

There was a stench in the room, something sharp, and it burned his nostrils. A familiar odor, but from where? And then he remembered. The summer he had worked on a ranch for board and room, to get him out of the city, his father had said, but then the cattle got some disease, and they didn't want it to spread, so—

"I asked you not to come down here, John."

She spoke softly from the top of the stairs, a glass of wine in one hand and a menacing expression accentuated by points of light reflected from her eyes.

"I thought you might need some help cleaning up," he said quickly, and started up the stairs, not looking back.

"It's all finished, as you can see. Please come up, now."

It was a command.

She reeked of wine, and the kitchen had smelled of the stuff during breakfast. I bet she drank all night, he thought. He brushed past her, close to the watery eyes, and she stumbled a little as she turned to follow him.

"You do *not* have the run of the house. I think you'd better leave for the rest of the day. I didn't sleep well last night, John. I'm going to bed for a while, and I don't want you prowling around the house. You have to earn trust, you know."

"I'm sorry. It won't happen again."

"I'm sure it won't, John. But leave now, please. Come back at seven, and I'll have a nice dinner fixed for us. As soon as I'm rested."

John Peterson hesitated. There was something scary about his grandmother; she seemed so calm. For some reason, he expected her to shout at him. Perhaps the wine had dulled her emotions.

"You'll be all right?"

"Yes, John," she said evenly. "Please go now."

He left the house, and Clara called to him from the doorway. "Remember—dinner at seven."

He did not look back.

Clara closed the door quickly, before he might answer, then went to the kitchen and filled her glass, taking two large swallows of wine before going to her room. She opened a drawer in her dresser, reaching under neat stacks of underwear to retrieve a plastic vial filled with tiny white tablets. It was Carolyn's prescription: Nitroglycerine. She wondered how many tablets would be necessary to kill a healthy, young boy.

It had taken only a few with Hanna.

* * * * * * *

John forced himself to walk away from the house, resisting the urge to go back again and apologize. A silent alarm was going off in his head, and he remembered again the sharp odor in the basement, and where he had smelled it before. The cattle had a contagious disease; they had to be destroyed. The men dug a giant pit, and herded the doomed animals into it, then stood on the edge with rifles and shot them one-by-one. The screams were awful, he remembered. Then they covered the carcasses with lye, and watered them down, and the smell from the pit burned their nostrils and eyes so bad they covered their faces and left quickly while bulldozers covered the pit with earth. He could never forget the smell of lye burning into those dead carcasses.

It was the smell in the basement.

The social security check for Hanna, and the others, the money in the closet and all the expensive wine his grandmother drank, it all fit. Hanna was dead, buried in the basement behind one of the newly painted walls. Perhaps others were there, all old people who had died naturally. Grandma buried them, and was collecting their social security money. It was wrong, but not murder. Dad said she was capable of anything when she was drunk. But she wouldn't murder anyone.

Would she?

John Peterson entered a park, and sat down on a bench to think about what he should do.

Two miles away, his grandmother had decided how she would kill him.

* * * * * * *

She spoke aloud to a darkened room that smelled like wine and fresh paint and a trace of lye now burning its way through dead flesh in the basement below. She was slumped over the kitchen table, face close to it, carefully counting the tablets she

had spilled out of the brown vial. The vial had rolled off the table, and rested near her swollen feet and a half-filled bottle of wine. She leaned back in her chair, sighed deeply before picking up the bottle and taking a long pull from it, eyes closed. Then she sighed again, fighting the terrible agony that filled her.

"You can have all the pills, John, crushed in a nice milk-shake when you come back. You drink them so fast on a hot day. It must be fast—I want it to be fast. Not like Hanna." She was crying now, but there were no tears. She was all dried up. "You shouldn't have gone in the basement," she cried out, then lurched to her feet and used the back of a large spoon to crush the tiny tablets on the table. She crushed two malt tablets, mixed the powders together, then filled the spoon, emptied it into a blender and took another swallow of wine.

"Nosy people," she declared. "Can't mind their own business. Parents teach them no manners, no respect for privacy. Teach them nothing! Let them leave home when they're too young! No responsibility!"

Another pull from the bottle, her voice rising in anger, and wine ran down her chin.

"I'll write him a letter," she said, "and tell him his son is dead. Then he'll know how wrong he was, and it won't be anybody's fault but his."

The wine suddenly tasted foul, and she suppressed an urge to vomit, stumbling into furniture as she crossed the living room and into John's bedroom, pulling open drawers, looking for an address to send her letter.

She found his diary in the nightstand drawer.

"Nobody's fault but his," she said, then opened the diary and began to read.

* * * * * * *

Clara sat again at the kitchen table, John's open diary and a small photograph in front of her. She was quite drunk, but the wine was nearly gone and she sipped a last glass slowly. She

stared vacantly at the diary and the photograph that had fallen out of it, her mind empty now, content, oblivious of the dry air or the hissing sound in the kitchen. The picture showed a man and a boy leaning against a car, grinning at each other like two old friends.

The boy was John.

The man was her son.

Her dead son. Her mind was so muddled she couldn't remember when or how he had died. It had been a long time ago.

She had locked all the doors, jamming them shut with chairs. The windows were closed tightly, and gas from the open stove burners and oven was rapidly filling the kitchen and living room. She didn't have the strength to seal the doors. No matter, she thought. The gas was working, drowsiness coming slowly, or was that the wine? It was too slow, and boring. She drained the wine glass with one swallow, fumbled for a cigarette and put it into her mouth. The matchbook on the table was empty; she searched for another one in her apron pocket.

There was the sound of a key in the front door lock, and then the rattling of the door knob, and then John's voice.

"Clara! I can't get in!"

The apron pocket was empty, and she needed a match.

"Clara, it's John! The door is stuck. Are you in there?"

The matchbook must have fallen out of her pocket. She looked groggily down at the floor beneath her. The matches were there. She pushed back her chair and leaned painfully over to retrieve them.

John was pounding on the front door, his voice rising. "I smell gas, Clara! Get out of there!"

Her fingers were swollen; it was difficult to open the matchbook, or even see it. What was all that noise?

"Grandma!"

I'm a grandma, she thought. My grandson lives with me, but he's a very nosy boy. His father didn't teach him manners, because he has been dead for many years.

The matchbook came open; she tore out a match and tried to strike it on the smooth cover.

The front door crashed inwards, John choking and coughing as he stumbled into the kitchen, grabbing her under the arms and dragging her towards the outside.

"I want to light my cigarette," she complained sleepily, but she had dropped the match somewhere and now her feet were hurting as John dragged her down the porch steps and away from the house.

"Don't go in there," he yelled to someone. "The place is filled with gas!"

He put her down on a grassy Bern, leaned over and put a hand on her forehead.

"It's all right, grandma. I'll take care of you now. Everything will be all right."

She reached up and touched his face.

"Oh John, I have something horrible to tell you."

"Not now, grandma. Just rest."

She caressed his face.

"John—your father is dead."

A crowd had begun to gather around them when the police arrived.

COLD SLEEP

The audience applauded as a band struck up the theme song of the show. David Leitner watched the picture on his monitor fade to a deodorant commercial, and was startled by the knock on the door of his little room. "One minute, Doctor Leitner," said a voice. "You're on after this commercial." Little creatures were suddenly flying around in his stomach again; the monster of stage fright kept coming back despite the hundreds of holovision interviews in his long life.

The band stopped playing and Larry Donnelly, talk-show host, was speaking again. "The books written by my next guest have been published in hundreds of languages on worlds across the inhabited part of our galaxy. Writer, explorer and Adjunct Professor of Galactic History at Colombia University, he has been likened to the fictional Indiana Jones of films a century past. He is a private man, and we are pleased to have him here on one of his rare holovision appearances to discuss his new book "Flight from the Coma cluster", which has just been published on cube and chip by Harcourt and Walsh. Will you please welcome, Professor David Leitner."

There was loud applause as he stepped out into the light. Women squealed like teeners seeing a holostar for the first time. It always embarrassed him. He walked to the dais as the band played the theme from a recent production based on one of his books, shook hands with Donnelly and settled himself in the green chair. The applause grew louder. He shook his head, smiling at his host, then stood up to wave at the audience and

sat down again.

"Nice to see you again," said David, leaning over and touching Donnelly on the arm. The personal touch, like they were old friends. Donnelly beamed.

"You haven't changed a bit," said Larry, "and it has been twelve years since you were last on the show. How do you do it?"

"I get a lot of sleep," said David. The audience howled with laughter.

"Ladies," said Larry, looking at his audience and holding up one hand, "how many of you would have an affair with a one-hundred-forty-year-old man?"

The reaction was expected; hysterical shouting from half the women in the audience. The response from a lady in the front row would have to be bleeped from the delayed broadcast of the show.

"They would find me a dull companion, I'm afraid," said David smiling. "I've spent nearly all my life in cryogenic suspension, I'm used to long silences, and when I go on a business trip it might be twenty years before I come home again. Not much of a life for a wife."

"Unless you can find a girl willing to spend a lot of time in cold sleep," said Larry. "Any volunteers, ladies?" There were a couple of shouts, the lady in the front row would have to be bleeped again, but the general reaction was nervous laughter and murmuring. The long sleep was always the turning point, thought David. There were disadvantages in being the oldest person on earth while walking around in the body of a thirty-five-year-old. Many disadvantages.

"Well, David, your waking hours have certainly not been idle. You're a recognized leader in the search for life beyond our solar system. Now you've traced the development of the human race back to a culture which you call the Andarian, a culture which itself had an extra-galactic origin."

"That's correct," said David. The audience grew quiet, respectful, waiting for him to tell them about themselves and

where they came from.

"What leads you to believe the human race originally came from another galaxy?"

The lecture began.

He told them about the discovery of the first cubic structures that never corroded, the runic inscriptions, clusters now found on several planets out to forty light years from Earth. The language was the same everywhere, built on thirty-six distinct characters, but so far untranslated. The digs were dangerous, with hostiles protecting what they considered to be ancient structures of their ancestors. Planetary archeology in the twenty-second century had indeed become a wild adventure and food for the media, and at the center of it was a handsome professor who was also the oldest human being on planet Earth.

The show halted momentarily for commercials and there was low murmuring from the audience as cameras were moved. Larry leaned closer, speaking softly, intimately. "You going to the Ramseth's party tonight?"

"I'll probably drop by for a while after the show. I'm not much of a party man."

"Karen Huseby will be there, with a friend," said Larry.

"Good. We can talk about the magazine business."

Larry chuckled, touched David's arm again. "Be honest with me, David. Is there anything to the rumors about you two?"

"You know show business and press people, Larry. There are always rumors. Karen and I are good friends, and she's interested in my work. We find a lot of things to talk about."

"I heard that you knew her grandmother," said Larry, still probing.

"Yes, but that was a long time ago." *And Karen might have been my grandchild*, he thought.

The red lights of the cameras were suddenly on again. "We're talking with explorer-author David Leitner about his new book 'Flight from the Coma Cluster'. David, in your book you describe a search for origins of the human race, a search that has taken you ten light-years from earth and led you to the

belief that we originally came from another galaxy. What has brought you to such a conclusion?"

David gave them the evidence for planetary settlements around yellow stars along a line chronologically ordered from the rim towards the galactic center with the initial number of colonists, as shown in glyphs, decreasing along the way. David's work now centered on the Andar system, the furthest yet explored by mankind.

"The most significant structure is a huge complex rising out of the jungles on Andar C, a tiny inner planet of the yellow star Andar. It's a veritable metallic crystal city, nearly inaccessible, unexplored, and I leave in just three weeks to study the place."

"The Andarian culture," said Larry.

"Yes, it's the earliest example I've found yet, perhaps extending back millions of years. If you arrange the known civilized worlds geometrically you will find they all lie in a distinct plane, until you near Andar. The last three, with Andar C at the extreme, are definitely above this plane, along a path curving up and out of the galaxy. It is this change in the migration path that leads me to the suspicion our origins are extra-galactic. It is possible, in fact, that Andar C is the earliest civilized world in our galaxy."

"And so we witness the start of another expedition, David, as our parents and grandparents have done before us, an expedition that might tell us where our earliest ancestors came from, why they migrated, and what they were looking for. Unfortunately most of us here tonight will not be around when you return. How long will you be gone this time?"

David thought for moment, feeling their eyes on him. "A little over sixty years," he said, and the audience groaned.

"I'm afraid you'll have to tell your next story to our grand-children," said Larry, "but perhaps by the time you return they will have migrated too, extending your line of civilizations still further towards the core of the galaxy. David Leitner, thank you very much for being with us, and good luck on your expedition."

The audience applauded with enthusiasm for the man they

admired and read so much about, a man who was with them only a few months each generation. *I would go to cold sleep with him*, thought the lady in the front row, not knowing her shouts had been bleeped twice from the show. She smiled to herself. He could thaw her out any time he wanted to, she decided.

* * * * * * *

The party was well underway when David arrived. It was loud. Nobody answered the door so he walked right in, found a closet and hung his coat in it. The house was filled with beautiful people having a good time. Some of them were already quite drunk; they stood closely packed in clusters, talking rapidly, looking intense. He elbowed his way across the room, searching for food and drink. A young girl, wearing a dress open in front clear down to her navel eased up beside and put a tiny hand on his arm. "And who are you?" she asked.

"Nobody, dear," he replied, and moved away. The girl watched him wistfully, then resumed her search for somebody who was somebody.

David found the food, an array of open-faced sandwiches, cheeses and little cakes stuffed with salty meat. He ate several, filled a glass with soda, then searched the room slowly with his eyes, looking for Karen. He found her in a secluded corner, standing with the ever-present Joel Kouri, talking to Larry Donnelly and a female companion young enough to be his daughter. Perhaps she was his daughter, but David didn't think so. Kouri saw him first, gave him a suspicious look, and then muttered something to Karen. She turned to wave at David, excused herself and began to negotiate her way towards him through a maze of people. The look on Joel Kouri's face was now a study in pure hostility.

Her blue dress was form-fitting, sleeveless and simple looking, yet somehow devastating. People noticed Karen Huseby as she eased her way past them towards David. And then she was standing close, looking up at him, holding an empty glass in

one hand. "Hi," she said.

David studied her for a long moment. "You look delicious this evening."

Several people had turned to watch them. David looked quickly around the room and noticed the stares, the faint smiles. "We should really stop meeting in secret like this."

Karen laughed.

He took her by the arm, guided her out of the room and away from the noise and the smoke and the stares. Outside the air was clean and cool; they passed a lighted pool surrounded by some of the more sober guests and found a marble bench under a tree near the edge of the light. They sat down on the bench and looked at each other quietly for a moment before they talked.

"Did you see the show tonight?"

"No, but I have it on chip at the condo. We put a magazine issue to bed tonight; I came directly from the office."

"I see," said David, smiling. "Fashion magazine publishers dress very fashionably in the office these days."

"This publisher has a very private office, dear." She withdrew an herbal spike from a slim golden case and sparked it, sucked gently and watched the thin vapor drift lazily towards the pool. "Donnelly said you were good tonight. An historic personage, he calls you. He also said half the women in the audience wanted your body. What ever did you do to provoke such a reaction?" She raised an eyebrow, looked at him closely.

"I just sat there and looked pretty. The women who go to those shows have very questionable tastes." He reached over to touch her face.

"Really? My tastes must be truly bizarre. I am a twenty-six-year-old professional woman, independent and successful, and I've fallen in love with a one hundred forty-year-old man who once made love to my grandmother."

"Not just once, Karen", he joked, but the memory was a painful thing. "I loved your grandmother. I wanted to marry her, but she—"

"Wouldn't climb into a cold coffin with you and share your

long sleep, wake up on another world she didn't know or understand and then return to earth and find her friends old and feeble or just plain dead while for her only a year or two had passed. That's what you wanted her to do, and that's what you want me to do, too." Karen's voice was calm.

It was suddenly very quiet. Was the party over? He looked at her closely. "Yes, I guess I do."

"Oh David," she moaned, taking his hand in hers, "I do love you, but don't you realize what you're asking of me? I have a career here, a successful business and work I love dearly. I feel the same way about this little planet I live on. It gives me warm beaches and an ocean to splash in, and in the winter I can go to the mountains and play in the snow."

"There's no snow on Andar C," said David. "There are lush jungles, and emerald lakes filled with fish. The human population is small; we could build a beautiful home anywhere there and live off the land. There certainly wouldn't be a lack of work to do, and once we were there we could live a normal life, raise a family. No more long, deep sleeps, waiting to wake up and find the world all changed and people you knew yesterday already years in their graves."

"You want to stay on Andar C?" Karen sat up straight, eyes wide, and her hand slipped from his grasp. "Never come back to Earth?"

"I think so," he said quickly. "I'll know when this next trip is over. The structures on Andar C are immense. It has to be at least one of the earliest settlements in the galaxy. It's untouched and remote, a sacred place. There's even a cult there that guards it. I don't think I'm going to find empty rooms this time." He could hear the excitement in his own voice.

Karen sighed and looked away from him towards the brightly lit pool. "You want me to fly away with you to a planet twenty-some light years out, leave my business and my friends and my world forever. Not to mention the little matter of cold-sleep, which I find to be a somewhat scary proposition."

"You know that's safe. It has been used safely and routinely

in hospitals for over a century now. There are no side-effects."

"No physical effects, you mean. What about mental? What about feeling like a displaced person in a primitive world with few people and living in a jungle the rest of my life with no creative work to do. I would go crazy within a year."

"You could help me with my work; I know you're interested in it, and there won't be enough hours in the day to get everything done. If what I think is true we'll uncover the earliest history of the human race, write about it, write about our life on Andar C, produce media material—"

"Maybe start up a magazine on jungle fashions," she said, and regretted it.

David looked down at his feet. *This has all happened before*, he thought. When would he learn to accept the loneliness?

Karen felt her face flush. *Now I'm a Viper-tongued female.* She slid over the bench, next to him, put her arms around his neck and pulled him against her. "I'm sorry, David. That was a stupid thing for me to say. It's just that your timing is so lousy, don't you see? Ten years from now I might fly away with you to your world without hesitation or regret, be your wife, have your children and help you with your work. But the magazine is just getting off the ground now. It was my idea from the beginning and I've got to see it through. That's my work, something I created. I can't just run off now and leave it all behind."

He kissed her throat and put his arms around her. "I'm not asking you to do it now. I'm asking you to wait until I get back from this next trip. Make your decision when I get back."

"Oh David," she said, wanting to laugh, "I'll be eighty-four years old when you get back."

"That doesn't have to be physically true."

So that was his idea, the long sleep on Earth, waiting for him to come back to her. She suddenly felt cold, and remembered her grandmother. The answer had been no. What else could it be? "I'll think about it," she said. "If you demand an answer right now I have to say no. I do love you."

"I'm leaving in three weeks," he said.

"I know."

"I'll leave it up to you," he said, and then pulled her to him and kissed her for what seemed to be a very long time. For one instant she remembered she was being kissed by a one hundred-forty-year-old man, but somehow it didn't seem to matter, and it was a very nice kiss.

* * * * * * *

They lived together for three days the week of David's departure for Andar C.

Karen called her office and asked Joel Kouri if he would please handle things for her so she could spend a little time with David before he left. No problem, said Joel, but he seemed in a hurry and hung up rudely on her before she had a chance to thank him for the favor.

The evening before he left, David crept up behind Karen in the kitchen, encircled her with his arms and kissed her neck. "What's for dinner?"

"Junk food," she said, and bent her head forward. "It's your last chance at it for sixty years."

"There are things I'll miss more than junk food." He kissed her neck again, and then bit it lightly.

"Ouch. You are the king of lecherous old men, sir."

David pulled a package out of a hip pocket and handed it to her. "For my favorite cook, a little something from Andar C."

Karen opened the package quickly, held up a long silver chain threaded through three pea-sized clear crystal spheres. "Oh David it's beautiful. Thank you."

David pointed to each sphere on the chain. "Man, woman, their God, all together", he said. "It's a gift the men on Andar C give to very special women in their lives."

Karen looked at the spheres sparkling in her hand. "I love it, David, but you know I can't promise anything about when you get back. I can't say that I'll—"

"I'm not asking you to promise me anything. Just remember

me. Remember me, Karen."

She looped the chain over her head and around her neck so that the spherical crystals nestled between her breasts. "I will, if you'll remember me too."

"You know I will," he said, and kissed her lightly.

They ate dinner in silence and went to bed before the sun disappeared below the edge of the sea. They did not make love, but lay comfortably in each other's arms until sleep came for both of them. Early the next morning, David arose in darkness, moving cat-like across the room and closing the door silently behind him. The high-pitched whine of a copter engine filled the darkness as the machine lifted off. Karen lay in bed, listening to the fading sound, and feeling a terrible numbness.

* * * * * * *

At twenty thousand feet he took over manual control and homed on the strengthening radio beacon. David brought the shuttlecraft down in a gentle glide through several thin layers of clouds and then the world below was suddenly green as he passed over steep hills and wandering canyons with rivers that sparkled in the light from Andar. His target was one of the larger villages known as Galuska.

There was a flash of blue from his left; he turned in time to see a massive cubic tower of metal rising above the gnarled trees of the jungle. It was three days back by foot or boat, he remembered. The territory was familiar now; he glided towards a triangular valley between three hills and saw the runway ahead. Plowed fields and scattered stone houses, cubic-shaped, passed below him. Nothing had changed, except the runway. It was longer now, and wider. He stopped well short of the end of the runway, and then turned the craft around and taxied back to a cluster of stone buildings past rows of small copters and several gliders. A small group of people stood in front of the largest building, staring at the impressive bulk of the approaching shuttlecraft. Some of them waved colorful scarves, motioning

David and his big machine forward. He stopped a few yards from them, turned off the engine and opened the bottom hatch of the craft.

Warm moist air and odors of vegetation filled the cabin, driving away the cold sensation he had felt since awakening from his long sleep. He lowered himself down through the hatch, hanging from his fingers for one dizzy moment, then dropped to the ground as a noisy open vehicle with oversized balloon tires pulled up to a screeching halt beside him. The driver was a young, good looking boy: chiseled features and blond hair that contrasted sharply with his deeply tanned skin. He grinned as David spoke to him in the guttural Andarian language that, curiously, resembled Arabic.

"I am David Leitner. Can you tell me where I might find Jaryl Vreen of Galuska? He was my friend and guide many years ago when I last visited your village."

"You are expected," said the boy, still smiling. "I am Devon, his youngest son. Please get in and I'll take you to my father. He is anxious to see you again."

They drove along a narrow winding road cut into the slopes of hills covered with ferns, trees with long slender leaves, and underbrush choked with red and purple flowers that smelled sweetly. Branches hung over the road in a high protective arch, diffusing the light of a hot Andarian afternoon. Birds screamed at their intrusion; a large white one crashed out of the under-brush, stumbled crazily ahead of them for several yards and veered back off the road. The young boy laughed.

"She draws us away from her eggs," he explained, and then looked at David. "Do you like this place?"

"Yes," said David, looking up at the trees. "I would like to stay here a long time."

"My father said it would be so." The boy nodded, smiling again.

"How is your father?"

"He's well, and content with his life. As he ages he stays closer to home these days. If you still wish to explore the metal

structures up-river I will guide you there this time."

"You know about the structures?"

"Oh yes. We've heard many stories about my father's adventures as a young man, and about you. Your name is familiar in our village, but only a few have seen you before now." He looked closely at David. "I know you are very old, but it seems you are not much older than my brothers."

"Did your father tell you how I do that?"

"Yes." The boy shook his head slowly. "I think it's a very strange way to live."

David laughed.

They stopped in front of a white stone house with a steep roof made from sheets of slate, and small windows covered with gauze-like cloth to keep out the many biting insects that hunted for blood in the night. The house was nestled in a natural hollow near the top of a hill, close to a stream that cascaded noisily down the slope into a deep canyon below. David was absorbed with the serenity of the place when Jaryl came out to meet them. David remembered the high-spirited eighteen-year-old adventurer who had guided his long river journey to the ancient metal structures hidden in the jungle. He was stunned by the physical appearance of the man. Jaryl Vreen was white haired, and very old.

They embraced, holding tightly to each other for a long moment, and then Jaryl stepped back to look at him. "You are as I remember you," he said, "and here I am, an old man." There were tears in his eyes, and envy for the man who remained so young. David leaned forward and looked into the twinkling old eyes.

"I think you also remain young, dear friend."

Jaryl laughed, took David by the arm and led him towards the house. "I have many children who are eager to meet you," he said.

They talked far into the night; the women served them fruit in large wooden bowls, and bread that tasted like honey.

The women were his daughters, explained Jaryl. His wife had

passed away the previous summer, and they had been married for forty years. The house seemed filled with children of all ages. David was introduced to all of them and quickly forgot their names, but he remembered Neela, a twenty-five-year-old beauty who hovered around the men protectively, hushing the others when they became too loud. David caught her gazing at him several times. Her smile was beautiful. Jaryl explained that Neela was still searching for a man. "Be careful of that one," he said, smiling. "She is like her mother."

When darkness came the house was illuminated with soft yellow light from transparent chemical filled containers of various shapes and sizes. Cooking was done with wood, electricity serving only for refrigeration of food in the hot climate, and produced by small turbines powered by underground streams. All organic waste was pumped to a small plant that synthesized enough fuel to power the few vehicles in the village. Nothing was wasted on Andar C.

They sat in the cold yellow light and talked.

"You returned alone," said Jaryl.

"Yes," said David.

"I thought there might be a woman."

"There is, or was; I hope she's waiting for me to return. I want to bring her back to Andar C and make our home here."

"She knows this?"

"She knows, but her business prevents her from leaving Earth now. Perhaps, when I return—"

"It's unfortunate I'll not be able to meet this woman of yours. Even if you must return alone, David, there are many women to choose from if you settle here. Maybe that would even be better for you."

David smiled at the man who could read the faint markings of loneliness on his face. "You might be right," he said. "In any case I have my work to do."

"Ah yes, your work. We'll begin plans for that tomorrow. There is danger in what you want to do."

"Danger? I don't understand."

"It's a man named Dorell, and a small group of fanatics who have appointed themselves guardians of the structures you want to explore. They wait for men to return from the stars and reclaim the place."

"If what I believe is true," said David, "then I represent the men they await."

"I believe you, and the village elders agree with me. That's why you've been given permission to enter the structures and make your studies. Dorell says you're an imposter; he has threatened physical harm if you come near the place, even though he knows any act of violence against you will be considered a serious crime, with an equally serious punishment. I fear the man is quite mad; he does not listen to reason."

"I'll have to take that chance," said David. "I've come too far to turn back now. The history of your people and mine is in those structures."

"I know. My son Devon will guide you there, and several of the village men will also go with you. That should be enough protection, but be careful. Any discovery you make isn't worth your life, and if you feel it is then you are as much a zealot as Dorell." His voice was suddenly grave. "We wish no trouble here."

"I understand," said David, and he swallowed hard. "I'll be careful for myself, your son and the other men."

"Good," said Jaryl, smiling again, "but first you sleep. The plans will wait until tomorrow, when our minds are rested. I'll take you to your room now."

David lay awake for hours that night, listening to the cascading waters behind the house and thinking about the people of Andar C. Karen intruded in his thoughts. When sleep finally came it was shallow and he remembered a profusion of dreams about metal structures, and his last night on Earth with a girl who lived on a hill overlooking the sea. He did not remember an earlier dream he had about Jaryl's daughter Neela.

* * * * * * *

Preparation and planning took six days and nights. David's respect for the people of Galuska grew rapidly; they worked hard, cheerfully, never complaining about the long hours, heat, or the biting insects that constantly hovered around them. The shuttlecraft was unloaded, pulled to the side of the runway and covered with a light tarp to protect its painted surface from the fierce heat of the day. Supplies, including recorders, laser torch and a month's ration of freeze-dried foods were piled in a heap on a wooden dock at the river and guarded day and night. David did not question the necessity for the guards on the dock, or the two men who drowsed in the shade of a tree near the shuttlecraft and slept beneath it at night. For reasons of his own, Jaryl had ordered the security.

The morning of David's sixth day on Andar C they began to load the four boats that would take them up the river. Flat bottomed, the twelve-foot long boats were powered by alcohol-fueled engines and rode high in the water with a full load. Four boats for ten men and a thousand pounds of supplies didn't seem like enough, but somehow they found a place for everything and in the afternoon of the sixth day they rested. David stood apart from the others, suddenly feeling very much alone and wanting to find a cool place for thinking. He walked away from them, along the river, in search of the place.

He had gone a mile along the river before he realized where he was. The hills were steep, and a stream cascaded loudly down into the dark river water, filling the air with mist. It was the stream that passed near Jaryl's house high on the hill. He climbed up along the stream and around large granitic boulders, feeling much alive and eager to climb further. The sound of the flowing water filled his mind, driving out all thoughts and giving him a kind of peace. Half way up the hill the waters formed a quiet pool beneath a rocky overhang before crashing onwards towards the river far below. He stood there for a moment, feeling the seclusion of the place, took off all his clothes and waded into the pool. The water was very cold. He splashed himself several times, working up courage, then flopped into the water with a

shout as the heat from his body was suddenly sucked away. He swam a few strokes, and then pulled himself up under a small waterfall and let water flow over his head and face. Mind blank, he sat there oblivious of the passage of a moment, then stood up and began to wade out of the pool.

Above him, somebody giggled.

David turned sharply, off-balance, tried to look up and sat down hard in the pool. Neela was sitting on a rock above him and laughed as he thrashed around in the pool trying to hide himself.

"What are you doing up there?" he shouted, angry with himself and feeling stupid.

"Watching you," she chirped. Her dark eyes flashed, teasing him.

"My God, woman, I'm naked," he said hoarsely.

"I know that. Don't you think I've seen a naked man before? I have six brothers, you know."

"Well I'm not one of your brothers. Turn around, so I can get out of here and get dressed."

"No." She gazed at him steadily.

David sat in the water, feeling ridiculous, and then looked at her mischievously as he stood up and thrust his hands above his head.

"Ta-dah!" he shouted, grinning as Neela threw her head back with a deep-throated laugh that echoed from the boulders and made his skin tingle deliciously from head to toe.

"'You're beautiful," she shouted gleefully.

God, what a creature. He waded out of the pool and began to dress. "Why don't you come down for a closer look?"

"No."

"Why not?"

"Father says I'm not supposed to bother you."

"Oh." David understood. He continued to dress himself.

"You've known my father for a long time?"

"Not really. We worked together for a year when he was about your age."

"And then you went away," she said.

"Yes, for a long time."

She sat quietly for a moment, thinking. "But you look so young now."

David smiled at her. "Has your father explained to you how I do that?"

"Yes, but I don't understand why you choose to live that way."

"My work requires it. I have to travel very far."

"Will you always live that way?"

"No. I'd really like to live here the rest of my life, but I have to make one more trip before I can do that."

"Father says you will return with a wife who is waiting for you now."

"I don't have a wife."

"But there is someone waiting for you?"

"Perhaps. I don't know for certain."

"And when you return, we will all be old like my father is now." Neela stood up suddenly, looking down at him sadly and making him wish she would come down from her rocky perch.

"I think it's a waste of your time to travel so far in search of a wife." She turned away from him, stepped back quickly from the edge of the rocky overhang and disappeared from his view.

"Neela?" he called.

She was gone.

He dreamed about her again that night, but this time the dream played at the edge of his consciousness and he awoke, startled by its intensity. Hew remembered the dream for a long time.

* * * * * * *

They traveled up the river for three days and part of a fourth. It was late in summer; the river was low, and a gentle current made travel easy. In the mornings they paddled the boats slowly, savoring the crisp air and the cries of the birds in moss-laden trees arching high over the river. It was a holiday for the

young men, taking them away from their everyday chores; they laughed and sang as they stroked the waters with their paddles. When they tired in the afternoons the motors pushed them towards their destination while they dozed or talked, enjoying each other's company. David felt very close to all of them, once they had forgotten how old he was and ceased to treat him like a village elder. Now they even shared their naughty stories with him during the night camps in clearings along the river banks. The stories were the same everywhere in the galaxy, he thought. It didn't surprise him. They were all one people.

In the morning of the fourth day the paddling rhythm increased as they neared their destination. David daydreamed and thought about Karen's condo on the hill. He imagined their house sitting in every clearing he passed, and compared views of the river and surrounding jungle. He could imagine a copter sitting on the deck beside the house. It would only be an hour or two flight back to the village, and when his studies progressed there would be other people living nearby and Karen wouldn't be lonely, and they would be working together.

His reverie was broken by the sight of a gleaming metal tower rising above the trees at a bend in the river ahead. He started to point towards it when Devon put a hand on his shoulder from behind him and spoke softly.

"Don't shout, David. We see it."

The men had stopped paddling, sat still in the boats and looked nervously towards the jungle on both sides of the river. Devon leaned forward and whispered into David's ear.

"We're being watched."

* * * * * * *

Karen paced back and forth in her living room, waiting impatiently for the copter to arrive. It was her birthday, her thirtieth, and she was feeling sorry for herself. The twenties were gone forever, and he couldn't be on time, she thought.

She watched as the copter descended a little too quickly and

bounced twice when it hit the deck. Joel leaped from the cab and hurried towards the house. Karen met him at the door.

"You're late," she said, looking at her watch.

He kissed her cheek, handed her a large envelope and pressed by her into the house. "I had to pick up your birthday present," he said smiling. He was excited about something.

She sat on the couch, Joel close beside her, and opened the envelope. She studied the papers inside for a moment, then looked at Joel in disbelief.

"You did it," she whispered. "You got them all to sign."

"Madam," announced Joel, "you are now a monopoly. You have in your hands the controlling interest of every fashion publication on this planet. How does it feel to be a powerful person?"

"Wonderful!" she cried, wrapping her arms around his neck as her hands clenched the documents that fulfilled her wildest dreams. "Oh, Joel, what would I do without you?" She kissed him lightly on the mouth, but he kissed her back long and hard, pressing her into the couch until she could hardly breathe.

"Marry me, Karen," he said urgently. "Marry me now, not later, no more talk about waiting for David to come back. I'm the one with you now, and I need you Karen. I need you badly."

"You just want me for my money," she said huskily, and laughed, but her breathing was heavy for a reason. Joel had done so much for her, was so important in her life, and she had given him so little in return.

"I have my own fortune," he said, grinning when he saw the sparkle in her eyes. "It's you I want." He kissed her face lightly: nose, forehead and cheek.

"Dinner is ready," she teased.

"To hell with dinner," he said, pressing her deeper into the couch. He brought his face close, saw her lips part, felt the heat of her breath.

Karen felt his desire, as she had felt it before, but now she gave herself completely to him. At first, in her fantasy, it was David who made love to her, but then the fantasy disappeared.

Their dinner got cold.

* * * * * * *

They set up camp near the river, in the shadows of two cylindrical metal towers. From the angular position of Andar, and stepping off the lengths of the shadows, David calculated their height at thirty-five meters. The towers were connected by a high arch with three small open ports. Probably a walkway, he thought. A door in one tower was sealed tightly, but David resisted use of the laser torch in cutting through it or any other entrance until he had explored the complex of structures before him. Beyond the towers was a natural bowl-shaped depression in the steep hillside, filled with rocky debris that showed signs of craftsmanship in a distant past. Perhaps it had been a meeting place, or a theatre of some kind. It lay before the yawning open entrance of the first tier of cubic modules stacked like children's blocks in terraces all the way to the top of the high hill, and ending in a single rectangular module that soared high above the trees. David remembered what he had seen from the shuttlecraft during his descent; he was awed by what the jungle had hidden from him.

Several men armed with knives and the skill to use them were left behind to guard the camp and boats while David, Devon and two others made the first probe into the unscarred remnants of an ancient civilization. David's heart pounded with excitement; where he walked was perhaps the beginning of galactic history for mankind. They moved at a snail's pace, David cautioning each step, taking pictures of seemingly bare walls and floors, talking to himself in a whisper. The men were amused by his behavior. Later on, they began to understand.

A wide staircase ran straight up through the center of the complex, connecting each level and narrowing gradually as it neared the top. The ascending pattern of hundreds of stairs drew David's gaze upwards, beckoning him to go further. At each level, pairs of hallways went off to right and left of the

stairs, at right angles to them, joining to form narrow loops that began and ended at the stairs. The halls were lined with sealed windowless entrances to rooms beyond. David picked at the seam of one with Devon's knife, then looked closely. Tiny flakes of waxy material lay on the shining blade; he dropped them into a plastic envelope, then turned to Devon.

"This place has been sprayed."

"How do you see that?" asked the boy.

"The seams in these doors are filled with something organic, and I'll bet that all this metal is impregnated with the stuff. That's why nothing has corroded."

"Perhaps the spraying has been done recently?"

"Yes, that's possible." David smiled at Devon, delighted with his quick observation. "We'll have to consider that possibility for everything we find here. But it doesn't seem likely that the inscriptions on these walls have been made recently."

The inscriptions were everywhere, in the same runic script David had seen on Earth, Mars and many other planets in still other planetary systems. They found them at the top and bottom of each flight of stairs, at the entrance to each hallway, and David was reminded of direction signs in office buildings back on Earth. No two inscriptions were the same; he took careful pictures of each one and sketched them in a notebook. On the twenty-third level of the complex he added up the number of different characters he had seen. Thirty-six, and maybe the entire alphabet was there. He began to make frequency tables.

They continued to ascend, level after level of dark hallways with sealed doors and secrets beyond, and myriad writings on the walls. The staircase became steadily narrower, the hallways shorter. And then there were no hallways, only a helical flight of stairs curving steeply upwards and out of sight, and a short inscription on the wall. David motioned the others on up the stairs, then stared at the writing. Something was there, in the back of his mind, he pulled at it, leafed through his notes and sketches, and then it was free.

There were thirty-six levels in the complex.

Thirty-six levels, and thirty-six characters. He turned the pages of notes with frantic excitement, looking for a pattern, and found it. The last character in each inscription was separated from the others by a single space, was different for each level. The alphabet was there, level by level. How nice of them, he thought.

He hurried up the stairs, looking for Devon, and found him looking out a narrow viewport towards the jungle far below.

"What a view," said the boy. "The river looks like a shining snake down there."

"I have the alphabet," said David.

"You can read the writing?"

"Not yet, but it's just a matter of time now. What's above us?"

"More of the same, four levels, tiny rooms and these little windows. This must be an observation tower; you can see everything from here."

David looked out of one of the narrow slots cut through the wall, saw the jungle stretching to the horizon and felt the heat from Andar on his face. He jumped convulsively when there was a shout from above him.

"Men running in the jungle!"

David pressed his face against the port opening, looked hard, and saw nothing but trees. "I see one," cried Devon, and David rushed to him for a look. Still nothing.

The other two men clattered down the stairs above them. "I saw four men running through the trees like they were being chased," said one of them.

"I saw one too," said Devon. "Our men?"

"I don't think so. They wore light shirts I didn't recognize. But they looked like they were running for their lives."

"We'd better get down there," said David, and they began the dizzying descent of the stairs. An alarm was sounding somewhere in David's head; only the first real day of exploration, and there was trouble already.

They reached camp and talked to the men who had been left to guard it. A stranger had tried to steal one of the boats, they

said, and then two others started throwing rocks at them with long slings and the men drew their knives and chased them away. Nobody had been hurt.

"It must be Dorell and his merry little band of misfits," said David. "We'll have to maintain a security perimeter day and night from now on." The alarm in his head was now loud. It had been an openly hostile act; there would be fighting, and someone was going to get hurt. They slept lightly and fitfully that night, and took turns manning a tight circle of guards around camp and boats. For the moment, David forgot about the alphabet of his ancestors.

They mapped the complex for three days before firing up the laser torch and cutting into the rooms beyond sealed doors. The towers at the base of the complex were empty, without furnishings. They cut into the rooms and discovered a Spartan environment for the people of the distant past. All were cubic hollows, three meters on a side, a single slab for sleeping, round table and circumscribing bench fixed in the center of the floor, a single shelf on the wall and what was probably a ventilation duct in the ceiling. There were no windows to the outside, each room a cell, isolated from the world, a place for quiet meditation. David's disappointment mounted as they went from room to room, finding the same thing.

In the evenings he worked on frequency tables with Devon while the other men prowled the camp, watching the darkness, listening for the sound of a footfall, the swish of a sling twirling and then releasing a stone towards them. The missiles fell harmlessly, but the attackers came back every night.

They discovered the library on the twelfth day.

Work was proceeding on the fifteenth level, and David was taking pictures of individual characters in an inscription when Devon called to him.

"In here, David. There are books."

He rushed to the newly opened room, looked inside, saw table, bench and a shelf stacked neatly with a long line of books that gleamed in the cold light of the lamps. His heart felt

squeezed, and he could barely breathe. He took pictures from all sides while the men watched him from the doorway, feeling his excitement in each move. He touched one volume, holding his breath, withdrew it from the shelf, opened it and stared at the words etched on thin metal pages. He sat down on the bench, turning pages slowly, delicately, like a buyer handling a rare first edition. There were pages and pages of writing, then maps and tables, and pictures.

Pictures of human beings.

David spread the book open on the table, gestured for the men to look at it. "Here are your ancestors," he said solemnly, "and mine."

They looked quietly at a picture of tall, handsome people dressed briefly for a warm climate, walking in a park with trees and strange flowers, and in the background buildings of a city soared high into the sky.

He knew there would be more, the entire history would be there on the shelf. The books had been left deliberately. The key to the language would be there somewhere, and he already knew the alphabet. He would begin like a small child in school, learning to read and count and spell, moving on to the history, geography, culture and science. He hoped that somewhere in the writings he would find the saga of a long journey to a planet known as Andar C.

There was a shout from the hall. Two men left the room.

The rest of his life was now clearly defined. And the only thing that could make it better would be to share it with Karen.

"Trouble below us!" Someone was shouting from the hallway. The men spilled out of the room, leaving David momentarily alone. Devon appeared at the doorway, leaning against it out of breath, voice urgent.

"There's fighting outside. Dorell and his people are trying to burn the boats!"

He was running, heart pounding and adrenalin flowing, and there was an anger he'd never felt before. Devon was just ahead of him, and David saw the flash of a knife in his hand. David

reached for his own knife, found he'd left it back at the camp. Stupid, he thought.

They reached the yawning entrance and saw men struggling with each other in a smoky haze near the ground. A knife flashed, followed by an agonized cry. A man lay near the entrance, eyes staring, his head split open and blood and grey matter spilling out onto the cold metal floor. Devon slammed upright into a man ahead, thrusting with his knife, the man's eyes widening in surprise. Another attacker rushed at Devon from one side, clutching a rock, one arm held high. David put his head down and crashed into the man shoulder first, feeling the ribs first give and then snap as the man screamed in agony and went down hard.

David picked up the rock, daring someone to come at him. There was sudden movement above him; he looked up over the entrance to see an apparition with blazing eyes, white hair framing his face Medusa-like, twirling a sling in a high arc, then pointing at him and something crashed into his forehead with shattering force. David felt suddenly cold and dropped to his knees, something warm running down his face and into his mouth. Not now, he thought. It's too soon for this to happen. What will Karen think? He fell over on his side and watched a bug scurrying along the ground. The bug didn't seem to notice him, and then the darkness came.

* * * * * * *

Light, then sound, and someone was crying far away. He blinked his eyes, and saw movement. Someone was squeezing his hand tightly. It hurt. He blinked again, the white fog clearing slowly, and then Jaryl and Neela were looking down at him, Neela's face wet with tears and her hand in his.

"Welcome back to life," said Jaryl. Neela released David's hand and began to sob softly, leaning against her father.

David turned to look at them and winced at the burst of pain in his head. "God, what a headache," he moaned.

"Not surprising," said Jaryl. "Your skull was badly split. It is maybe fortunate; there was room for the swelling of your brain. We have waited a long time for your return."

"I remember fighting," said David, "and a crazy man with white hair and a sling. He hit me with a rock."

"Dorell," said Jaryl, looking down at the floor. "He has been dealt with."

"How do you—?"

"Dorell and two of his followers survived their treachery. Devon and the men brought them back with you many days ago. At the time we were certain you were going to die. The villagers were angry, they took the criminals down to the river and stoned them to death."

David closed his eyes. "I'm sorry," he said. "I didn't want this to happen."

"Dorell doesn't deserve your pity. He was a fanatic, a madman, a disgrace to all of us. The village is safer without him."

When David looked at Jaryl he saw tears in the old man's eyes. "Did we have any casualties?"

"Only bad bruises, and a minor concussion. Your injury was by far the most serious. We almost lost you."

The old man began to cry, and Neela clung to him, burying her face in his shoulder.

David felt a strangling sensation in his throat, and swallowed hard. His thoughts came quickly, now. "I've brought you nothing but misery," he said. "I should go home, as soon as I'm able to."

Jaryl looked at him through a mist of tears, breathing slowly to regain control of himself. "Home?" he said in a whisper. "Your home is here, David, with us. There's no need for you to leave; the structures and books you want to study are still there, safe, and guarded day and night. You have a lifetime of work to do here, and the people regard you as one of their own. There was rejoicing when they heard you would survive your injuries. You are an ancestor, returned to us. Your place is here."

David reached out and touched the man's shoulder. "Not yet,

not this time. I have to return to Earth just one more time, to show them my pictures and tell them about what I have found. There are scholars there who must be told about this, and others who—"

"You're returning to Earth to find your woman and bring her back here with you," said Neela, face still pressed against her father's shoulder. It was said coldly, and when she spoke again there was bitterness in her voice.

"She will be old, David."

He lay back in the bed, looking at the ceiling. "Maybe," he said, "but I have to be certain about that. Do you understand?"

"Yes," she said softly, then added "I would wait for you if I could."

"No Neela," said Jaryl.

"I agree," said David. "Things are just beginning for you here. It would not be right for you to live in a way I've chosen freely for myself. If Karen still waits for me, as I hope, she has had plenty of time to think about it and make her decision wisely and without regrets."

The fear that she would be old suddenly struck him.

"Then it is settled," said Neela, without emotion. She turned, walked gracefully to the door and opened it. "I will see you again, David, before you leave." The door closed, and she was gone.

"Thank you, David," said Jaryl, "for understanding."

* * * * * * *

He recovered from his wound, swam in the river and tanned himself brown in the light of Andar. Work began on a road through the jungle, linking the village with the place of their ancestors, and the home David might someday build. Many people worked willingly, even with the knowledge that only their children and grandchildren would ever see him again. And he loved them for it.

On the morning he pulled the nose of the shuttlecraft up

towards the yellow disk of Andar, the entire village was there, shouting and waving, and Jaryl waved to him for the last time from the top of a hill. David cut the main engines in, there was an explosion of birds from the jungle below and a brief glimpse of something metallic towering above the trees. As he lifted towards the mother ship far above he looked back at the blue and green planet for a long while, certain that it would all be the same when he returned. But as he neared the start of still another long cold sleep, he wondered if someone else would be returning with him.

* * * * * * *

The people of Earth welcomed him. Word of his arrival had sped ahead at light speed; the oldest man in the human race had returned. Reporters surrounded him like hyenas around a piece of seasoned meat, asking rapid-fire questions, pushing against each other for position. David answered graciously, but kept moving, anxious to get away. He promised them an evening interview to tell about what he had discovered. The police intervened, spiriting him away to a conference room to meet the mayor of the city and his staff. More reporters, in a room packed with holo-cameras and hot lights. The mayor gave a speech, smiling broadly for the cameras. David searched the room frantically for familiar faces, and saw none. More promises of a later interview, and then he asked the mayor for a favor.

A police hovercraft sped him across the city over darkly stained buildings thrust up into a hazy sky filled with aircraft. The quality of life had decayed with the city, he thought. They approached a building that soared high above its neighbors, and David gasped. On top of the building, white block letters proclaimed HUSEBY CENTER. They landed on the letter S. David found the main lobby on the top floor and read the directory there. His face flushed as he read the name at the top: Joel Kouri, Publisher and Editor-in-Chief. He scanned the directory quickly, desperately, looking for Karen. He found her name at

the bottom: Karen Huseby, Consulting Editor. What the hell was going on? Had she sold out? At least she was still alive.

He found Kouri's office and burst into a large reception room staffed with three secretaries who looked up, startled, as he entered. He walked up to the desk of a pretty, young woman who smiled at him expectantly.

"My name is David Leitner, and I'm looking for Karen Huseby. Can you tell me where I can find her?"

"David Leitner?" the woman was momentarily stunned into silence; she looked for help from someone, and found it. An older woman, in her fifties or early sixties, got up from her desk and walked over to David, extending her hand. "My name is Kathy, Mister Leitner. Welcome home." She looked sincere, thought David. Her handshake was firm and dry.

"I want to see Karen Huseby."

"I understand," she said, smiling. "I'll tell Mister Kouri you're here." She turned away, walked quickly to an intercom and punched it. "Mister Kouri? Kathy, here. David Leitner is in the outer office, and he wants to see Karen right away. Do you want to talk to him first?"

David suddenly felt a tight knot form in his stomach.

There was a croaking sound from the intercom. "You can go in now," said Kathy, motioning him towards a closed door, and smiling at him. But as he passed her, David saw tears welling up in her eyes and the knot in his stomach tightened further.

The office was dimly lit, the only furnishings a large desk, and behind it a swivel chair turned towards the picture window looking out on the murky city. David stepped up to the desk and leaned over it. "Mister Kouri? I'm trying to find Karen."

The chair turned slowly.

David stepped back with a shock as the shrunken figure of a dissipated old man glared back at him from the deep embrace of the chair.

"So the hero returns at last," the old man said, his eyes burning into David's.

"I want to see Karen."

"You might be too late; it has been a very long time, as you can see by looking at me." Joel Kouri cackled, then coughed a deep rattling cough and wiped his mouth with a handkerchief. He peered at something in the handkerchief, then folded it and put it back neatly in his pocket.

"Just tell me where she is," said David.

The old man babbled, gesturing around the room. "You see all of this, David? It's an empire, the largest publishing conglomerate in the world. Karen and I built it together. I got them all to sign. I got them to go along with Karen's leadership, and now they know how right I was. I gave her the world, David. While you were out there running around on some planet, I gave her the world. Me!"

David leaned over, grabbed the lapel of Joel's coat with one hand and pulled at it. "Where is Karen?" he whispered, close to Kouri's face.

"Mercy Hospital, fourth floor Geriatrics, room 407." The old man muttered, eyes closed.

David dropped him back into the chair. *Oh, my God.* He hurried towards the door, Kouri shouting bitterly after him, "Hurry, David! You may not get there in time!"

David crashed his way through the outer office and left the hall door open. The flight to Mercy Hospital was a short one. His feet hit the landing pad before the copter had landed, and he started to run. The copter pilot screamed angrily at him, he returned and stuffed all the money he had into the astonished man's hand and ran again.

The elevator was occupied. David took the stairs down three at a time, threw open the doors to the Geriatrics ward as people jumped away from him in fright. Rooms 400-425 were to the left, and he was running again, straight down the middle of the hall past nursing stations, shriveled faces gaping at him from doorways. There was a laundry room, cryogenics storage, and an old man tottering along with a walking aid. David burst through the doors of room 407, grunting as he collided hard with a heavily built nurse who glared angrily at him and pushed

him back towards the door.

"What the hell do you mean, barging in here like this?" she said hoarsely, trying to catch her breath. "This area is restricted to doctors and—"

"I'm David Leitner, and I've got to see Karen Huseby right away."

"I don't care who you are," she said, pushing him hard. "You can't just come in here—"

"Let him in, nurse," said a male voice softly behind her. "I'll handle this."

"Yes, doctor," she said, glaring at David again. She left the room and closed the door softly behind her. As the light from the hall disappeared, the room was engulfed in darkness, David's pupils dilating rapidly to accommodate it. A shadow moved.

"Over here, by the bed," said the shadow.

David moved cautiously, feeling his way across the room. A hand touched his.

"I'm Doctor Meyer. The news about your pending arrival came quite late. She's still pretty sleepy, I'm afraid." The man stood up, moved to the shade-covered window. "We can try a little light, I think, but only for a short time. Too much exposure might be traumatic right now." He opened the shades a crack; light spilled into the room. David sat on the edge of the bed, looked at Karen, and then his body was shaking and the doctor's hand was on his shoulder.

"Easy, man, take some deep breaths and then look at her again, because I think she's nearly awake now. She really has come through it all quite well.

David looked. He reached out, touched a cheekbone, felt moist lips, pouting, and brushed soft hair back away from her eyes. He leaned over and kissed her lightly, feeling her lips move at his touch and hearing her moan like a child in sleep. Her eyelids fluttered; he sat up straight, studying her face, loving it.

The doctor consulted a chart on the end of the bed. "It says here she wants children. Better not wait too long; physically she's about thirty-four years old now."

"I don't intend to wait," said David, as Karen opened her eyes and looked at him. Her smile made him want to shout.

"David," she said.

"I'm here, Karen."

"Hi," she said.

THE DEPTHS OF LOVE

Elise cried when he left her, and said she would never love another. They had been together only a month, their lovemaking intense and satisfying, yet Eric could not make the emotional bond she needed to have with him, his soul trapped in a dream about someone else. Always it was the same, one woman after another, none of them matching the illusion that haunted his nights, and even daydreams. An illusion that swam with him in the sea. Often he would taste salt, and awake gasping for breath, but when sleep returned she was still there and he felt a rough texture when their skins touched.

He had always been attracted to the sea, even as a child, but in a strange way it frightened him, calling to him for some sinister purpose, suffocating him when his head was beneath the waves. The sea beckoned to him again after he had left Elise sobbing her grief. He was stricken by the sorrow he had caused, and returned again to the place he had found when he was a boy.

He caught the Long Beach boat to Catalina at seven on a foggy morning with rain expected. Mostly locals on board, the beautiful people, the ones he waited tables for. It was raining when the boat pulled into Avalon. He left the paved road near the botanical gardens, and was soaked when he turned south near the west cliffs of the island. The wind blew in cold from the open sea, and he covered himself with a poncho. In the cave there would be peace, perhaps serenity. He had hurt another person terribly again, and his life was going nowhere. He wondered if it was time to end it.

Eric reached the cave in late afternoon as sunlight exploded overhead, quickly drying him. Seal Rocks were straight ahead, but most of the animals were in the water, and a nearly empty tourist boat had pulled up to watch them. He turned to his right, out of sight of the rocks, and climbed down a goat trail to the main entrance, a five-by-five hole crammed with tumbleweed. A hundred feet below him, foamy waves crashed against sharp rock. A simple push from the rock, and it could all be over. Would there be pain? He pushed his way inside, then replaced the tumbleweed plug and turned on his light. The cave was a ten minute crawl away, down tubules blown out by an ancient, higher sea, and already he felt safer. It was quiet, except for the distant pounding of surf. Others rarely came to this place, but left garbage behind as proof. It seemed unlikely he'd see anybody in the next day. Time enough to make some decisions, about life—or death.

The cave was egg-shaped, high ceiling punctured by three holes through which light streamed to warm the slowly undulating pool below. He came out ten feet above the pool, onto a series of rock shelves leading down to a tiny sandy beach at water's edge. An empty, crushed beer can was on the sand. He filled it with water, tossed it into the pool, watched it sink into darkness. As usual, he had no desire to swim here, the inky water hiding anything below the surface, yet connected with the open sea, breathing with it. Only once had he gone in, a year ago, had imagined something touching his leg, grabbing at it as he thrashed his way to the little beach. A piece of kelp— perhaps.

Eric stowed his pack and took off his boots, wiggling toes in sand. He sat quietly for only a few minutes, his life whirling before him in a dream-like state before his grief struck hard again and tears were running down his cheeks. He let out a whimper of despair, and then choked it down. I want to die, he thought. He fumbled in his pack, took out a skinning knife sheathed in leather. Pressed the point of the blade into the back of one hand until a tiny bead of blood formed there. It hurt. It

hurt bad. He couldn't take the pain. It suddenly occurred to him that he was afraid of dying. He groaned aloud, and the sound caught in his throat.

Something had surfaced in the pool.

At first he thought it was a seal, but the color was too light for that. It surfaced, submerged again for an instant, then slowly rose, two eyes flickering golden points of light just below the surface.

They were human eyes, moving towards him, a white shape beneath the water, drawing close. He stood up, panicked and ready to run, until he saw it was a woman. A beautiful woman, and horribly familiar. She swam languidly to the edge of the pool, and pulled herself out with long arms. Light brown hair, long, strong legs, small breasts barely covered by the black bikini she wore. Tall. Up close she looked straight into his eyes, licked her lips and smoothed hair back from her face. "Hi," she said. "I'm glad you came back again."

"What?" said Eric. The quivering had started in his legs and now reached his chest.

"I feel your agony, and I can help. My name is Halena, and I think you might remember me. What do you want me to do?" She stepped right up to him, reached out to unbutton the top button of his shirt, pulled it aside to inspect the flesh underneath and rubbed it with a long finger. Her eyes were golden and dreamy, looking slowly back to his face. His heart pounded beneath her moving hand.

"My God, you are beautiful," he said.

Her voice was like the moan of wind in the cave. "There is no God but Eros, and he is here with us. He has created us."

"You look so familiar. I think I've dreamed about you or someone like you."

"Of course. You left me a long time ago, and you've forgotten. Have you had a good time?"

"I don't understand."

Halena laughed, her head tilted back, and Eric saw long scars running under both her jaws from ear to chin. "Swim with me,"

she said, and the scars beneath her jaw seemed to redden for an instant.

"Ah, I'm not much of a swimmer, and I didn't bring a suit."

"You don't need one," she teased. "Swim with me. You'll like it. Come on."

"I said I don't want to swim. What's down there, anyway? How did you get in here?"

"Another cave, not far, and still another where the seals keep their pups when the black-eyed predators are close. I live from the sea, and the fish offer themselves to me, but it is not enough. I have been without another of my kind, my lover, and now Eros has smiled on me at last. You are here, and the spirit of my God is in you. I felt it when I sat alone in my cave, and now I see it in your eyes." She tilted her head back as she spoke, eyes closed, and the long scars beneath her jaw flared red, opening for an instant into gashes of raw, bony tissue before closing with a snap. At the sight of it, Erik's heart skipped a beat, then pounded hard. He grabbed her arms, squeezing fiercely.

She opened her eyes, close to his face, golden orbs in a field black as the pool she had come from. "Ahhh," she gasped, writhing against him, and then her fingernails were biting into his hands.

Who was holding who? "I don't know you," he said, and tears came again. "I have no feeling for you or for any other woman." His voice was a snarl.

"Then remember me," she said and kissed him deeply, hotly, draining him liked blood from a wound. "Again and again I want this, for eternity," she murmured.

Moments later they fell back exhausted on the cool sand. She leaned over to kiss his chest, her long hair spilling over his side and shoulder. For the moment, Eric felt a strange contentment, without wonder at what had just happened. "I don't see how anyone could forget you," he said.

"It has been a thousand years," she said, "or so it seems. Time alone passes slowly."

He touched her lips with a finger. "Have there been others,

like me, who have come here?"

She smiled faintly, looked away from him. "I've had only one lover, a long time ago. It was good for awhile, but then he changed. I've been alone since. And what about you? This is a secret place, known to few. You come here to think, to hide, or is there something else that draws you here?"

He spoke without thinking. "I've had some trouble on the mainland. I've hurt good people who only wanted to love me. The world would be better off if I died, or stayed by myself, or never left this cave." Eric could hear the anger in his own voice.

"The world judges those who are different," Halena said softly, running a fingernail up his chest and around a nipple. "You have learned a harsh lesson, my darling. Those of us who are out of Eros and receive our powers from him may be rightfully considered dangerous to others, and so we must seek out our own kind. I have experienced many forms, and always it has been the same: judgment, persecution, and banishment from those who do not understand. With our own kind we are safer, though not totally so, and we are understood. Not loved, perhaps, but desired, and it is desire that is commanded by Eros."

"I don't know this Eros you talk about," said Eric. "And I don't believe in a God."

"It's not necessary for you to consciously believe, but to accept yourself, for he has possessed you long ago, and now you are again with your own kind. We are alike, you and I. We share the spirit, the desire, and for this we must stay apart from others unlike us. Stay with me, Eric. Swim with me."

"How do you know my name?" Had he said it?

"Your mind cries out," she said tenderly.

He reached up to touch the scar beneath her jaw, but she lowered her chin to hide it and so he touched her lips again. "I can't swim with you," he confessed for the first time in his life. "The water closes me in, and I can't let myself be closed in by things, or by people. I have to be free and in control."

"Even in lovemaking?" she said softly.

"Yes. Especially then."

"Freedom is trust," she said, "and control is an illusion. When you trust me, you will swim with me. And I will show you our home." She stood up and stepped towards the pool on long, muscular legs.

"Don't go," pleaded Eric. "Spend the night with me. You can use the sleeping bag, and I'll cook up some freeze-dried stuff I've got in the pack."

Halena stopped at water's edge, considering, then answered without turning around. "If you wish it. I'll be gone only a moment. My skin is getting dry." She dove cleanly into the pool, disappearing in blackness, and he waited long moments, listening to his heart beat. He checked his watch. One minute, then two, then five. He stood up, peered into the water and saw a white shape rising towards him, a slash of gold, a flash of red, and her head eased above the surface, only the golden eyes showing as when he had first seen her. She held up a hand, grasping a fat Garibaldi Perch by the gills, and he took it from her. "This has given itself to us," she said, climbing out of the pool. She took the fish from him, bit down hard behind its head. The fish shuddered, and died. "I promised you would not cook it."

"Raw fish? I don't know—"

"The flesh is yet pure. It is a gift. Do you have a knife?"

He handed Halena the knife tipped with his own blood, watched her expertly fillet the fish, and then she fed him pieces of raw flesh, tasting sweet on her fingers, and there was nothing left but head and bones when they were finished. They curled up together on the sand, and went to sleep before it was dark, Eric awakening twice during the night to find her cuddling anew with him, her body and hair dripping water. And towards morning, he awoke to find her riding him, pressing his hands to the sand, holding him down, her head tilted back in pleasure as he moved with her. The skin beneath her jaw flared darkly, outwards from her neck as she gasped and rocked, and he squirmed beneath her, uttering a soft cry. And then she was gone again, returning wet and smelling of the sea a few minutes later. They slept again

until the cave was well lit by a sun nearly overhead. She lay close, ran a finger over his lips. Salty. "Swim with me," she said.

"No," he said.

"Then I must leave you. You won't trust me, and I want to go home." She pointed down into the pool, pulled away from him and stood at the edge of the water.

How can I let her go, he thought, and where else can I go? He looked at the dark water, and took a deep breath. "Okay, I'll swim, but not for long."

She smiled, waited while he pulled off his underwear and stowed his pack on a rocky shelf. He joined her naked at water's edge, took her hand and looked into her golden eyes

"It is only a little cave, but it is well hidden and safe," she said.

Her grip was strong. He took a deep breath, then another.

They jumped feet first into the pool.

She pulled him with her, down and down, his head ringing from the sudden pressure in his ears. He opened his eyes in stinging salt water, blinked at her, long legs kicking, body undulating, hair flowing behind her like the blooms of a sea-flower. There was light below them, coming from two sides, and he could hear a pounding that could only be surf breaking. As they moved into the light, she turned back to look at him, and that was the moment of his panic, the moment he breathed in water in a sudden burst of fear and surprise. For her eyes glowed golden beneath the sea, and the flesh beneath her jaws had opened up into a fan of richly red, bony gills, flaring and closing with her movement. He sucked water, saw her eyes widen, and then blackness came.

He awoke in near darkness, and blinked his eyes. Around him rock walls glowed green, the air thick and salty. Halena stood over him, and smiled. He remembered the gills, and was afraid, and she seemed to see it in his eyes. "You nearly drowned," she said, "but I pushed all the water out of you in time."

"I don't know where we are," he said.

"Only for a while, my love. I'm not yet sure of you, and you

must learn to trust me. Here, I brought you some sweet meat from a bottom crawler." She fed him pieces of crab with her fingers, straddling him. Even in near darkness her eyes were still golden, but softly so, as if dimly illuminated from within."

"You're not human," said Eric. "You're some kind of fish."

Halena rocked back and forth gently, and smiled at his reaction. "Does it matter, Eric? Does it really matter? Do I not feel like a human?" She smiled again when he groaned. "I have lived since Eros, and have chosen many forms, but the ones that please me the most are of the sea. Only in the sea is there true freedom. I want you to go there with me, to swim and make love in the depths. I want you to share that life with me."

"I couldn't even get to this cave without drowning. You've made a bad choice, Halena."

"I don't think so," she said, her breath quickening as she moved, and in seconds it was over. She leaned forward so that her hair was in his face. "You are a gift," she said, "and I will cherish you forever."

* * * * * * *

They lived together in their cavern for nearly a year before the change came.

Halena gradually coaxed him into the water again, slowly, patiently teaching him how to swim strong against surging currents, taking him to a nearby cave filled with barking sealions and then outside under a setting sun, where they spent a hundred evenings chasing each other around the rocks like playful otters.

The loss of his job, his apartment, the small accumulation of personal possessions, did not bother him. His life was Halena. In less than half a year he knew he had come to truly love her, wanting to be with her constantly, yet respecting those times she seemed to go within herself, desiring to return alone to the sea for hours at a time. Even then she would return with a special delicacy, rewarding him for his patience. And gradually, her

sexual demands of him were not so intense. They spent much time sitting close, with idle talk or in silence. It seemed enough that they were together in a slow, easy life they both wanted, sharing each day as if it was their last.

After several months of cavern living and swimming in the sea Eric felt happy with his simple life but began to feel drained of all energy by the end of each day. His stomach swelled strangely, and there was pain in his hands and feet. When he complained about it, Halena just smiled and said his body was adapting to their seafood diet. As his vitality languished, and the pains grew worse, he feared she would splash away to find a new lover. But always she returned, flaring her gills wide when surfacing, holding a new treasure aloft for him to see.

The symptoms of whatever ailed him grew rapidly worse, frightening him; the day came when it seemed his body was on fire, and he could barely move his arms and legs. "I think I'm dying," he said, but Halena didn't seem concerned.

"It will pass soon, darling. For us, death is only change."

"I don't want to leave you. I love you, Halena," said Eric.

Halena smiled, and stroked his forehead with a cold hand. "And I have always loved you," she said softly.

"I don't know what's wrong with me, but if I have to die, let it be here. You're here, and that's all I need. There's nothing for me outside of these walls."

Halena thought for a moment, and caressed one gill with her hand. "I've been in this form too long. It is time for me to change. Tell me what I should become, my love."

"You've stayed with me longer than anyone, yet you've always wanted to be free. When I'm gone, you must be something totally free."

"In the sea," she said.

"Of course," he said, then grimaced at a squeezing pain in his lower abdomen.

Halena frowned. "I will need to leave you more often, but I promise I'll be here when your time of change comes. I promise you will not be alone."

"You are always in my heart." He nestled his head on her firm shoulder. Was she immortal? He wondered, but would not ask.

In the last week of his life she floated him to a place where they watched a sunset, and then to the cave where they had first met. She returned only three times in that last week, eyes golden as she popped from the water, but different in other ways. Her gills were gone, and there was a gray pallor to her skin, though it was still smooth and warm. His own skin had also turned gray, but was rough and pealing. His vision was now blurred, and his hands and feet felt misshapen.

On the night before his death, she cuddled him in her arms until he slept, and they said nothing to each other. And the following afternoon, alone, his breathing was shallow and he had just closed his eyes, content to begin his eternal sleep when there was a loud splash beside him, cool water showering his dying body.

He opened his eyes and found a large Dolphin half-beached beside him, nuzzling his leg. The mammal chirped brightly and looked at him with golden eyes. He stroked her nose and back with difficulty, felt her press against him in an awkward embrace. And then, as he took another deep, strong breath, she slid from beneath his hand and he saw her beautiful, symmetric tail thrusting her beneath the water, propelling her towards a new life of freedom in the sea.

The sight of it opened something within him and triggered the final surge of energy to complete his change. He heard a strange sound when he called out to his love, pulled himself into the pool on awkward appendages, and with a mighty thrust of his suddenly powerful tail, surged into the depths to join her.

ABOUT THE AUTHOR

JAMES C. GLASS is a retired physics and astronomy professor and dean who now spends his time writing, painting, and traveling. He made his first story sale in 1988 and was the Grand Prize Winner of Writers of the Future in 1991. Since then he has sold seven novels and three short story collections, and over fifty short stories to magazines such as *Aboriginal S.F.*, *Analog*, and *Talebones*. Jim writes science fiction, fantasy, and dark fantasy. He now divides his time between Spokane, Washington and Desert Hot Springs, California with wife Gail, who is a costumer and healing dancer. There are five grown children and eleven grandchildren scattered around the country. Jim also paints mountain, desert, and red rock scenics in oils and pastels, and is often heard playing didgeridoo and Native American flute. For more details, please see his web site at:

www.sff.net/people/jglass/